Cora's perspective

Chapter 1

"God damn it, Cora! Get out of bed, you promised you'd go on a run with me last night!" Megan's voice shrilly wakes me up.

Shit…why did I promise Megan that? I'm not a morning person at all. "Uuuugh, hold on, let me try to wake up and get some coffee at least." I tell her.

"I told you I wanted to be out the door at seven, it's a quarter till, you better hurry up or I'm leaving without you." Megan whines.

With sleep still in my throat, "Perfect, go without me, then I could sleep more," I say with a silly sleepy smile on my face. I know she won't leave without me, not since the recent disappearances of a couple women our age. It's all over the news. First, it was Jessica McSorely, who disappeared after leaving her work at the 'Downtown Haven', one of the local bars. Then, it was Penelope Guzhar, who went missing after leaving the library. Now, the most recent is Kristy Webbing, a girl we went to school with. She went for a run and never returned.

"Bitch, you know I won't. We promised our parents we'd stick together, and after Kristy, I'm scared." Megan says. *I don't blame her, I'm scared too. All of the missing women are similar to us. Twenty to twenty four years of age, brunettes, and on the small side. Except Megan is skinner than me, I'm a little bit chubby but I flaunt it.*

"You're lucky that you're my best friend or I wouldn't be doing this….I'm coming, Megan, just let me get dressed. Start the Keurig please, double caramel cappuccino." I tell her while rubbing my eyes.

"Right away!" she says like a robot, "Now get your ass out of bed," she slaps my butt, "the run will wake you up more than the coffee will." She says while walking out my bedroom door. I fucking hate running. I'd rather go for a swim but its spring in Michigan. The lakes are either still frozen or way too cold to swim in, for other people that is. The water temperature never bothered me. I can't wait for the warmer weather. The water is where I feel alive. My whole body buzzes with excitement when I'm submerged. I put on some leggings, an over-sized sweatshirt, socks and my shoes. Megan is holding my cappuccino, all decked out in her runner gear. She was a track star in high school, and has loved her morning run ever since. Me? I was on the swim team, and has hated running ever since they made us do the mile run in school.

"Thank you!" I say as I grab my cappuccino and take a sip. *My god! It's so good!*

"Hurry and drink up, we're leaving in five minutes." She tells me with evil eyes and a sickly sweet smile. Dear, sweet Megan, she's so bossy and whines if she doesn't get her way. I don't want to deal with her attitude later, so I down my coffee fast and grab my cell phone. Megan grabs her house keys. We are roommates, in a nice little three bedroom house that we were gifted. It was a graduation present from our parents, her parents bought the house, and my parents furnished it for us. We have been best friends since third grade, and have been inseparable since.

Running sucks, I seriously can't wait until it warms up a bit and the lakes unfreeze. I can swim in any temperature, but no one else I know can, besides my dad. Megan cries the whole time and gives up before even getting her ankles in the water if it's not summer.

"Cora, you're slacking!" Megan yells at me, while running back to me. I guess I'm going to slow for her. "We are supposed to stick together." She says.

"Sorry, you know I hate this shit." I tell her.

"We'll turn around and run back now then, I have to take a shower before work anyways. You work tonight?" she asks me.

"No, I have the next two nights off." I tell her. Today is my Saturday, even though it's Wednesday.

"Any plans for tonight?" She asks. Megan is always trying to get me to go out on dates. She dates around a lot, one night stands mostly. Good thing we have our own house, if her parents knew about her sleeping with half the guys in town, I don't think they'd be too happy.

"You know me, just planning to relax, read my book, and watch 'the office' on Netflix, maybe go for a swim." I tell her. I don't like to talk much when I'm running, takes up too much energy.

"Did you ever text Shawn? Or Brandon? I told you I thought they'd be perfect for you. You need some sexual release." She tells me with a smirk on her face.

I roll my eyes at her, "No, I'm fine, plus I don't want your sloppy seconds." I say with a grin on my face. Megan play slaps my arm. It's been a while since I've been with anybody. I don't like the whole one night stand thing like Megan does, tried it few times but it wasn't for me. I like being committed to someone. My last relationship ended badly. He was my high school boyfriend of three years, and he cheated on me with a co-worker of his. He tried to lie about it but I figured it out.

"Well, you are never going to meet anyone locked up in your room. Let's go out tomorrow after I get off work." She proposes.

I tell her "Sure." Just to shut her up for now, I'll think of an excuse later. We get back to our house. Megan jumps in the shower, does her make-up for thirty minutes, and then leaves for work. I'm cuddled up on my couch in my mermaid blanket, with my steamy cup of cappuccino and my even steamier book. *Man, this book is so hot, now I know why Megan said I needed some release. I actually do with this book. Maybe I should go out with her tomorrow. But for now, maybe a swim in the cold lake will do me some good.*

I grab my swim bag, and text Megan that I'm going swimming. You can never be too careful with letting people know where you are, especially with all these disappearances lately. I grab my keys and lock up the house. My little car isn't the greatest but it runs, for now. I drive out to my favorite little lake, Prism Lake. *No cars in the parking lot, that's how I like it.* Solitude is something I really appreciate, and don't get enough of. I go to the little bathroom to change, it's locked but I have a key. My parents talked the grounds keeper into letting me have one since I needed a place to practice for the swim team. I've had the key since high school, I guess they never change the locks. I do my stretches. My body is already buzzing and I haven't even got to the water yet. I run into the water and dive.

Yes! This is what my body's been missing. The flow of electricity in my veins, from the water, is amazing. I get goosebumps all over my body. I swim to my heart's content, doing breast strokes, butterflies and flips in the water, and then float when I get tired. Letting my body soak up the water. I see something out the corner of my eye. I stop floating, and look. It's a shirtless man.

He's doing stretches in his bathing suit. Which is pretty weird because I thought I was the only crazy person who swims in February. His body looks to be sculpted out of clay. You can see every line of ab and muscle of his skin even from the distance apart we are. His dark black hair going in all directions. He looks out to me and waves with a big grin on his face. *I might have been staring, and drooling, or is that just the water?* He's fucking gorgeous. How is it even possible or fair for him to be this good looking? When I get 'plain-Jane' Cora for myself? I wave a little back, embarrassed and go back to my floating, trying to ignore him walking into the water. I start treading water, mystery guy is swimming towards me. *There goes my solitude.*

"I thought I was the only crazy person who swims in early spring around here." He says.

"I was going to say the same thing." I politely tell him.

With a sexy little smile he says, "I just moved into town a couple months ago, the name's Jett."

"I'm Cora." *I know I'm blushing, I can feel it.* He's even more gorgeous up close. His baby blue eyes, are piercing and look me over. His jaw is chiseled and covered in stubble that I just want to nibble on. My sex clenches, *god he makes me wet just looking at him. I wanted a swim to fix my frustrations, not add to them!*

"I'm going to get back to my swimming." I tell him after a few minutes of us just staring at each other.

"Mind if I join you? It's been awhile since I've had any competition." He says.

"What, like a race?" I ask, smiling because I know I'm an excellent swimmer. He may have picked the wrong fight here.

"Yea, a race. Let's see what a crazy girl who swims in the cold can do! How about from that buoy to the next one." He suggests.

"Or we could do across the whole lake?" I say with my eyebrow cocked. I'm taunting him.

"Alright, across the lake it is." He says with a laugh. *Is he blushing too or is that my imagination?* "I'll throw a rock up in the air, as soon as it hits the water, we start, ok?" He asks.

"Sounds good to me." I say all smug. *I'm determined to win this race, I think he underestimated me.* We go to the one side of the lake to get ready. The lake is not huge, but most people in this town cannot swim across it. I'm one of the few who has, on many occasions.

"You ready, Cora?" He asks. *I'm excited!* My face splits into a huge grin.

I nod my head, "Yup! Let's go Jett!" I tell him. He throws the rock high up into the air and gets into position. As soon as I hear the splash, I take off like a rocket. Everyone in high school called me 'Ariel', or 'mermaid girl'. I have always joked that I was part mermaid. I don't know why but I'm amazing in the water. I make it across the lake in record time. I see that Jett is right beside me. *We tied, that doesn't happen, not to me.* I feel a little defeated.

"Why the sad face?" He says in concern, "It was a tie. You're really fast! I didn't expect that, but what else should I expect from crazy Cora, who swims in the semi-frozen lake."

"I've never tied before, I always win." I say with a playful pout. "I don't like it, feels like losing." We tread water. "Well, I think I'm done swimming for today. That race tired me out." I tell him, feeling slightly disappointed. And looking at him is not helping me like this swim was supposed to.

"Yea, me too." He says and we swim to shore together. While toweling dry, I'm sneaking peeks of his body from behind my towel. I can't really help myself.

"Nice to meet you, Jett." I tell him once I'm done and dry.

"Same to you, Cora, hope to see you around." He says and there he goes with that sexy smile again.

"Uh, bye!" I wave and walk away from him, feeling like an idiot. I get to my car and see no other cars in the parking lot. I wonder how he got here then. *I'm definitely going to have nice new mental images for myself and my vibrator later*, I think in my head with a smile. I make it to my house, unlock the door and get into some comfy house clothes. I have a few hours before Megan will get home. I grab my laptop and set it up to watch Netflix.

I'm watching 'the office' when I hear the front door close. I pause the show because I know Megan will come in and want to talk.

She knocks, "Cora? Are you home?"

"Yea, come on in!" I yell out.

She walks in still in her uniform, "Work was a drag, barely made eighty dollars." Megan is a waitress at a restaurant in town. She makes good money, and it helps that she's pretty and a natural flirt.

"Wednesdays are slow, eighty dollars is good." I laugh at her. "Anything happen today?" I ask her.

"Nothing except a weirdo texting me that she is going swimming in the middle of February. I can't believe you don't get cold, that shit literally hurts me." She jokes.

"Speaking of weirdos," I say, her eyes perk up at me. "There was this guy that was at the lake too, swimming with me. We had a race and we tied." I tell her.

Her eyes get gigantic. "You didn't win? And there is another person who swims in this weather? What did he look like? Was he hot? What else happened?" I'm bombarded by her questions.

"His name is Jett. He is the single most gorgeous male I have ever seen in real life. He looked like a male model. I swear Megan, he is a fifteen out of ten. And he stayed with me the entire race. Then we just said goodbye and I left." I explain.

"What kind of a name is Jett?" She asks.

"I don't know, what kind of a name is Coral? Maybe his parents are hippies like mine." My full name is Coral Marina, everyone calls me Cora for short.

"He didn't ask for your number?" She asks another question.

"No, I kind of left real fast after the race, it was weird to lose and I was embarrassed." I respond.

"Well, you didn't lose, it was a tie." She chastises me. "How about we go out tonight instead of tomorrow?" She asks.

"Depends on where you want to go." I say.

"What about the 'Electric Stick'?" She suggests with a shoulder shrug. I immediately get heated and pissed off. She knows that's the place I don't go to. I haven't been since my break up, it is my ex's hang out.

"Seriously, Megan?" I say while giving her my best pissed off glare.

"Yes, seriously Cora! You need to get past all that shit. It's been two years, Kevin rarely comes in anymore. Not after he had his kid." She says. Yea, my ex knocked up his co-worker, that's how I found out he cheated. Megan is starting to whine.

Ugh, I roll my eyes. All I wanted to do was finish this season of 'the office', not go out, but if I don't, I won't hear the end of it. "Fine, Megan, let's go, why not." I say with a shrug.

Megan's face lights up. "Yes, Cora! You will not be disappointed! It's changed quite a bit since you've been!" She is practically bouncing up and down on the bed. "I'm going to go get ready!" She quickly says before running out my bedroom door.

It gives me time to mentally beat myself up for agreeing with this. I look in my closet for something to wear. Something that shows off my plump cleavage without showing too much. I find my sparkly blue low-cut top. It accents my blue eyes, and of course my handy black leggings. Next is my make-up, little accents of blue and brown to highlight my eyes. I don't really do the whole make-up every day thing, like Megan. She even does YouTube make-up tutorial videos. I just simply do eye make-up. I can't stand foundation and lipstick. Once my eyes are perfect, I start on my hair. It has a slight wave to it from the lake, I straighten it. Next, I put in my black headband with purple sequins and check my finished look. I look pretty damn good. My brown hair is slick straight and out of my face so you can see my make-up. My top fits me well. It really shows off my curves. I may not be the skinniest of the bunch but my curves are perfect for me. "Megan! Are you ready yet?" I yell down the hallway.

"Two minutes!" She screams after me. That gives me enough time to check my phone. I go to Facebook and search for Jett. I see a couple of Jett's but they don't look like him. He must not have an account. Megan comes out in her little black dress. *I know that dress, it means she's not coming home tonight.* She looks so glamorous in her high heels and brown perfect curls. I can't wear heels, I'm in my fancy black flats.

"Now, I'm ready. Let's go, can you drive?" She asks. I roll my eyes. *When I saw her dress, I knew I was driving already.*

We arrive to the club. Megan is re-applying her lipstick in the rear view mirror. The building looks the same as it did a couple years ago. "Come on, Cora. Let's get inside before all the tables are gone." She says as if I wasn't just waiting for her. I roll my eyes at her and follow her inside. It's really not that different inside. Now there is a dance floor. Other than that, everything looks the same. The pool tables are still lit up neon. The bar is still in the back. I'm not really a big dancer unless I'm hammered. I guess Megan really wanted to go dancing. We find a pool table that is empty and start a game. I'm decent at pool but Megan is better. We make a better team than opposing each other. The waitress comes over to us and hands us a drink each.

"These are from the guys at table three." She says while she points to the table. Two guys are looking our way. We wave a little thanks and continue our game. She beats me and I still have three solids on the table. I need another drink so I head to the bar. I get Megan and me a 'sex on the beach', our favorite drink. I'm headed back and I see Megan is chatting with one of the guys who bought us the drinks. He's hot, he's got the surfer look going for him. Long blond hair, tan skin, and with a Hawaiian shirt un-buttoned all the way down. He's falling for her little black dress routine.

"Hey Cor-bear!" I hear a voice say. I immediately stop frozen. *I know that voice and I fucking hate it.* Dread hits my face. I turn around and Kevin is there. My fucking ex, and the reason why I didn't want to come here anymore. He looks a little drunk. "I haven't seen you around in years! You're looking great!" He says while checking my body out, up and down. "How have you been?" Kevin smiles.

"Umm. I've been fine, just working a lot. I've got to get this drink to Megan." I say. I try to get out of this situation. Things didn't end well with us. I don't want to see his stupid face. I fucking hate what he did to me.

"Megan's fine and has a drink already. She's talking to the surfer dude. Are you still working at the aquarium?" He asks.

Guess I can't get out of this that easily. "Yes, I love that place, I don't know if I'll ever leave." I tell him. I sip my drink, it's good. Kevin's downing his beer fast. I look over at Megan, she's dancing with surfer boy. He's probably the lucky guy tonight. "I'm going to go outside for a breather." I say, still trying to get away from Kevin.

"Oh, I'll join you, I need a smoke." He mentions.

God damn it! Go away Kevin! "When did you start smoking?" I ask, he never smoked when we were together.

"A little after Camden was born. Parenting is fucking hard work and stressful." He says. His son, Camden, is two years old. We broke up two years ago. I was so stupid to not have realized he was cheating on me. He came clean about everything on the day his son was born. We step outside. "Like old times, huh." He comments while taking a puff.

"Sure." I say, this is awkward. I have a bad feeling about this. I want to leave. I have to tell Megan that I'm leaving, make sure she's alright, and doesn't need a ride home. "I'm going to check on Megan." I blurt out and try to make my getaway.

"Wait, first. I wanted to say, I'm so glad I ran into you. I've been meaning to call you actually. I really wanted to talk to you." He's slurring his words a bit, "I really miss us. Things aren't going well with Tiffany. I wanted to see if maybe you wanted to relive old times." He says while wiggling his eyebrows at me.

My face probably has disgust written all over it. "Are you fucking kidding me, Kevin?" I yell at him.

He tries to wrap his arms around me. "Remember all the fun we used to have?" He says. I'm trying to push him away and he's trying to kiss me. I can smell the beer on his breath. *He's too fucking close to my face.*

"Kevin, you fucking cheated on me, and lied about it. The only reason you got caught was because you knocked her up. And now you don't want to deal with those consequences? No, absolutely not! Never again, Kevin. Go run to Tiffany, it's what you do best." I scream at him. My body starts to feel weird. Like, hotter than normal, and my hands start to prickle some.

"I think the lady said no. Let her go." A voice says. I turn to see my savior. *It's Jett!* Kevin drops me and winces. *Did I hurt him?*

"Mind your own business, pal." Kevin drips with apprehension.

"Hey Jett, thanks for meeting me here." I say while giving him the 'run with it' eyes.

"Hey baby, are you alright?" He asks as he puts an arm around my shoulders and kisses my forehead.

"Who's this guy?" Kevin growls at us.

"I'm her boyfriend." Jett tells him with a smile. *What? Did he really just say that?* I try to keep my face from showing my surprise.

"I thought you were still single?" Kevin asks defeated.

"Nope, you thought wrong. Bye Kevin, go home." I tell him while Jett escorts me into the bar. Once we get inside, I say loudly over the music, "Oh my god, Thanks for that! That was awful."

Jett smiles, "No problem, it looked like you needed help. Who was that guy?" He asks.

I sigh, "He's my ex, and he cheated on me and got the girl pregnant. That's how I found out." I tell him, he's really easy to talk too.

"So what, things got hard and he wanted you back?" He muses.

"Seems like it." I say with an eye roll.

"Good for you, for saying no. I know too many women who would have taken scum like that back." He says.

"Thanks." I smile. He smiles back. *God, he's gorgeous.* I almost forgot about Megan. I frantically look around for her. I can't find her anywhere. "I have to go look for my friend. Let me go check the bathroom, I'll be right back." I say.

"Trying to get rid of me already?" he says in mocked shock.

"No seriously, I don't see Megan, I'll be right back, I promise." I tell him.

"I'll get you a drink, what would you like?" He asks.

"A sex on the beach, please" I say with a cocky smile.

"Ok" he grins "will do Cora."

I love the sound of my name coming out of his mouth. *And sex on the beach, with him? Yes fucking please! I'm wet just thinking about it. I better go look for Megan before I forget again.* I run to the bathroom. "Megs! Megs!" I shout.

"Over here bitch!" She screams from one of the stalls.

"Dude, hurry up, I have so much to tell you!" I say. She comes out. "Kevin was here." She gasps while I say this. "He tried to kiss me and, naturally I refused."

"Oh my god Cora, I'm so sorry! I never would have made you come here if I thought he'd be here." She apologies to me.

"It's okay, Jett stopped him." I tell her with a smile.

"Jett's here?" She exclaimed.

"Yea, he's waiting for me at the bar!" I say.

"Oh my god, I just have to see this gorgeous god you keep talking about!" She smirks at me. We walk out of the bathroom, arms linked, and walk to the bar. Jett is talking to the surfer boy. "Oh that's Jake, I'm going home with him tonight." She whispers and smirks.

"Have fun with that. The tall, dark, and handsome man Jake's talking to is Jett." I tell her.

Megan's jaw drops, "Damn, Cora, he's fine as hell!" *Yea, I know, my body does crazy things just from looking at him.*

"So, you found her." Jett passes me my drink.

"Thank you," I tip my glass to him, and take a sip. "Yes, I found her."

Megan has her new drink from Jake. "So, you must be the famous Jett I keep hearing about!" *Real smooth Megan*, I give her a pointed look.

"Oh, you've heard of me." He gives that devilishly good smile.

"Yea, the only other weirdo to swim in February." Megan says. I laugh. It's true.

"That's me!" He smiles. His face is perfection. I drink my glass almost gone. "Woah, there killer, slow down." Jett chuckles at me. Megan and Jake go to the dance floor. "You want to dance?" He asks me.

"Me? Umm, no, I only do that when I'm drunk and it's not pretty." I laugh.

"Finish that drink and I'll be the judge of that." He's says.

Holy shit! He wants to dance. With me? Why? I'm so nervous. I shakily finish my drink. He grabs my hand and brings me to the dance floor. I don't even know the song that is playing but it has rhythm. He wraps his arm around me and our hips swing to the beat. Our pelvises touching, I'm so turned on and I'm sure my face is beet red. He's either turned on too or that's a big cell phone in his pocket. He's a good dancer, better than me, that's for sure. The song ends and a slow beat comes on. Now this, I can do. Our hips sway, I wrap my arms around his shoulder and back. Sure, my face is still red but I'm enjoying myself.

Jett whispers in my ear. "Do you swim in that lake a lot?"

"Yea, it's my happy place. I'm part mermaid." I joke.

Confusion on his face, "How do you know?" Jett whisper asks.

Now it's my turn to be confused. *What does he mean?* "It's a joke, my nickname in high school was Ariel. I'm just an excellent swimmer." I tell him.

His smile returns, he chuckles, "Oh, I know you are. No one's ever come close to beating me in a race before."

"Yup, same here, still feels like I lost." I deadpan.

"Wow!" He laughs, "It was a tie, and you didn't lose. You've never lost a race before?" He laughs again.

'No, never." I tell him. The song ends and Jett drags me back to the bar.

"Want another drink?" He asks.

"No, thank you, I have to drive home tonight." I look around and see Megan sucking face with Jake. Looks like I'm in the clear, she's definitely going home with Jake.

"Your friend looks to be having fun." Jett remarks with a huge grin on his face.

"That's Megan for you." I say with a little head shake. "So, what made you move to North Creek?" I ask.

"Work." He smirks.

"And that would be?" I smirk back.

"Fisherman." He replies.

"Oh. That's funny, I also work with fish." I tell him.

"You're a fisher-woman?" He asks with a smile.

"No." I laugh. "I work at the aquarium downtown. I do a little bit of everything there. Cleaning the tanks, feeding the fish, educational lessons for the kids."

"So, I kill the fish and you take care of them?" He jokes.

"Yea, I guess so." I laugh again. I check my phone. It's one in the morning! I guess we were dancing for longer than I thought. Megan texted me that she will be home in the morning.

"Am I boring you already?" Jett asks.

I look up from my phone. "No, sorry, just checking my texts. It is real late though. I have to get home and sleep. It was real nice to see you again." I tell him.

"Yea, I'm real glad I came out tonight. I got to see you again. Think I could get your number?" He asks. *Seriously?! This golden god wants my number? Mine? Why in fucks name does he want my number when there are plenty of better looking women here?* I get flustered.

"Yea, uhh here let me text you, what's your number?" We exchange numbers and he walks me out to my car.

"I'll text you Cora, and maybe I'll see you swimming again." He says while I step into my car. My chameleon skills are working on my face, I can feel the heat of my blush in my cheeks.

"Ok, yea, I go to the lake quite often so it's possible, bye Jett!" I shut my door and drive off. I can see Jett out my rearview mirror, watching me pull off. *After tonight, I might have to replace the batteries in my trusty vibrator. It's going to get some use.*

Jett's Perspective

Chapter 2

I've been in this town for months. I shouldn't even be here. I'm a mer-man from the Halcyon tribe. If mer-people are on land, we have legs. Once in the water, we can summon our scales and fins to grow over our legs. It's an evolutionary trait that some people with the right genes have. Some mer-people choose to live on land and never go back to the water. That is how the traits get passed down generations. And that is why there are guardians like myself. It's my mission to find a Lunafriya, if possible. Lunafriya's have been extinct for one hundred and fifty years. They are mermaids who have special powers, who are supposed to keep the peace among the tribes, instead of the constant wars that we are in now.

My tribe wants to find her first. That's why I'm on land. I actually enjoy being on land, but not for this long at a time. I miss my home. A Lunafriya has been thought to be in this town of North Creek, Michigan. The great lakes state. Of course, I've been bar hopping, going to any and all places where I might find her. I can't find what I'm looking for. If I don't find her, these disappearances in town will continue. I'm sure it's another tribe, looking for exactly the same thing as I am. It's my job to protect the Lunafriya from the other tribes. But the only Intel I've got is that she will be a brunette, and a swimmer. They sent me here in the winter. Even if it's a lake town, no one goes swimming in winter, in Michigan. All the lakes are frozen. I've gone up to the local pool, but have not seen the one I'm searching for. I'm doing a real shitty job at this guardianship.

The weather is starting to warm up. It's not quite warm yet, but the water on the lake behind my house is almost thawed. I have to admit, this house is awesome. It's my tribe's property, dating back to the 1920's. We have land all over the globe. *Maybe I should go to the water. My body is missing its contact.* I put my suit on and head to the trail that leads to the beach. The water looks so peaceful, a few ripples of waves. There is still some frozen parts by the edges of the lake. I see movement in the middle of the water. Something is in the lake. It looks to be a person. But the water is too cold for normal people to be swimming in. It's a woman floating. I see a face, tits, and toes poking out of the water. Then movement, like she saw me. I start stretching my body so it doesn't look like I'm staring at her. I can see her watching me out of the corner of my eyes. I don't need to stretch, but I want to give her a little show. She's still looking at me so I give her a wave. She waves back and starts to float again.

I make my way into the water. *Fuck, the current of the water on my body feels good. I really needed this. I haven't been in the water for over two months and I could feel my energy wavering. The mystery girl, who's swimming in February, might be exactly who I've been looking for.* I get so excited, I get closer to her by the second. She has brown hair, I'm guessing, it's hard to tell when wet.

"I thought I was the only crazy person who swims in early spring around here." I say to her.

"I was going to say the same thing." She says warily. Damn, she's fine. She has blue eyes just a little lighter than mine. Her tits are big, I'd say two handfuls per tit. I can't stop sneaking glances at them. I feel a chub starting. *She has to be the one I'm looking for, no doubt about it.*

"I just moved into town a couple months ago, my name's Jett." I tell her.

"I'm Cora." She blushes, I have that effect on women. She's fucking adorable, biting her lip. We just kind of stare at each other until she says, "I'm going to go back to my swimming."

"Mind if I join you? It's been awhile since I've had any competition." I say.

"What, like a race?" Her face lights up. *Perfect! Let's see if she's really the one.*

"Yea, a race, let's see what a crazy girl who swims in the cold can do. How about from that buoy, to the next one." I tell her. *I don't want to make it too hard. I know I'm going to win. Duh...mer-man here!*

"Or we could do across the whole lake?" She says with one of her eyebrows cocked. *She's got some spunk. I like that in a woman.* She's cocky. It makes my dick even harder.

Luckily, we are in the water and she can't see my boner. *Oh, the nasty things I would do to this girl, but if she is the one I'm looking for, that can't ever happen.*

"Alright, across the lake it is." I say with a laugh. "I'll throw a rock up in the air, as soon as it hits the water, we race, ok?" That sounds like a fair start.

"Sounds good to me." She says all smug. *I just want to shove my cock between those tits. I have to stop thinking about her like that, racing with a hard-on isn't going to work.* We go to the one side of the lake to get ready.

"You ready, Cora?" *Let's see what she can do.*

"Yup, let's go, Jett!" She yells.

I throw the rock and get into position. As soon the rock hits, I see how fast she is. I have to try to win, but I don't win, it's a tie. *She's definitely a mermaid, even if she doesn't know it. I'm ecstatic! My search might be over! Now the hard part begins. Trying to tell someone that they are a mermaid, never goes well.*

"Why the sad face?" I ask in concern. "We both won, it was a tie. You're really fast! I didn't expect that, but what should I expect from crazy Cora, who swims in the semi-frozen lake!" I exclaim.

"I've never been tied before. I always win." She says with a playful pout. *I want to taste those lips.* "I don't like it, feels like losing." She's biting her lip again. *I'd like to try that.* We tread water. She's nervous, I can tell. I need to get closer to her. "I think I'm done swimming for today. That really tired me out." She says.

"Yea, me too." I reply. *Damn it! She's leaving! Now that I think I've found a Lunafriya, I can't let her get away.* I'm also glad I remembered to bring a towel down with me to the lake.

We dry off and she wraps up in her towel and sighs, "Nice to meet you, Jett."

"Same to you, Cora, hope to see you around." I say and flash her my lady killer smile.

"Uh, bye." She waves and turns. *I was going to ask her for her number, but she ran off.* I finally get a view of her ass. It makes my dick jump. *I wonder if she wants me as badly as I want her. I seriously have to stop thinking these nasty thoughts.*

I run to the house, grab a shirt and my leather jacket. I bolt to my car and drive quickly out of the garage. *I have to catch up to her. I can't lose the Lunafriya.* I drive past the parking lot, a little red Neon is driving further ahead. *That has to be her.* I catch up to Cora but stay a little bit back so she can't see it's me. I don't want her to know I'm actually stalking her right now. That wouldn't freak her out or anything. She turns into a driveway with a cute little house attached. There is even an anchor on the front porch. I find a spot to park. Now my job can actually begin.

A car has parked next to Cora's car in the driveway. A cute waitress, I'm guessing by her outfit, goes into the house. I'm still waiting and watching for Cora. I need to follow her wherever she goes. I have to protect her, it's my mission. About an hour goes by and I see the two of them all dressed up, walking to Cora's car. *God damn, that outfit she's wearing is sexy as hell. Her friend is just as fine, a little too slutty for my taste though.* My dick twitches. I wait for Cora to drive away and I slowly follow.

They stop at a bar. 'The Electric Stick' must be a pool hall or something. I find a spot where I can see the entrance door, and wait. I can't just go in right away. I need to take my time and not blow this, but also watch and see that she doesn't leave. *I'm glad I always have a change of clothes in the car. She'd be weirded out if I was still in my swim suit.*

Two hours later, I See Cora step outside. She's with someone. It's a dude. He's smoking a cigarette. They are talking, it seems. She looks uncomfortable. I don't like the looks of it. I start to get out of the car and head her way. The guy wraps his arms around her so fast, I'm practically running at this point. She's pushing him away.

I hear her say, "And now you don't want to deal with those consequences. No, absolutely not. Never again, Kevin. Go run to Tiffany. It's what you do best." *She doesn't want him.* This makes me proud.

"I think the lady said no. Let her go." I say with authority. The dude drops her.

"Mind your own business, pal." Kevin snarls at me.

Her face lights up when she sees me. Cora is giving me pleading eyes, just asking me to save her. "Hey Jett, thanks for meeting me here." She says.

"Hey, baby." I put my arm around her shoulders and kiss her head, to play the part, of course. And to protect her, the kiss was just for fun.

"Who's this guy?" Kevin growls to her.

"I'm her boyfriend." I say, *I hope this is the direction she wanted me to go.*

"I thought you were still single?" Kevin asks.

"Nope, bye Kevin. Go home." She sighs. I steer her into the bar. The music is loud. Poppy bullshit, but I can dance to anything. *I love to dance. It's just so sexual. My hands and body all over a woman, in front of people no less. Yes please!*

"Oh my god, thanks for that!" She says loudly over the music. "That was awful!"

I give her a smile, *I like being the knight in shining armor.* "No problem, looked like you needed help. Who was that guy?" I point my head back.

She sighs, "He's my ex, and he cheated on me and got the girl pregnant. That's how I found out."

Wow, what a fucking dick, and an idiot! He had Cora, who's the fucking Lunafriya maybe, and threw that away? His loss but my gain. "So what, things got hard and he wanted you back?" I muse.

"Seems like it." She says with an eye roll.

"Good for you, for saying no. I know too many women who would have taken scum like that back." I say.

"Thanks." She smiles. *It's a perfect smile. I want to see that smile more.* I give her a big grin. *Poseidon, she's beautiful. She's shaped like an hourglass. Her tits are huge and her top is low-cut. It turns me on.* Her eyes snap wide and she starts frantically looking around.

"I have to go look for my friend. Let me go check the bathroom, I'll be right back." She says.

"Trying to get rid of me already?" I say in mocked shock, trying to make her laugh.

"No, seriously, I don't see Megan, I'll be right back, I promise." She tells me. *Well, she promised, she'll be back.*

"I'll get you a drink, what would you like?" I ask her.

"A 'sex on the beach'." She says with a cocky smile. *Fuck, yes. She's giving me bedroom eyes.*

"Ok." I grin devilishly, "will do, Cora." *And I really wish we could, but I'm her guardian.* She turns and runs to the bathroom. Her ass is deliciously plump. *I want to smack it, with my hand and my dick.* I head off to the bar to get us drinks.

The bar has neon lights all around, it hurts my eyes. I wait for the bartender to see me and order a Corona with lime and a sex on the beach. The surfer looking dude next to me says, "Women sure do love to have us order that drink, I think they think it's funny or something."

"It's better than having to order a blowjob shot." I reply.

"I've never heard of that one, what is it?" Surfer dude chuckles.

"It is Baileys Irish crème and Kahlua and Amaretto topped with whipped cream. You are supposed to pick it up with your mouth and with your hands behind your back." I explain with a laugh.

His laughter is deep, "Now that is something I'd like to see a women drink." He says.

I grin. *Maybe Cora would like a shot.* I get our drinks and tip the bartender.

"Name's Jake." Surfer dude says while extending his hand out.

"Jett." I reply and we shake hands. I turn and see Cora arm in arm with the waitress from earlier. Megan, I think Cora said her name was. "So, you've found her." I say while giving her the drink.

"Thank you." She says, taking a sip. "Yes, I've found her."

Her friend Megan looks at me and says." So, you must be the famous Jett I keep hearing about!"

I grin. *So, she's talked about me, good.* "Oh, you've heard of me." I say while giving Cora a grin.

"Yea, the only other weirdo to swim in February." Megan remarks. We all laugh, it's true.

"That's me!" I smile. Cora drinks her glass almost gone in one shot. "Woah, there killer, slow down." I chuckle at her. Her friend follows Jake to the dance floor. "Do you want to dance?" I ask her.

"Me? Ummm, no, I only do that when I'm drunk and it's not pretty." She laughs.

"Finish that drink and I'll be the judge of that." I say. *Fuck yes, I am touching that body. I will make her want me, I but can tell she already does.* She's blushing and nervous. She downs her glass.

I grab her hand and take her to the dance floor. I wrap my arm around her and pull her to me, making our hips swing to the beat. *Her body feels good against mine.* I really can't help it but I get an erection. I push it against her hip, wanting her to feel what she does to me. The song ends and a slow beat comes on. Cora grips me tighter, she's enjoying this and not a bad dancer, like she seems to think. I need to talk to her more, find out more about her.

I whisper into her ear, "Do you swim in that lake a lot?"

"Yea, it's my happy place. I'm part mermaid." She says with a grin.

My brows furrow, "How do you know?" I ask. *Has another tribe told her?*

"It's a joke, my nickname in high school was Ariel. I'm just an excellent swimmer." She says. *Duh, it was a joke. Now I feel like an idiot.* I have to change the subject.

"Oh, I know, no one's come close to beating me in a race before." I tell her.

"Yup, same here, stills feels like I lost." She deadpans.

"Wow, it was a tie, you didn't lose. You've never lost a race before?" I laugh, *I think she might be a sore loser.*

"No, never." She says. The song ends and I take us back to the bar. We've been dancing and talking for a while now.

"Want another drink?" I ask.

"No, thank you, I have to drive home." She looks around and I'm sure she's looking for Megan. I spot her making out with the surfer.

"Your friend looks to be having fun." I remark with a huge grin on my face.

"That's Megan for you." She says with a little head shake. I get us some waters at the bar and head to a little table. "So, what made you move to North Creek?" She asks.

"Work." I smirk.

"And what would that be?" She gives me an eye roll. *I can't tell her my real job yet. I need her to trust me first.*

"Fisherman." I reply. *I know a lot about fish, that's something I can easily lie about and not get caught up.*

"Oh, that's funny, I also work with fish." She says.

"You're a fisher-woman?" I joke.

"No," She chuckles, "I work at the aquarium downtown. I do a little bit of everything there. Cleaning the tanks, feeding the fish, and educational lessons for the kids." She smiles. *Of course, she knows about fish. She's a Lunafriya.*

"So, I kill the fish and you take care of them?" I joke.

"Yea, I guess so." She chuckles and checks her phone.

"Am I boring you already?" I ask. She's been on her phone for a few minutes. She looks up from her phone.

"No, sorry, just checking my texts. It is real late though, I have to get home and sleep. It was real nice to see you again." She's nervous and wants to leave. *I need to get her digits so I can stop following her around.*

"Yea, I'm real glad I went out tonight. I got to see you again, think I could get your number?" *Real smooth Jett, hopefully she can't read the desperation on my voice.*

She blushes deep red, and stutters for a second. "Yea, uhh here let me text you, what's yours?" We exchange numbers and I walk with her to her car.

"I'll text you Cora, and maybe I'll see you at the lake again." I give her my smoldering smile. Her face gets even redder than before. *I can tell she wants me. How did I get so lucky to find a Lunafriya, who's smoking hot and wants me back? I can't wait to see her full potential.*

"Ok, yea. I go to the lake quite often so it's possible, Bye Jett!" She hurriedly jumps into the car.

I watch her as she drives off. I have her number and I know where she lives. She shouldn't be in any immediate danger. I should be safe to go home. I will text her in the morning. Now I have to figure out how to break the news to her that first, she's a mermaid. And second, that she's a Lunafriya, a women warrior, who has powers.

I have my work cut out for me.

Cora's perspective

Chapter 3

Brrrrrring…bbbbbrrrrring…bbbbbrrrrring.

Ugh, why is my phone ringing this early on my god damn day off? I check my phone. It's my mom, and it's only eight thirty in the morning.

"Hello?" I say sleepily.

"Hi, honey! Did I wake you up?" My mother sounds too cheerful for this early in the morning.

"Yea, you did. I got home late and then couldn't sleep much." I tell her.

"Do you want me to let you sleep? I can call back later." She says.

"No, it's ok mom, I don't think I could get back to sleep, I'm up now. How are you and dad?" I ask.

My mother likes to talk and will go on and on about anything. I actually like talking to my parents though, you appreciate them more when they get older.

"We are doing great, enjoying retirement. Your father took me to Keego Harbor last week and wouldn't you know it, he went swimming in the frozen lake!" She tells me.

I laugh, "Like father, like daughter, I went swimming at Prism Lake yesterday."

Mom chuckles, "Oh, my crazy fishy family, speaking of fish, do you have to work today?" I was thinking of having you over for dinner."

Home cooked meal? Hell Yes! "I have today off, I would love to come over for dinner! What are you making? Please say meatloaf." I say.

I can hear the smile in her voice. "Mom's miracle meatloaf it is!" She comments.

I feel my phone vibrate on my face, which means I got a text message. "Hold on Mom, I got a text." It's probably Megan letting me know she's ok and on her way home. I check the text, it's Jett!

'Good morning beautiful. I had a lot of fun last night, and since I'm new in town, I don't really know what to do with myself. Let me know when you are free.'

My heart does a somersault. I gasp. *I didn't expect him to text so soon.*

"Who was it, honey?" Mom asks.

"Oh, just a guy I met yesterday" I smile.

"Oh yea? Was he hot?" She jokes.

"Very. We met at the lake. He went swimming too, actually." I say.

"Oh geez, he sounds perfect for you." She replies.

"Yea, well, we'll see. But I'll see you later for dinner, Mom. I have to go, love you." I tell

her.

"I love you too, sweetie." She says then we hang up the phone.

Jett texted me! I have to respond to him but what to write? I wish Megan was home. She would know what to do. I shoot Megan a text, but she's probably just still sleeping.

'Hey, just checking up on you, also Jett texted me this morning!'

I decide to get up and drink some coffee first before I deal with anything. I turn my Keurig on, and it heats up quickly. Double caramel cappuccino, my favorite. My phone buzzes, I check it, and it's Megan.

'Hi, I'm ok, be home soon, got to get ready for work.'

We have been checking up on each other a lot lately. These disappearances have us freaked out. I'm going to wait till Megan gets home to text Jett back. Today is my only other day off this week, besides Sunday. The aquarium is closed on Sunday. So if I am going to hang out with him, it has to be today. I already promised my mom I'd come over for dinner though.

I jump in the shower quickly before Megan gets home, she's going to need one too. She's still not home when I finish. I apply some black eyeliner and mascara, you know, just in case I see a sexy guy. I hear the front door open and shut.

"Hey Megs, I'm up here!" I yell. I hear her coming up the stairs.

Megan knocks on my door, "You decent?" She asks.

"Yea, come on in." I tell her. She opens the door and she looks like shit. Her hair is a crazy bird's nest, and her make-up is smeared across her face. "Well, aren't you a looker." I tease her.

She yawns and smiles. "I may look a mess but it was worth it. Last night was so amazing, Jake knows what he is doing in the bedroom. I know I have a strict one night rule but I might have to break it for him." She says.

"Wow, really! That's surprising!" I say, *it really is not like her. She's always one and done.*

"Have you texted Jett back yet?" She asks.

"No, I was waiting for you, I need your expertise." I tell her.

"Ok, what exactly did he say?" She asks.

I unlock my phone and bring up my text messages. I tell her everything that he said and explain that today is my only day off this week.

"Well, it's obvious, text him that today is the day you're free. If he's not, then you have to wait till next week." Megan yawns. "I need to get ready for work, I won't get good tips looking like this, and hopefully the shower wakes me up." She leaves the room.

Ok I need to text Jett back.

'Good morning! I had fun too. Today is my only day off until next week. I was also planning to go to the lake, want to join me?'

Hope that doesn't sound desperate. A few seconds goes by and my phone buzzes. I check and Jett texted back.

'Yes, see you there.'

I have a big stupid grin on my face. *That was fast! I didn't expect him to answer so quickly.* Now I'm a little nervous. *I get to see him without a shirt on again!* I smile and find my most flattering swim suit, it's a brown swim dress that resembles a scuba suit, with a zipper down the front. I can make it as revealing as I want. I change into it and find my cover all and put that on as well. I grab a change of clothes and my little make-up bag to re-touch after. I want to look nice for my parents. I hear the shower running so I text Megan that I went swimming with Jett and I'll see her after dinner.

I jump into my car, start it up and head to the lake. The drive isn't far, about fifteen minutes. There is no other cars in the parking lot. *I wonder when he'll show up.* I decide to wait for him at the beach. I find my favorite picnic table, it's right under a willow tree, I could just sit here and relax all day and be perfectly happy.

I am reading a book, Harry Potter, to be exact, when I hear his voice, "Nice little nook you got here. I can see why this is your happy place." Jett flashes me a sexy grin. He really is gorgeous with that flashy smile, black spikey hair and well defined body.

I blush, "It's really nice in the winter with all the snow, the tree makes a sort of igloo, I hide in here for hours and nobody ever finds me. Peace and quiet is something I don't really get with Megan as a roommate." I confess.

"That sounds pretty awesome, actually." He says. We are just looking at each other, *I could look at him all day.*

"Want to go swimming?" I ask.

"Most definitely." He replies.

I strip off my cover-all and I hear him sharply inhale. That makes me smile. I have my suit zipped down enough where I have a good amount of cleavage showing. Jett takes off his shirt and I swear he's flexing more than he should be but I like it. *He's so tasty looking. I want to run my hands down those abs to his cock that I know is a decent size, I felt it on my hip while we were dancing yesterday.* I shake myself out of my daze and head to the lake, Jett beside me.

The current of water immediately sets my skin abuzz. *I love this feeling.* My face lights up with my smile. Jett is smiling just as big as I am. He's enjoying it too. I swim around, nothing fancy, just playing around. Jett is watching me and staying near. He's even hotter in the water. His hair is flowing in the waves, his muscles rippling, and glistening. It's enough to make me squirm and tighten my thighs together. He turns me on. I go up for air and he joins.

"This is my true happy place." I say.

"Any water is my happy place." He smiles. We are treading water. I float on my back so I don't look at him too much. Jett floats beside me. We stay like this for at least thirty minutes, letting the water soak into our skin. I really needed this.

"I packed a picnic lunch for us, if you want any food." Jett says.

That's like really sweet, and makes my heart flutter. "A picnic sounds perfect. I didn't eat this morning so I'm getting a little hungry." I smile.

We swim back to shore, I try to out swim him again but we wind up at the shore together. Back at the table under the willow tree, I see the basket. We grab our towels first and dry off a bit before we sit to eat.

Jett opens the basket, "I didn't know what you liked so I made a turkey and cheese sandwich and a peanut butter and jelly sandwich. Some grapes, cheese cubes, crackers and water. You pick what you want."

Wow! He went all out. "I will take the peanut butter and jelly, thanks for this." I say with a smile.

"You're welcome, I knew I'd get hungry so I packed enough for both of us." He replies.

I take a bite of the sandwich and it's good. Normal peanut butter and jelly. I take some grapes and pop one in my mouth. I look at Jett. He looks at me like he has something to say.

"I have to tell you something but you have to promise not to freak out." Jett blurts out.

"Well, it really depends what you are about to say, I can't really make that promise." I reply.

He breathes in deep. "Ok, this is going to sound crazy but…You are in fact, a mermaid, and quite possibly a Lunafriya, who are mermaid warriors with powers." He says.

I laugh, a deep belly laugh. *That's exactly what I am. So Jett' got jokes, does he?* "Well I hate to tell you, but you are a vampire." I joke with a cocky smile.

"Cora, I'm not joking. You seriously are a mermaid." I'm rolling my eyes, he continues. "The water temperature doesn't bother you, you almost beat me in a race, one of your parents is a mer-person, I can guarantee it."

This isn't funny anymore. "Jett, mermaids aren't real, this isn't funny anymore, and you're kind of freaking me out." I say.

"You have to believe me Cora, I'm telling the truth. I am, in fact, a mer-man, and most importantly your guardian. I am from the Halcyon tribe, my tribe are the ones who get assigned as protectors. The other tribes are behind the disappearances in town. I'm not sure which tribe though, they are looking for you. I'm glad I found you before they did." He explains.

My head is spinning and I'm really freaked out at Jett, he's talking crazy. "I'm leaving Jett. Don't follow me, you are scaring me." I manage to say before hurriedly grabbing my stuff and running full blast to my car.

I jump in and slam the door and lock it. I look around and see that he didn't follow me. I can still see him at the picnic table. I start the car and drive away. *Why is it every time I think I meet a new guy, he turns out to be a creep or an asshole?*

I make it home and am still feeling a little weird about everything. I go to my bedroom. Megan is at work so I can't really talk to her. *What the fuck did Jett mean, that I'm a mermaid? It's fairy-tale bullshit. Plus I have legs, dumbass, last I checked mermaids have fins and a tail.*

I grab my laptop and turn it on. Once it loads up, I google search 'are mermaids real?' a bunch of articles come up, some I can tell are bullshit from their web addresses. I did see one article from a mermaid lore book that said that mer-people can have legs while on land and even marry and have children with humans. Some of the humans don't even realize what they married. I gasp. *My father is a swimmer where the temperature doesn't bother him as well. I always just figured that I inherited that trait from him. Maybe I got a lot more from my dad. Good thing I'm going over his house for dinner, I've got a lot of questions for him.*

It's only one in the afternoon so I decide to take a nap, my parents don't expect me until six. I go to set my alarm on my phone when I see I got a text from Jett.

'Please Cora, I didn't mean to freak you out. I am telling the truth. Ask your parents if you don't believe me, they should have some answers.'

I plan on it Jett; I don't reply to him, I just ignore the text and try to take a nap. I toss and turn, trying to get comfortable. My mind won't stop racing. *I've always wanted to be a mermaid. Dreamed of it every night of my childhood. My dad used to tell bedtime stories about mermaids to me. Actually about one in particular. A mermaid named Lunafriya. Is that the name Jett said?* I finally fall asleep but am riddled with nightmares about someone trying to abduct me when I'm leaving work.

I wake with a fright. My heart is racing and tears are falling down my cheeks. I look at my phone and it's nearly time for my alarm to go off. I hate waking up right before the alarm, feels like I get cheated out on more sleep. I actually am glad I woke up from that dream though. It was very vivid, felt almost real. I get up and go look in the mirror. My make-up is a little smudged, I quickly rinse it all off. I want to go bare faced. It's only a quarter till five but I am just going to leave for my parent's house. I'm anxious to talk to my dad.

My parents live about thirty minutes away from my house. I jump into my car and start my journey. The drive takes longer because it's rush hour. I arrive at the time my mom said dinner would be ready. I don't knock on the door, this was my childhood home after all. The house smells amazing. You can really smell the meatloaf.

"Honey! I'm home!" I yell loudly. It's something we always said when we got home.

"I'm in the kitchen, dear!" I hear my mom yell. I walk down the hall into the kitchen.

"Hi mom, meatloaf smells great." I say happily.

"Everything just got done, will you set the table while I get your father." Mom says.

I get the plates, forks, and knives, enough for three. While setting the table, my dad walks in the dining room.

"Hi sweetie! How is everything?" Dad smiles and asks.

Mom is still getting everything from the kitchen so I just blurt out, "Dad, are you a mer-man?" *I couldn't think of a better way to ask. If it's nothing, I can pull it off as a joke.*

My dad gives me the biggest widest eyes ever, "How did you know?" He asks. Mom is coming down the hall, "We will talk after dinner, no more in front of mom." Dad says.

Seriously? My dad is a fucking mer-man? How the hell did I not know this? So Jett might not be crazy after all. Maybe I am a mermaid? That thought makes my heart flutter. *That's been my dream ever since I was a little girl.* Mom comes in with the meatloaf and biscuits.

"I still have to get the mashed potatoes and broccoli, don't start without me." Mom says with a wink.

Mom leaves the room again. I'm about to ask another question when dad says, "Honey, after dinner, I promise, we will talk." And it immediately stalls my questions. Mom comes back in with the rest of dinner. I make my plate and dig in. The food is amazing. I really miss my mom's cooking. Now I have to do all the cooking by myself; Megan is not a good cook, so no help.

"How's everything at the aquarium?" Mom asks.

"It's great! They are letting me do more show feedings and educational lessons. I love it when I get to clean the big tanks. It's like I'm in the ocean." I exclaim.

"That sounds wonderful." Dad says. I continue to eat. The broccoli is perfect, I've always liked broccoli, even as a child.

"How was Keego Harbor?" I ask.

Mom answers, "It was wonderful! There was blue ice formed on the docks, it was really beautiful."

Dad responds, "The water was nice and refreshing. I really needed that soak."

Mom shakes her head, "You guys are crazy, and you can catch a cold swimming right now." I smile, because I understand now. I look at dad and he's not smiling, he actually looks sad.

"What's wrong, dad?" I question him.

"Oh." He shakes his head, "nothing, just a stomach ache." *That sounds like a lie.* I shrug it off and we finish our plates without another word.

I help my mother with clearing the dishes and putting away the leftovers. Mom is putting the dishes in the dishwasher. She doesn't need my help anymore so I go try to find my dad. We desperately need to talk. I find dad in the living room, getting his shoes on.

"Want to go for a drive with your old man?" dad asks

"Yes, I really do. I'll go tell mom." I reply. I go back into the kitchen, mom is still doing the dishes, probably going to be for a while. "Hey mom, dad and I are going to go for a drive." I tell her.

"Ok dear, enjoy your daddy-daughter time, reminds me when you guys used to go to the lake after dinner." She sighs with a smile, eyes glossing over, remembering past events.

"Just like old times I guess, bye mom!" I run out the door. *Finally I will get some answers.* Dad is waiting for me in his car. He has a 2016 ford focus. It's a really nice car. "Where are we going?" I ask.

"The lake, of course, one of the only places around here that is befitting this conversation." Was his response. My pulse quickens. I'm excited yet nervous.

We arrive at Prism Lake. My favorite little lake, my happy place. Dad parks the car and gets out, grabbing some towels from out the back seat. Luckily, I wore a swim suit under my clothes. *I was secretly hoping we'd come here, like old times.* We walk to the beach, it's seven o'clock and already dark, *I hate daylight's savings time. It shouldn't get dark until 9pm.* Dad walks over to the willow tree table, he knows it's my favorite. We set our stuff down and I take off my top and pants. I head to the lake, dad behind me.

The water electrifies my pulse. It feels like I've been missing this my entire life. I look over at dad. He has a sad frown while looking at my glowingly happy face.

"Seriously dad! What is wrong?" I demand.

"This wasn't supposed to happen to you, it's supposed to skip generations when mixed with humans." He replies.

"What is happening to me? Am I turning into a mermaid? Why are you sad about that if you are a mer-man yourself? Does mom know?" I bombard him with questions.

Dad smiles a sad little half smile, "Well, it seems you are not 'turning' into a mermaid, you have been one your whole life. You just didn't know it and I refused to see the signs. I was hoping that you would never really find out the truth. I'm sad because the water is not a good place to be. That is why I left in the first place. Then I met your mother and I decided to never return and live on land. The mer-tribes are in constant war with each other. People die every day. And to answer your last question. No, your mother doesn't know and cannot find out about this. I brought you out here tonight to finally show you the truth."

Dad closes his eyes and scrunches his eyebrows together for a few seconds, then his eyes pop open and his smile widens. He splashes me with his fin. *Wait? HIS FIN?* I look down, it's hard to see in the dark but dad definitely has a tail and no legs.

"Oh my god! Dad, you weren't joking! Oh my god, oh my god." I am freaking out! I feel light headed and dizzy. Dad swims closer and grabs me by the shoulders, holding me lovingly and with concern in his eyes.

"Sweetie, I'm sorry I didn't tell you sooner. Nothing has to change for you if you don't want it too, but I want you to know the other half of who you are now." He says, calming me down. I don't feel dizzy anymore. "Now Coral, close your eyes and focus. Think about your fin, instead of legs. Picture it in your mind. It may take a few times but you will eventually get the hang of it." Dad tries to teach me to summon my fin.

I try, I close my eyes and think real hard. I imagine a fin and not my legs. It feels like nothing happens. I open my eyes and look down. I still have legs. I try again. I close my eyes tight and scrunch my eyebrows like dad did. Still nothing happens. Dad is watching me. I'm getting impatient. "I don't think this is going to work." I say.

"You need to really focus. You should have learned this when you were a toddler but like I said earlier, I didn't want this life for you. It's supposed to skip generations or be non-existent when mixed with humans. I refused to see the signs but now I see they have been clear since you were little. Now, learning all of this while an adult will be tricky. Just focus real hard on your fin." Dad says.

Ok, let's try this again. I shut my eyes tight. I take a deep breath, focusing on a fin instead of legs. I'm trying real fucking hard, squeezing my face, gripping my hands into tight fists. Still nothing seems to be happening. I open my eyes to look down at legs again. I groan, frustrated! *One last try before I give up.*

This time, I think of a repeating dream. One that I have had since I was little. In the dream, I was a mermaid. I had a beautiful purple and green fin. I was catching fish with someone. I remember feeling ecstatic. Every time I have the dream, I get so over-joyed that I wake up. I think about this dream and focus real hard. Something inside me stirs. This gets me excited and I try harder. I hear me dad gasp. I open my eyes and look down.

I have the fin, the fin in my dream, I gasp! Then I look at my dad with a huge smile. He's smiling too but not as happily as I am. I'm so ecstatic, my heart is pounding in my chest. I decide to test out my new fin. I swim about and make a huge splash.

"I know you're excited but you have to keep it quiet, we don't want anyone seeing us." Dad exclaims. *I didn't even think of that.* I look around to make sure nobody is around when I see movement out on the beach, I gasp.

"Dad! Somebody's here, just over there, near our table." I tell him. Dad looks with me, it's hard to see in the dark but I swear I saw something.

"Try to summon your legs again, just in case." Dad whispers to me. I try to think about legs. It didn't work the first couple of tries but eventually I got my legs back. I look and see the person is now making their way over to us, just starting to get into the water. It's a guy, that's about all I can tell right now with him so far away.

"Well, looks like we have some company, stay behind me." Dad says. The guy is getting closer, and now I can now tell that it's Jett, with a huge smile on his face.

I gasp, "Its Jett!"

"Now, who is Jett?" Dad asks.

"He's the one who told me the truth. He said that he's my guardian. He told me to ask you the truth because I didn't believe him.' I explain.

"Guardian? Why would you need a guardian?" Dad questions.

"I don't know, he also said something about a Lunafriya. Which I remember is the name of the woman from your bedtime stories." I tell him.

He gasps, "You remember that? You were so little at the time, I thought you would forget. That's why I told you those stories. He thinks you are a Lunafriya?" Dad asks with concern.

"I don't know, I'm new to all of this. You ask him, he will be here in a minute." I say while watching Jett's fine form coming towards us.

Jett has a huge smile on his face, "So, do you believe me now?" He asks.

I can't stay mad at him, and give him a flirty smile back, "Why, yes I do. My dad has told me the truth." I say with a head nod in my dad's direction.

"Nice to meet you, sir. I'm Jett, your daughter's guardian." Jett shakes my dad's hand.

"And why is it that my daughter needs a guardian? What tribe are you from? Why did you feel the need to tell my daughter that she is a mermaid? She was perfectly fine, not knowing. I wanted a human life for her." My dad is getting an attitude with Jett.

"I'm sorry, sir. I'm from the Halcyon tribe. I was sent here to find a Lunafriya and I believe your daughter is a Lunafriya. I'm sure you remember the stories. She had to know truth if she is going to save our people from the madness that we currently reside." Jett explains.

Wait…I'm meant to save mer-kind? How? I just learned that I am a mermaid, I'm not going to be able to save anyone. I laugh out loud, both of them look at me with bewildered faces.

I blush red, "There is no way I am going to be a savior." I chuckle with embarrassment.

"I'm sure you are." Jett says with a small smile.

"I have to get home now, your mother will wonder where we got off too. Cora, are you ready?" Dad asks. *I don't want to leave so soon, I'm just learning everything. I want to use my fin again.*

"I'm not ready to leave just yet, dad. I want to use my fin some more. I'm sure Jett will give me a ride home." I look over at Jett, pleading at him with my eyes to say yes.

"Of course I will, your wish is my command. She's in good hands with me, sir. I am second in my rank." Jett says to me and my dad. *Whatever that means, I don't get it but my dad seems to understand.*

"Ok then, Cora, please be careful. We will talk more later on. Don't forget to grab your car at my house." Dad replies.

"Thanks, dad. Bye, I love you and I will call you soon." I say while giving my dad a hug.

"Bye sweetie, I love you too." Dad says while swimming away from us. I watch my dad get out of the water and go to the picnic table to dry off.

I glance over at Jett, he is smiling his super sexy smile at me. I smile right back, I can't help it. I'm so fucking happy, my heart could burst. *My childhood wish came true.*

"I'll show you mine, if you show me yours. Your fin that is." Jett says with a cocky half smile.

I raise my eyebrows, "Ok, I'll try." I close my eyes and focus on my dream. I feel the same weird motion in my legs, and I know that I summoned my fin. I smile and open my eyes. Jett is right in front of me, eyes big and round. *I want to kiss him so badly. He's making me want him, right here, right now.* I look down and he has his fin too.

I gasp, *his fin is orange and green, with a hint of black, I think. It looks exactly like the other person in my reoccurring dream.* "I think I've dreamed about this since I was little." I tell Jett.

"What do you mean?" He gives me a questioning smile.

"I've had a repeating dream, ever since I was a toddler. That I was a mermaid, with my exact fin, catching fish with a mer-man, with your exact fin." I explain.

"Well, that is interesting." He chuckles and thinks for a few minutes, I can see the wheels turning inside his head, so to speak. "Let's see what your new fin can do!" He says out of the blue.

Yes! This is what I want. I smile and start swimming away from him fast. Jett is right behind me, trying to grab my tail playfully, but I keep just out of his reach. *I'm having the time of my life, right now.* I can see in the water better when I have my fin summoned. I notice that, and I'm swimming twice as fast as I do with my legs.

Finally, Jett grabs a hold of me and pulls me back to him. We are laughing while he wraps his arms around me. *I'm surprised that I can laugh and talk in the water but I guess that comes with the whole mermaid package.* I can feel his heartbeat in his chest. Its beating sort of fast. I look up at his face and he looks down at me. *'Kiss me,'* I plead with my eyes. He leans his face down to mine, it feels like we are about to kiss. Then he shakes his head and lets go of me.

"We can't do this. I'm sorry. I am your guardian. It doesn't matter how badly I want you. We can never be. I took an oath, not to fraternize with my charges." He says with sad eyes.

I scoff at him. "First of all, I don't need a guardian, so fuck off on that one. Second of all, no oaths are going to tell me who I can and cannot be with."

"Cora, you don't understand. Down in the ocean, it's a complete war-zone. None of the tribes get along, and are constantly fighting with each other. Many people die, or leave to live on land, to get away from the wars, like your father did. You will need a guardian down there, especially if you are a Lunafriya, like I think you are. We have to go down to my city and the council will decide if I made the correct choice. I am very lucky to have found you first, before the other tribes did. They are the ones behind the disappearances around town." Jett explains.

I gasp. *The disappearances, they were trying to find me?* "What do you mean, Jett? About the disappearances, I was the person they, the bad guys, were looking for? Why?" I ask.

"Like I said before, you are a Lunafriya, the first one in one hundred and fifty years. I am sure of it, that's what all the tribes are looking for. Some tribes for sinister reasons, others, like myself, we're looking to save you, so you can save us." Jett says.

I'm getting frustrated, "How am I going to save anyone lest of all the whole mer-people population? I don't know a thing about war or the world of mermaids." I tell him.

Jett smiles his stupid sexy grin, "I will tell you the stories another time, now I think it's been enough of an exciting new day for you. Let's call it a night and I will drive you home."

We swim to the shore and I stop to summon my legs again. They feel like jelly, while walking onto the beach. *I swear, I feel like a baby deer.* I get my towel and dry off. Still feeling a little disappointed that Jett didn't kiss me.

"Where's your car?" I ask because I still don't see a car in the parking lot.

"It's at my house. I live right over there to the side of the lake." He says.

"Well, that's convenient." I reply. I follow Jett through the bushes to his house.

"This is my tribe's property, not really my house, mine is in the ocean." He say with a smile. *I love that smile.* We get to the house and it's a beautiful little ranch style house. "It's really not that late. Want to hang out and watch something? The house has a very extensive DVD collection in the theater room." Jett asks.

"Sure, let's see what you got." I say. He takes me to the theater room as he called it. It's really just a big screen TV and loveseat couches. One of the walls is filled with shelves of DVDs. I'm in awe, I have never seen this many movies or TV shows in one place. "Why is there so many?" I ask.

"We don't get movies down in the water so my tribe stocked the house up. We have every genre. Go ahead, pick one. I haven't seen much of them." Jett says with a smile.

I look at the wall, it's too intimidating. I see some seasons of 'The Office', my favorite show, so I grab the first season. "Let's watch this, it's my favorite." I state.

He pops it into the DVD player and I get comfortable on the couch. The show starts and Jett plops down on the couch next to me. Our legs are touching and it's driving me wild. *I want him so badly. I have to distract myself because if I don't, I will jump on him. Plus I actually have some more questions.*

"Sorry to interrupt the show, but why are the tribes in war with each other?" I ask.

Jett responds, "There are lots of factors but mostly right now, it's about boundaries. Also two of the tribes think we shouldn't go on land ever. They will kill on sight."

He laughs, he's still trying to watch the show while talking to me. I stop asking questions and just watch with him. I've seen all of the episodes but I love the early seasons, where you get the sexual tension between Jim and Pam. We are laughing at the same parts. We watch like ten episodes and I'm getting tired. I end up just closing my eyes for a second and drifting off to sleep. I had a dream that night about Jett and me. It was very hot and heavy and realistic. *Let's hope that dream comes true too.*

Chapter 4

Jett's perspective

I wake up with a massive boner. *God damn morning wood. Well I shouldn't let it go to waste.* I pull my dick out and start stroking. Thinking about Cora in that low-cut blue shirt from last night. *I shouldn't even be thinking of her like this but fuck it. I can't get in trouble for jerking it.* I come fast and hard. Something about Cora just does this to me. I don't know if I can stop myself and keep my hands off her.

I decide to text her, *I need to keep a close eye on her and to tell her the truth of what she is, since her parents haven't yet.* I grab my phone and type, 'Good morning beautiful. I had a lot of fun last night, and since I'm new in town, I don't really know what to do with myself. Let me know when you are free.'

Now it's a waiting game. *I'm awake so I might as well work out. Nothing much else to do around here except watch movies and I don't want to do that right now.* I work out for about an hour and still no text back. I jump into the shower quickly. I hear my text notification while I'm drying off. I check it, and it's Cora.

"Good morning! I had fun too. Today is my only day off till next week, I was planning to go to the lake, want to join me?"

I text her back right away, "Yes, see you there."

It's about ten in the morning, and I haven't eaten yet so I decide to pack us some sandwiches. I'm always hungry and eat one instead of packing it. Then make another. I don't know what she likes so I make a peanut butter and jelly sandwich and a turkey with cheese. Two safe sandwiches that anyone should like. Some crackers, cheese cubes, grapes, and water bottles should be enough for the both of us. I grab my swimsuit and put it on. Cora never said what time to meet at the lake. I get the picnic basket and fill it up with the food, grab a towel and decide to head down to the lake and wait for her. I walk down the trail from my house to the bushes that open up to the lake. I see Cora sitting on a table under a willow tree, reading a book.

"Nice little nook you got here. I can see why this is your happy place." I say once I reach her and flash her my lady killer smile.

She is so beautiful, with her sweet face and plump breasts. She blushes, "It's really nice in the winter with all the snow. The tree makes a sort of igloo, I hide in here for hours and nobody ever finds me. Peace and quiet is something I don't really get with Megan as a roommate." She confesses.

"That sounds pretty awesome actually." I say. We are just staring at each other, I could look at her all day.

"Want to go swimming?" She asks.

"Most definitely." I reply.

She strips off her clothes and I sharply inhale. *Damn, her body is sexy. I want that body against mine.* I take off my shirt and flex my muscles to give her a little show, I swear I hear her gulp. I look at her and she's checking out my body, this makes me smile. She shakes her head and starts heading towards the lake, me beside her.

I never get tired of the feeling of the water on my skin. It warms my entire body. I look over at Cora and she is smiling just as big as I am. *She's enjoying it too.* She swims around. I watch her and stay close to her. Her hair is flowing in the water. *It's long and I would love to grab it and fuck her from behind. I really have to stop picturing her in those situations. It's against my oath for me to get involved with my subject.* She comes up for air and I join her, not really needing any, but I have to play the part.

"This is my true happy place." She says.

Because you're a mermaid. I say in my head, but out loud I say, "Any water is my happy place." I smile.

We are treading water. She floats on her back. This just makes me zone in on her tits so I float beside her, to stop my staring. *Hopefully I don't have an erection right now.* We stay like this for at least half an hour, letting the water soak into our skin, *I really needed this, it would be better with my fin though.*

"I packed a picnic lunch for us, if you want any food." I say.

Her eyes glaze over, "A picnic sounds perfect, I didn't eat yet this morning so I'm getting a little hungry." She smiles.

We swim back to shore, she tries to out swim me but I won't let her win, we tie again. Back at the table under the willow tree, we grab our towels first and dry off a bit before we sit to eat. I open the basket, "I didn't know what you liked so I made a turkey with cheese and a peanut butter and jelly sandwich. Some grapes, cheese cubes, and crackers, and water. You pick what you want." I tell her.

Her eyes get big and she smiles, "I will take the peanut butter and jelly, thanks for this." She says.

"Your welcome, I knew I'd get hungry so I packed enough for both of us." I reply. She takes a single bite of her sandwich while I devour mine. *It looks like it's now or never, I have to tell her the truth. Hopefully she doesn't think I'm a crazy person and I don't fuck this up.* I'm staring at her. She looks at me with a questioning look.

"I have to tell you something but you have to promise not to freak out." I blurt out.

"Well, it really depends what you are about to say, I can't really make that promise." She replies.

I take a deep breath, *here it goes, all or nothing.* "Ok, this is going to sound crazy but you are, in fact, a mermaid, and quite possibly a Lunafriya, who are mermaid warriors with powers."

She laughs, a deep belly laugh. *She thinks I'm joking.* "Well, I hate to tell you, but you are a vampire." She jokes with a cocky smile.

I put my serious face on. "Cora, I'm not joking. You seriously are a mermaid." She's rolling her eyes, I continue, "The water temperature doesn't bother you, you almost beat me in a race. One of your parents is a mer-person, I can guarantee it."

She is getting frustrated, I can tell. "Jett, mermaids aren't real, this isn't funny anymore, and you're kind of freaking me out." She says.

"You have to believe me, Cora. I'm telling the truth. I am, in fact, a mer-man, and most importantly your guardian. I am from the Halcyon tribe; the other tribes are the ones behind the disappearances in town. I'm not sure which tribe though. They are looking for you, I'm glad I found you before they did." I tell her.

This is not going how I hoped it would. She needed to know the truth but she is freaking out right now.

"I'm leaving Jett, don't follow me, you are scaring me." She says before hurriedly grabbing her stuff and running full blast to her car. She jumps in the car and slams the door, I can hear it slam from the beach. I am watching her from the picnic table. She starts the car and drives away. *Great Jett, you fucked this up too. Hopefully she will see the truth eventually and come back to me.*

I text her, *just one last try*, 'Please Cora, I didn't mean to freak you out. I am telling the truth. Ask your parents if you don't believe me, they should have some answers.' She doesn't text back.

I decide to go back into the water and summon my fin. *I need to tell the council about my discovery.* There is a portal at the very bottom of this lake that connects to the Atlantic Ocean, which is where my city is. I go through the portal and arrive in a cave. I swim to the opening, checking my surroundings.

The water is a very dangerous place. You have to worry about the wildlife trying to eat you and the other tribes trying to kill you. I don't see anything around so I make my way towards the city gates, still constantly looking about. At the city gates are two armed guards, with armor and spears. I recognize them as Krill and Beck, guys that were in training with me. Beck is a lot of fun, and a great funny guy. Krill is always serious and to the point. He and I never really got along, plus he has a thing for my sister, so it makes me hate him even more.

"Hey guys, I've got news for the council." I state.

"Alright, Jett, go on through." Beck remarks with a smile.

I push the gate open and swim into the city. Nothing has changed since the last time I was here, but it has only been two months since I was home. All of the buildings are pearlescent and crystal like. I swim to the council chambers inside town hall, waving at people I know.

Caol is guarding the door. Caol is my best friend. He waves and says, "Hey Jett! How's the mission going? Been awhile since we had a report."

I smile, "I think I've found her Caol. I need to report to the council." I tell him. *I can't help but tell him, he's stuck by my side through everything.*

His eyes get wide. "The elders are in the council room, go on in." He says.

I clap his back while walking into the council room, all of the elders are at the head table. Master Zale speaks first, "Jett, my boy! Do you have any news for us?" Master Kae, and Master Yarrow are both just staring at me, waiting.

"Sirs, I think I have found a Lunafriya. I have found a women, about twenty-two, who is a mermaid but didn't know it." I tell them.

Master Yarrow speaks now, "That does not mean she is a Lunafriya. Has she shown any powers?"

"No, sir, but I only met her yesterday. I have a really good feeling about this one. I told her the truth of what she is today and she freaked out and left. I implored her to ask her parents the truth. I'm sure one of them is mer-kind. She should be back." I reply.

Master Zale nods his head, Master Kae asks his brothers in arms, "Who do we know that could be the parent of this young woman? Caro, Finn, Ray?"

Master Yarrow answers him, "She could be the offspring of any of the tribes."

"Master Yarrow is right, she could be from any of the tribes, but I do hope she is Ray's. It would be wonderful to have a granddaughter. Jett, I would like you to find out as much information about this woman as you can. See if she develops any powers, answer all her questions, and persuade her to join the Halcyon tribe." Master Zale says to all of us.

"You have my word, it will be done." I bow, "Let the water flow freely." I chant.

"Let the water flow freely," all three masters say in unison.

I'm dismissed so I leave the room. Caol is still standing guard outside the door. I say goodbye to him and swim away. It's been awhile since I've been home so I stop by before heading back to land. My sister Meri is home, I can see her through the window. I scare her while swimming into the house.

"Damn it, Jett! Don't do that!" Meri screams at me.

I laugh, just like old times. "Hey sis, good to see you." I give her a hug.

"How have you been? You've been gone for two months. How is the mission going?" Meri bombards me with questions

"I've been fine, enjoying myself, but I've recently found someone who quite possibly could be a Lunafriya." I tell her

Meri squeals, "Really! I would love to meet her!" She is zipping back and forth excitedly.

"Hold your seahorses, I just met her yesterday, and possibly fucked everything up. I freaked her out by telling her that she's a mermaid. Hopefully she'll still talk to me." I try to calm her down.

"I'm sure she'll come around, what's her name?" Meri asks.

"Cora." I sigh with a smile.

"Uh, oh big brother, you catching feelings? I know that look." She gives me a cheeky smile.

"She's the fucking most beautiful woman I've ever met, but she is my subject and I will not break my oath." I state with a serious look. "I really need to get back to land and watch out for her. I just stopped by to see you before I left." Our parents died in the war when we were little. We are the only family we have left.

"Please be careful." Meri says.

"You too." I reply. We hug one last time and say "Let the water flow freely," to each other before I swim out the door and out of the city. I look around before heading back to the portal. Once I'm at Prism Lake, I summon my legs and swim to the shore. I grab my phone from its hiding spot and check for messages from Cora, there's nothing.

I pop her number into the GPS on my phone to get a location on her cell. It's at a house. I look up the address and see its Ray and Nancy Marina's property. Further investigation showed they are the parents of a Coral Marina. *Cora must be short for Coral. It's such a perfect name for her.*

Ray, isn't that the name Master Zale mentioned? She is at her parents' house and should be safe. I get all my stuff and head home. *I'll make a quick dinner and wait for her to contact me, or...comes to the lake, whichever is first.* I keep watch on my phone and on the beach from my window. It's dark but I can see if she is there. A couple of hours go by, and nothing.

Finally, I see two people swimming in the lake. *It has to be Cora and one of her parents. No one else would be swimming in this weather.* I make my way down to the beach and set my stuff at the table under the willow tree. I take off my shirt and head for the water. Right to Cora. *I saw her jump out of the water on my way down here. I know she has her fin.*

I have a huge smile on my face, "So, do you believe me now?" I ask.

She gives me a flirty smile, "Why, yes I do, my dad has told me the truth." She says with a head nod in her dad's direction.

"Nice to meet you, sir. I'm Jett, your daughter's guardian." I shake her dad's hand.

"And why is it that my daughter needs a guardian? What tribe are you from? Why did you feel the need to tell my daughter that she is a mermaid? She was perfectly fine not knowing, I wanted a human life for her." Her dad is being hostile with me. *I have to defuse this situation.*

"I'm sorry sir, I'm from the Halcyon tribe. I was sent here to find a Lunafriya and I believe your daughter is a Lunafriya. I'm sure you remember the stories. She had to know the truth if she is going to save our people from the madness that we currently reside." I explain.

Her dad even looks like Master Zale. I'm sure he is his son. Cora starts to laugh out loud. I look at her with bewilderment.

She blushes red. "There is no way I am going to be a savior." She chuckles with embarrassment.

"I'm sure you are." I tell her with a small smile.

"I have to get home now, your mother will wonder where we got off too. Cora, are you ready?" her dad asks.

I don't want her to leave yet. "I'm not ready to leave yet, dad. I want to use my fin some more. I'm sure Jett will give me a ride home." She looks over at me, pleading with her eyes to say yes.

"Of course I will, your wish is my command. She's in good hands with me sir, I am second in my rank." I say.

"Ok then, Cora please be careful. We will talk more later on. Don't forget to grab your car at my house." Her dad replies.

"Thanks, dad. Bye, I love you and I will call you soon." She says while giving her dad a hug.

"Bye sweetie, I love you too." Her dad says while swimming away from us.

I look at Cora. *It's just us now and I'm turned on. I have a stupid grin on my face but so does she so I don't care.* "I'll show you mine if you show me yours. Your fin that is." I say with a cocky half smile.

She raises her eyebrows, "Ok, I'll try." She closes her eyes and smiles.

I summon my fin as well. *Her fin is amazing, all purple and green with swirl patterns.* I can't help it, I swim right up to her, just inches from her face. *I want to kiss her so badly.* She opens her eyes and stares into my eyes for a minute before she looks down and notices my fin.

She gasps, "I think I dreamed about this since I was little." She tells me.

"What do you mean?" I give her a questioning smile.

"I've had a repeating dream, ever since I was a toddler, that I was a mermaid, with my exact fin, catching fish with a mer-man, with your exact fin." She explains.

"Well, that is interesting." I chuckle. *I wonder if that is a power she has. She can maybe dream of the future. I will have to tell the council of this and of Ray.* I snap out of my daze.

"Let's see what your new fin can do!" I say to change the subject. She smiles and starts swimming away from me fast. I am right behind her, playfully grabbing at her tail, but she keeps just out of my reach. *This is a fun little game but I need her.* I grab a hold of her and pull her back to my chest. We are laughing while I wrap my arms around her. *I really need to stop and think about what I am doing but my dick is running the show right now.*

My heart is beating so fast inside my chest. She is so near to me. I am loving this skin to skin contact. She looks up at me and I look down at her. She is giving me bedroom eyes, she wants me bad, too. I lean my face down to hers, ready to kiss her and fuck her breathless.

Then I come to my senses*, I can't do this*, and let go of her. "We can't do this, I'm sorry. I am your guardian. It doesn't matter how badly I want you, we can never be. I took an oath, not to fraternize with my subject." I say with sad eyes.

She scoffs at me. "First of all, I don't need a guardian so fuck off on that one. Second of all, no oaths are going to tell me who I can and cannot be with."

"Cora, you don't understand. Down in the ocean, it's a complete war zone. None of the tribes get along, and are constantly fighting with each other. Many people die, or leave to live on land, to get away from the wars, like your father did. You will need a guardian down there, especially if you are a Lunafriya, like I think you are. We have to go down to my city and the council will decide if I made the correct choice. I am very lucky to have found you first, before the other tribes did. They are the ones behind the disappearances around town." I explain.

She gasps, "What do you mean Jett? About the disappearances, I was the person they, the bad guys, were looking for? Why?" She asks

"Like I said before, you are a Lunafriya, I am sure of it. That's what all the tribes are looking for. Some tribes for sinister reasons, others, like myself, we're looking to save you, so you can save us." I say.

She is getting frustrated, I can tell. "How am I going to save anyone least of all the whole mer-people population? I don't know a thing about war or the world of mermaids." She replies.

I smile, "I will tell you the stories another time, now I think it's been enough of an exciting new day for you. Let's call it a night and I will drive you home."

We swim to shore. She stops to summon her legs and I help her walk to the table, *her legs are sure to feel weird now.* I get my towel and dry off.

"Where's your car?" She asks.

"It's at my house. I live right over there to the side of the lake." I say.

"Well, that's convenient." She replies and follows me through the bushes to my house.

"This is my tribe's property, not really my house, mine is in the ocean." I say with a smile. *She really is sexy wearing her wet suit under her clothes.* "It's really not that late, want to hang out and watch something? The house has a very extensive DVD collection in the theater room." I ask.

"Sure let's see what you got." She says, I take her to the theater room. "Why is there so many?" She asks once she sees the DVD wall.

"We don't get movies down in the water so my tribe stocked the house up. We have every genre. Go ahead, pick one, I haven't seen much of them." I say with a smile.

She picks one quickly, "Let's watch this, it's my favorite." She states.

I grab the DVD from her and pop it into the player and she gets comfortable on the couch. The show starts and I plop down on the couch next to her. Our legs are touching, on purpose. *I want to feel her.* This show is pretty good, it's funny.

"Sorry to interrupt the show, but why are the tribes in war with each other?" She asks.

I respond quickly, "There are lots of factors but mostly right now it's about boundaries. Also two of the tribes think we shouldn't go on land ever. They will kill on sight."

I laugh, still trying to watch the show while talking to her. We watch six episodes and I notice that she fell asleep. She is still in her wet clothes but I don't want to invade her privacy. I carry her to my bed and wrap her in my blanket. She looks so peaceful sleeping. I lay down next to her and let her sleep. *It's better to be with her, for her protection. I try to tell myself that but really I just want to snuggle with her.* I wrap my arm and legs around her and fall asleep myself.

Chapter 5

Cora's perspective

I wake with a fright. *Where am I?* I feel heavy arms around me. I look and it's Jett. *I must be in his bedroom. I must have fell asleep and he must have taken me to bed.* I look at the clock. It's nine in the morning, I have to be at work in two hours. I shake Jett awake. "Hey sleepy head" I say once he stirs.

"Good morning, beautiful!" He says with a smile.

"Sorry I fell asleep." I reply sheepishly.

"Don't worry about it, you had a big day yesterday." He says with a yawn. *It really was a crazy day. It's not every day that you find out your dad is a mer-man and because of that, you are a mermaid.*

"I have to go to work soon, so I'll need a ride to my car, please." I inform Jett. "Have you seen my phone? I ask him.

"It died so I plugged it in for you, over there." He says while pointing to the nightstand.

I grab my phone and it's off. I turn it on, while sitting on his bed. Once it's on, I see seven missed calls and several texts, all from Megan. She's freaking out because I didn't text her where I was yesterday and I didn't come home last night. I quickly call her. It only rings half a ring before Megan picks up.

"Cora! Cora, are you alright? Where are you?" She asks slightly hysterical.

"I'm ok Megan, sorry, I forgot to text you. I fell asleep at Jett's house on accident." I tell her.

"You slut." She says and I can tell she's smiling.

I blush, not knowing if Jett could hear her over the phone. He is getting dressed and I can't help but watch a little. "It's not like that. I'll be home in a bit, just didn't want to worry you anymore." I say to her.

"Ok, bitch, see you soon." She says.

"Bye." I hang up the phone.

"Do you want any coffee or breakfast before I take you to your car?" Jett asks.

"No, thanks, I have to hurry home and get ready." I tell him.

"Ok, let's go if you're ready then." He says.

I grab my phone and swim bag, then follow him into the garage. His car is a rental, makes sense though. I tell him how to get to my parents, and he nods in understanding.

"I know I don't really have to say this but just in case, do not summon your fin in front of anyone except your dad and me, for now. And don't tell anyone about you being a mermaid, even jokingly. We don't know who is behind these disappearances yet, so you have to be careful around everyone, understand?" Jett explains and asks.

"Yes, I understand." I say with a head nod. He smiles and I smile right back. *I am falling for this guy and I can't even be with him. This isn't fair at all. Finally, I found someone and he's untouchable.* I get a little sad, and a frown appears.

"What's wrong?" Jett asks, he noticed my mood shift.

"Nothing" is my response.

He pulls up to my parents' house, where my car is. He turns to face me, grabbing my cheek with his hand lightly, so I'll look at him. "Seriously, what's wrong? You look so sad and I don't like it." Jett asks again. The sexual tension between us is getting stronger.

"It's just...not fair. I found someone that I actually like and nothing can become of it." I tell him, just letting my heart out to him. He makes me feel safe. He gives me his sad eyes now.

"Oh Cora, I'm sorry, I feel the same way. It's killing me, not being able to touch you, kiss you...and make you come." He says with a hungry look in his eye. I inhale a bit of air, *he is making me so wet right now.* I bite my lip. "I've been dreaming of it every night since I've met you." He says.

"Actually, I have too." I tell him while squirming in my seat trying to release this pressure in my groin. We have gravitated towards each other, getting closer by the second, staring into each other's eyes. *I want this so badly,* I can't help myself. I pounce at him, smacking my lips against his. We kiss passionately, swirling my tongue against his. He tastes good. I break the kiss. "I'm sorry." I say.

"Get back here." He grabs the back of my neck and brings me to his lips again. Sucking and nibbling at his lips, my hands rubbing his muscles over his shirt and in his hair. *We shouldn't be doing this, it will get him into trouble, but I can't help myself, I want him too badly.* We kiss until we are out of breath. We pull apart and breathe heavily.

"Fuck, Cora." He says while resting his forehead against mine and tugging my hair a bit, it feels good.

"Yes, please." I whisper, he sucks in a breath and exhales slowly.

He unlocks the car door, "You better go before you're late for work." He sighs out.

"Yea, you are right. When will I see you next?" I ask.

"When is your shift over tonight?" He asks me back.

"Seven." I tell him.

"Do you want to come over after work? I can make you dinner and we can watch more of 'the office', that was a really good show." He says.

"Sounds like a plan." I reply, "Bye Jett!"

"Bye, beautiful." He says.

I shut the door and head to my car, start it and back out the driveway. I watch Jett out of the rear-view mirror. He is running his hand through his hair, while staring off into space. I drive off, with only an hour to get ready and make it on time. *I will have to be quick.* I make it home and run to the house. The aquarium is about a thirty minute drive from my house. That means I only have about twenty minutes to get ready. I quickly take a shower, probably the shortest shower I've ever taken, just washed my hair. While I am getting dressed, Megan knocks on my door. "Come in!" I call out.

She opens the door and sits on my bed. "Hey bitch." She says.

"Hey, how was work last night?" I ask her.

"It was good, I made two hundred. Jake came in, but he was being weird though. Just kept asking questions about you." She replied.

"About me? Why?" I ask confused.

"I don't know, he asked if you liked to swim a lot. What your parents did for a living, if you had a boyfriend. It was enough to the point I called him out on it. Asked him why he was so curious. He said no reason and dropped the conversation. I don't think I will see him again. He was just creeping me out." She explained.

"That is kind of creepy. I agree, stay away from him." I say and mentally remind myself to tell Jett about that.

"When do you work today?" She asks.

"At eleven, I have to hurry out of here very soon." I respond.

"Want to have a girl's night in after work?" She asks.

My face deflates, "I'm sorry, I already made plans with Jett after work. How about tomorrow after work?" I say.

"I work a double tomorrow, damn our work schedules. I feel like we never see each other anymore." Megan states.

I give a little chuckle, *she is so over-dramatic.* "We just went out two days ago. I will hold Sunday open just for you, how about that? We could go for a run, or whatever you want." I say.

"Ok, Sunday. We will wake up early and go for a run, then out to breakfast, then we will have a movie marathon all day!" Megan is jumping on my bed while telling me her plans for our Sunday.

"Sounds good, now I have to go to work or I'll be late, bye Megan!" I give her a hug then run out the door. I hate being late to anything, it gives me anxiety. I usually arrive at least fifteen minutes early. Looks like today I will arrive just in time to open the aquarium, and that's if I speed the entire way down the freeway. Luckily I make it to work with five minutes to spare.

I run to the building. Jenny, my boss and co-owner of the aquarium with her husband Steve, is holding the back door open for me. "Late start today, huh, Cora?" She smirks. *She knows I'm always early.*

"Yea, but I made it on time!" I tell her.

"That you did. Hurry, let's get this place open. I see some people waiting to get in the front door." She says.

I hurry inside and put my stuff in my locker and head on to the touch pool area. This is where I'm starting my day. Jenny usually works the front desk and her husband Steve does some educational lessons, but mostly works on feeding the fish and maintaining all the tanks.

Today, Steve is doing a lesson and feeding on the sharks. The aquarium is not that large but we do have a couple sharks and some sea turtles. Mostly fresh water fish but the largest tank is the salt water tank. That's the tank I like to clean, it feels like the ocean and I actually have to get inside the tank to clean it. I've been working here since my junior year of high school. I've been the only constant worker, except for the owners, of course. Everyone else seems to leave after one season. I like working the touch pool because of the kids. It's really funny to see some kids grossed out by touching the starfish, crabs, and such. Then some other kids love it!

There are a few families that are regulars, meaning they have paid a yearly membership and come in any time we are open. Most of the regulars know me by name. I see Ashley walk in with her twin boys, Mark and Adam. She's a stay at home mom, who's boys love the touch pool, and one of our regulars. The boys usually like to hang out all day at the touch pool, which is okay with me because then Ashley and I get to talk all day. She's a few years older than I am but we hit it off instantly.

"Hi Cora!" Mark screams, while both the boys are running and waving at me. "We're going to McDonald's for lunch!" Adam tells me.

"You are! Well that sounds very yummy." I say while looking at Ashley, she's rolling her eyes and smiling. The boy proceed to touching the starfish.

"How have you been, Cora?" Ashley asks me. She doesn't get much adult time so her getting to chat with me is a god send to her. She tells me this all the time.

"Well, since the last time we talked was about four days ago and not much has happened, I'm going to say I've been good." I laugh and tell her *but if only she knew, a lot has actually happened. I just can't tell her though, Jett warned me not too. Thinking of Jett, that's something I can tell her.* "Actually, something did kind of happen, I met a guy." I smile while telling her.

She smiles too, "Well, that's exciting! What's his name? What does he look like? Give me the details, sista!" She asks with gusto.

I chuckle. "His name is Jett and he's so gorgeous. Looks like a mix between Channing Tatum and Robert Downing Jr. Super buff with black hair." *And an awesome looking fin,* I add in my head.

"Oh man, that does sound hot! Be careful though, don't want to end up like me!" She says while holding her belly.

"What? Are you pregnant again?" I ask happily.

"Yes, I am! It's too early to tell but I am hoping it's a girl this time!" She says.

"Oh yea, I bet, being outnumbered with all boys. Congrats Ashley!" I say while giving her a hug. The boys are still playing in the touch pool. *Three kids, I don't know if I could do it but good for her.*

"Thank you! It wasn't planned but a very happy surprise for us." She says.

"Momma, I want to go see the sharks now." Mark whines to his mother.

"Alright, alright, let's go see the sharks." Ashley says to the boys. "I'll see you probably in a couple of days, Cora. You know these boys love this aquarium."

"They sure do, bye Ashley, bye boys. Have fun and enjoy your happy meals!" I tell them while they leave my area.

A bunch of families are coming in now and I make my best expressions to the new kids enjoying the touch pool. "Look everyone! The starfish are moving. You can pick up the crabs but please just touch the other fish, do not pick them up, for it will hurt them." *I love the smiling faces of kids looking at fish. It reminds me of myself at their ages.*

The rest of the day goes by pretty quickly up until lunch. I take my lunch break while the new girl fills in for me at the touch pool area. I think her name is Jean but I could be wrong. After my lunch, I am scheduled to do an educational lesson on the seahorses. I'm eating my lunch, just a salad from home, when my boss Steve walks in.

"Hey Cora, Jean has to go home, she's not feeling well. Can you cover the touch pool the rest of the night? I will do the seahorse lesson for you." Steve says.

God damn it, that sucks. I was really looking forward to the lesson. "Yea, Steve, that's fine." I tell him even though I'm a little disappointed.

"Ok, thanks, sorry. I know how you like to do the lessons for the kids. Want to do the feeding and lesson on the rays tomorrow instead? I will cover the touch pool then." He asks.

"Yea, that will be fun." I say with a smile. *I like feeding all the creatures but the manta rays are my favorite. I just feel like they actually listen to me, and do what I want them to do. Even though, that's crazy. Then again, if someone told me mermaids were real, I'd of said they were crazy. In fact, I did tell Jett he was crazy. It's hard to know what's real or not now.* "I'm on lunch for another ten minutes, then I'll go to the pool." I tell him.

"Thank you." Steve says while leaving the break room. I pull out and check my phone. I have a text from Jett.

"Hey beautiful, do you like spaghetti?"

I do like spaghetti, it's one of my favorites. Whenever I make it, I have leftovers for days and it's so filling. He really needs to knock off the flirting crap if he won't allow us to be together. I text him back, 'Hi, yes I love spaghetti. You need to stop calling me beautiful. It's not fair if we can only be friends. Going back to work and I won't have my phone on me.'

I push send and put my phone back into my locker with my purse. I head back to the touch pool. Steve was covering the area. *Jean must have gone home already.* I go to Steve to let him know I'm back.

"Hiya kids! Want to see something cool? I say loudly.

"YEAH!" A bunch of kids shout.

We are kind of busy today. I reach my hand in the water and try to see if the starfish will crawl on my hand. I wait for about thirty seconds, willing the fish with my thoughts and the starfish actually crawls on my hand. It has done this several times before. It's just a friendly starfish, who of course, I named Patrick. It's a cool party trick for the kids. I lift my hand out of the water to show them the starfish on my palm. Some kids say wow and some others are scared a bit. I let them touch the fish for a little bit before putting him back into the water.

I see a cute little curly headed blond boy, around two years old, squealing at the horseshoe crabs. I go over to him and pick up the crab out of the water to show him a better look. He squeals again and touches it. He laughs and looks at his dad, I look up and it's Kevin, my ex. My heart drops and my face immediately frowns. *He knows I fucking work here.*

"Hey, Cora." He is blushing and looking slightly embarrassed. "Camden really wanted to see the fishies. He is really into 'Finding Nemo' right now." He says.

"Hi" is all I manage to say. *I'm looking for a way out, I don't want to talk to him any longer than I have too.*

"How's the boyfriend?" He asks.

I smile a big fake, but one that doesn't look fake smile. *At least, I hope.* "Jett is wonderful, thanks for asking. He has asked me to move in with him." I lie. *Why did I lie to him? Whatever, it's a harmless lie.*

"Oh, wow. I didn't know you guys were serious." Kevin says.

"Yup, life is pretty good right now." I tell him. *Life is pretty good right now, I'm a mermaid. An actual fucking mermaid, but I don't tell him that.*

"That sucks, I always thought of us as Jim and Pam." He says to me.

I chuckle a bit. "I am Pam, but you are no Jim Halpert, you are Roy. Jett is my Jim, get that into your head. We will never happen again, do you hear me?" I whisper to him so his son doesn't hear. *He is looking so sad but I don't give a fuck.* "Well, I have to attend to the other guests. Bye Kevin, bye Camden, nice to meet you." I say to his son. I even give him a little high five. *I am not going to be mean to a child because I hate his father's guts.*

I can't wait to get off work to see Jett. I also want to text Megan and tell her about Kevin coming into my work but that will have to wait till I clock out. A couple hours go by, it is an hour before we close now. I am busy with the kids at the touch pool, when I hear someone say my name. I turn around and it's Jake. *The guy that Megan went home with the other night. The one, who was being weird and asking her all those questions about me. She must have told him I worked here or something.*

"Hi, can I help you?" I ask him. I'm playing nonchalant, even though I'm a little freaked out right now. All of my senses are going haywire, telling me to get away from this man.

"I don't know if you remember me but it's Jake from the other night." He says.

I'm just going to play dumb. "Oh, yea. How are you? What bring you here?" I ask him.

"Oh not much, Megan told me you worked here and I wanted to check it out. Me being new here and all." He tells me.

"Lots of new people in this town, all of a sudden. It's weird." I laugh at him a bit.

"It's a nice town, why not move here." He retorts.

I'm getting a major bad vibe from this guy. I don't know why but he makes my skin crawl. He's not a bad looking guy, quite the opposite. He's very attractive with his long blond waves of hair, tan skin, and buff body. I can see why Megan slept with him, but something inside of me is screaming to get away from him. I look around and see my boss, Steve, watching the area in the doorway.

"My boss needs to see me, bye Jake." I say while hurriedly walking to Steve. I hear him grumble bye. I ask Steve to walk with me into the back room. Once we get in the back, I tell him the situation. *I am getting creeped out by the guy.* "This guy out there is just giving me a bad vibe, do you mind if I stay back here till he leaves?" I ask Steve.

"I'll cover the area for you, do you want me to kick him out?" Steve asks.

"No, nothing that harsh. Just let him leave on his own. Thanks." I say.

Steve leaves me in the back room. *Today has been a weird day. Two people that I really didn't want to see decided to come into my work. I've got a lot to tell Megan. Too bad I won't see her till Sunday.* Steve lets me know when the creep leaves. He waited for around ten minutes, then went through the aquarium, and then left. I waited in the back room till he was gone out of the building. Meanwhile, I was texting Megan.

'So you'll never guess who came in here today. Kevin…with his kid…and Jake…Today has been a weird one.' I hit send. I notice I have a text from Jett.

'I can't help but flirt with you. I'm sorry, I know it's not fair. I will try harder to be professional from now on. See you for dinner.' *Well, that's just great. I like his flirting but it is true that it's not fair, to either of us.* My phone buzzes in my hand. I got a text back from Megan.

'Woah, dude. Sorry about that. I accidentally told Jake you worked there. Kevin knows you work there, he could have at least gone on one of your days off. Still it's weird that Jake went. Is he like stalking you now?'

I text her back right away. 'I know, dude. He was giving me a bad vibe too. I hid in the back room till he left. I might fall asleep at Jett's again tonight, just giving you warning now so you don't freak out later.' Send.

A few seconds later, my phone buzzes again. It's Megan, again, all she says is 'whore' with a winking face emoji. I roll my eyes. *I wish dude. I have to let her think that though. Since I can't tell her anything about him being my guardian.* I put my phone in my pocket this time, instead of my locker.

It's about thirty minutes till closing time and most of our patrons have left. There are still a few stragglers but they look to be on the way out, they are in the gift shop. I am checking on all the fish in the touch pool area. Then I cover the tanks with the specialty designed tops. We only use them at night while we are closed. Before we didn't cover the tanks and some of the crabs kept sneaking out at night. We would find them on the floor all dehydrated. Some died. Since the covers, we've had no deaths, I'm happy to say.

The touch area is pretty new to this aquarium. They only built it last year. I start the walk to make sure no one is still in the aquarium. *I love this part of the day. It's just me and the fish. I swear they follow me whenever I walk through tunnel and in all of the rooms. They just look so happy to see me. I know that's nonsense, just something I've always thought of with fish. Ever since I was little.* Every room is clear, no more guests. I go up front to Jenny.

"Hey girl, what was up with that guy today? Why did you hide?" She asks me.

"I just had a bad feeling about him, First he hooked up with my roommate, then just started asking her all these questions about me, and then shows up to my work. He just creeped me out." I tell her.

"I get ya, listen to your gut. Everything all clear?" She asks again.

"All clear and I put the tops on the tanks." I say.

"Thank you Cora, you can punch out now, have a good night and see you tomorrow." She says.

"See you!" I say while walking to the back room to grab my stuff out of my locker. "Bye, Steve!" I yell across the back room. *I hear him back there, probably checking the tanks.* "Bye, Cora." I hear him yell.

I punch my time card into the machine, and head on outside out the back door. It's dark already even though it's only seven. *I hate daylight's savings time.* I fish for my keys in my purse while I'm walking to my car. I found my keys and hold them in my hand.

All of a sudden, someone grabs me from behind. They hold their hand over my mouth, so I can't scream. I still try my hardest to scream the loudest I can. It's muffled because the person, who I'm guessing is a man because he's big and muscular, is holding my face hard. He is dragging me away from my car, I'm wriggling and trying to get out of his grasp. I still have my keys in my hand. I get my hand loose from his grasp and jab my keys up into his face. I hear him scream in pain and he releases me. I bolt to my car which is luckily unlocked and jump in. I lock my doors, start the car and drive off, all in record time. My heart is pounding and all I can think about is getting to Jett. *He will keep me safe.* I race to his house. Luckily, I remember where he lives. I park my car in his driveway and run into his house without knocking.

He's standing in the kitchen, surprise etched in his expression, then fear once he sees my face. *I'm sure I look scared out of my mind.*

"What happened?" He asks.

"Someone just grabbed me from behind and covered my mouth and was dragging me away from my car while I was leaving work. I got free by jabbing my keys into his face, then drove off as fast as I could." I say in between deep breaths.

He gets serious while I said all of that, and grabs my face. "Are you all right?" He asks while looking deep into my eyes.

"I'm fine, just shaken up. Will you hold me for a minute?" I ask him. *I can't stop shaking.* He grabs me into a big bear hug. We stay like this for a while. *I love the feel of his body.* My body starts to shake less and less as time goes on. *This hug is really comfortable. We mold together, kind of like puzzle pieces, and we fit perfectly. He smells good too, like salt and woodsy, I guess. I don't know how to describe it other than its wonderful.* I pull away first. "Should I go to the police?" I ask him.

"Honestly, I wouldn't because it could be another mer-tribe. They might have found out who you are, too. I'm just really lucky I found you first. From now on, I go where you go." He tells me.

"What like, twenty four seven? You have to go to the bathroom with me too?" I roll my eyes at him.

"Please, Cora, this isn't a joke. Do not fight me on this. I will not get in your way but I will do my job." He says.

"Fine." I say with a pout, *I like my alone time, but so far I like hanging out with Jett too. Maybe this won't be such a bad thing.* "So, is dinner ready? I think all this adrenaline made me starving." I say.

"Yea, everything but the garlic bread. I waited to make that so it's fresh and hot for you." He exclaims.

"Why thank you, good sir." I say with a little curtsy. He chuckles. We walk into the kitchen together. I sit on one of the bench stools in the kitchen while Jett pulls the garlic bread out of the freezer. He pops it into the oven, should only take about five to ten minutes. "So, guess what happened today." I say.

"Something else happened? Eventful day, huh?" He asks.

"You have no idea, first my ex comes in with his kid, then remember that guy, Jake from the bar? The one that Megan went home with?" I ask him.

"Yes." He says with a head nod.

I continue, "He also came to the aquarium. Megan was telling me this morning that he came into her work and was asking her all these questions about me. What my parents did, and about my swimming habits. It really creeped her out. He gave me a bad vibe while he was talking to me so I hid in the back room until he left." I explain.

He thinks for a minute then says, "What if he was the one who attacked you? What if he is from an enemy tribe? It would make sense, why you got that vibe, your powers are developing."

"Wait, what? Powers? Like Spidey sense?" I ask.

He smiles a big sexy smile. "Well, I don't know what 'Spidey sense' is but, yes, powers. You are one of very few, if not the only one, who has them. As a Lunafriya, your DNA possesses the perfect balance so you develop powers. You should have known about them ages ago, but I understand why your father did what he did." He states.

"How do you know I'm a Lunafriya? How can you be so sure?" I ask him.

Beeeeeeeeeeeeeep. The timer goes off and the bread is ready, dinner is ready. Jett doesn't answer my question and gets the bread out of the oven. *Everything smells delicious. I can't wait to eat, I'm pretty starving from just eating a small salad today.* Jett gets us some plates and he actually serves me. We sit at the kitchen island and eat. He is eating so fast.

"It's not a race, you know." I say with a small lip twist.

He smiles, "It's just so good. First time I've ever had spaghetti." He says.

"Really? It's one of my staples, I make it once a week." I tell him.

"What would you like to do after dinner?" Jett asks me.

I think about it. *You* runs through my head. *But I actually would really like a swim, it would be perfect to ease my anxiety from the attack.*

"Can we go to the lake?" I ask him.

He gives me a wary look. "I don't know if we should. Since you were attacked tonight, some other tribe has to know who you are. They could be watching all the bodies of water around here. I just don't want anyone to find you." He says.

I give him a defeated look. "I understand. I just thought the water might help me. I guess, you want to watch a movie?"

He stares into my eyes. *His eyes are a beautiful blue, they look like little pools of water.* "Ok, lets swim but only for a little bit, then we'll watch a movie, your pick." He says.

I light up with happiness. Bouncing up and down in my seat. "Ok, can we go now?" I ask excitedly.

Jett laughs, "Let's finish our dinner first."

I immediately start shoveling my spaghetti into my mouth. *I'm not one of those shy girls who's afraid to eat in front of guys.* He laughs again, he's almost done with his plate. Only a couple more huge bites and I finish my plate as well.

We walk to the beach together. *I'm really mad at myself when I remember that I don't have my swim bag in my car. I took it out to wash my clothes and never replaced it. At least I wore my pretty panties and matching bra.*

I smirk, "I didn't bring my suit."

He smirks right back at me, "Neither did I, but we aren't going to need them. We have tails remember."

I didn't think he'd let us use our fins! I thought he wanted to be inconspicuous. But I guess, it is dark and no one is around.

"Easy for you to say, you don't need a shirt." Again with my little smirk. *Oh well, my bra will do.* I whip off my shirt and slowly take off my pants. Jett is staring at me with hunger in his eyes. I smile a knowing smile at him.

"This is hard." He says, rubbing a palm over his face.

"What is?" I say with an eyebrow raised up and a smirk.

He shakes his head at me with a sexy smile. "Are you always this sarcastic?" He asks me.

"No, not always. Just most of the time." I say with a chuckle.

He smiles at me again, "Let's swim." He says.

We walk to the shore together after putting our clothes on the picnic table under the willow tree. Immediately the water soothes my anxiety. The current of water in my veins feels like electricity and it feels great. Once my lower half is in the water, I summon my fin. *I still can't get over how beautiful my tail is. The purples and greens and blue blend together almost artistically. I see that Jett also has his fin. It's quite wonderful how different his fin is to mine. His is more of a striped pattern while mine is swirls. His is mostly orange and green with a hint of black, again I think, it is still hard to see it at night.*

I start swimming around, just playing, seeing what my fin can do. This is only the second time I have been able to use it. I put my head under water and I can see clearly. Jett joins me, watching my every move.

There are many fish out tonight. I try something. The fish at the aquarium always seem to listen to what I tell them to do. I focus on a school of fish. I think, *swim to Jett and circle around him.* To my surprise and astonishment, they actually listen. The fish start to swim around Jett in circles. He has a surprised look on his face and looks at me.

I smile and say, "So, I think I found one of my powers. I told the fish to do that. The fish at the aquarium always have done what I wanted them to do."

He smiles the biggest smile I've ever seen. "I knew it! I fucking knew it!" He says while swimming fast to me. He scoops me up in his arms and we spin around and around, laughing while we spin. He lets me go. "I can't wait till your other powers develop. We need to go to Halcyon and see the council."

"Wait, Halcyon? What is that? And how many powers will I get? Do you know what they are?" I bombard him with questions. *I feel like I could explode with questions. We are still under water and I'm still surprised that we can talk fine under the water.*

He smiles and chuckles a bit. "Halcyon is my city and also my tribe name. It's where all Halcyons live. The city is my home. I don't know how many powers you will get but the stories have listed a few. You should be able to have will over sea life, your 'Spidey sense', as you called it, and the power of electricity."

Holy shit, that's awesome! We know I have at least two of those things now.

"Oh, and I'm pretty sure your grandfather is on the tribe council. He said his son's name was Ray. That's your dad's name. Just makes sense."

Holy fucking shit! I have a grandpa! A mer-man grandpa! I have to talk to dad about all of this. I mentally note to call him tomorrow. "WOW!" is all I can manage to say.

"I know this is a lot to take. I'm sorry, to have to tell you all this. You really should have a talk with your dad. I will join you if you want."

"No, that's ok. I want to talk to him alone." I tell him. I get back to swimming, but lazily. I try to understand everything that has been thrown at me. *Ok so, I am a Lunafriya, whatever that means. I am a mermaid that has powers. I have a grandpa that lives in the sea. Someone tried to* abduct me tonight. *What's next? I have a pet dragon or something? My life had turned into a crazy comic book or whatever.* "So, can we do something to take my mind off of all this crazy stuff happening? I need to chill the fuck out." I tell him.

"Let's fish." He says with a crooked smile. I follow behind him. He is looking so fine. *I hate that stupid oath. I want to jump his bones right now. His muscles are rippling in the water and his V lines in his abs are to die for. I want to lick them.* He is trying to catch a fish with his hands but he's moving too slow and the fish are making a getaway. I will the fish to go lay in Jett's hand. That gets a laugh out of him.

"You know what? You're a lot better at fishing than I am. You could just tell these fish to get into a net and they would do it no problem. It's a very helpful skill when your main food source is fish." He says with a chuckle.

"Yea, I guess that would be useful." I say with a smile. *I dreamed of this. What is happening right now, is the recurring dream I had been having since I was little. I guess that might be another power I might have. I can maybe see the future in my dreams.* "I think I just realized another power." I say.

"Oh, yea? What's that?" He asks.

"This is the dream I have been having since I was a toddler. Us, catching fish together, the fish swimming right into your hand, all of this, I have dreamt, many, many nights. I think I can see the future in my dreams, sometimes." I explain to him.

"I thought of that yesterday, when you mentioned that. We should take your dreams seriously from now on, just in case." He says. I smile. I remember my dream last night. *It was very dirty. Jett and I had passionate sex in my dream. Should I tell him about that one?* "What are you smiling about?" Jett asks with a smile of his own.

"Just remembering my dream from last night, I sure hope that one comes true." I say.

"What happened in your dream?" He asks again while getting closer to me. We are staring into each other's eyes deeply. I am searching to see if he really wants me as much as I want him.

I lick my lips and say, "We happened."

That was all it took. He grabs me by the nape of my neck and kisses me deeply. I am moaning into his mouth. Our tongues are twirling together. *He tastes so good.* I am rubbing his arms and back while we make out. *His muscles are firm and oh so sexy. I wish we were on land for this. I pull away though, because I don't want him to get into trouble. He said there were laws against us being together.* We are taking deep breathes.

"Sorry." He says.

"No, I'm sorry. I don't want to get you into trouble." I tell him.

"Doesn't really matter now, I think. It is bound to happen, you dreamed of it. We both really want it, might as well go for it." He says while pulling me into another kiss. *I'm enjoying myself but if we are going to do this, we have to do it right.* I pull away again.

"Can we go to your house?" I ask him. My clit is throbbing and I need release; *having my fin, that wouldn't be possible. We need to go on land to have sex and it's been over a year since I've had any.*

Jett smiles widely at me, "Yes, let's go home." We swim quickly to the shore and will our legs back. Jett scans the area to make sure no one is around and we get our stuff from the table. Jett brought two towels and we quickly dry off and head back to his house.

I don't bother putting my clothes back on since we will be taking them off anyways. As soon as we get inside, Jett pick me up and backs me against the wall. He passionately kisses my lips and neck. I am so wet right now. I can feel his hard-on against my hip. I reach down and stroke his dick. He groans into my neck. He gives me little nips and I fucking love it.

Again, this is turning out exactly like my dream last night. He starts to carry me into his bedroom and throws me lightly onto the bed. He jumps on top of me and kisses me again. We are both still in our wet underwear but he is rubbing his dick against my clit and it feels amazing. I moan loudly. *I missed this feeling, it feels so much better than just doing it myself.* I pull his boxer briefs off of him with my feet while he is unclasping my bra in the back.

Next, he sucks my nipples once they are free. I moan again. He lifts my hips up and pulls my panties off of me. He rocks his cock against my clit again. It feels even better this time with no barriers in the way. *I know I should ask him if he has a condom, and I know exactly what to say,* "Do you have any protection?" I ask him.

He stops what he's doing. "No, actually I don't. I'm not supposed to be having sex on this trip to land." He says. He starts to look defeated. I smile, *because this was all in my dream, I know what to say.*

"Don't worry about it, I'm on birth control." I say while guiding his cock to my opening. He gently puts his tip in and I gasp. *I haven't been filled in a long time and I really needed this. What better stress relief than sex.* He starts to go deeper, I start to moan louder.

Soon, he is pumping and I am groaning. He grabs my breast and squeezes while flicking his thumb over my nipple. I feel the pressure building in my abdomen, it's intense. My breaths are short. Jett is moaning into my ear. It is such a turn on that I explode with sensations. I moan loudly and come. Jett slows his pace and then stops to flip me around. *I love this position.* I get on all fours and stick my ass up for him. He licks his hand and rubs my clit. I groan and squirm slightly at his touch. He positions himself behind me and shoves his whole cock inside of me, to his hilt.

I gasp, not expecting him to do that and he starts pumping fast. I am rubbing my clit and touching his balls while he fucks me. He starts to moan loudly and I can feel him coming. He lays his head on my back while breathing heavily. Soon, he pulls out of me and cuddles me close. We both fall asleep fast cuddled in each other's arms. *We probably shouldn't have done that but I'm so happy that we did.*

Chapter 6

Jett's perspective

Cora fell asleep on me while watching the TV show. She had a busy day so I can't blame her. I carry her into my bed, *I don't want her to sleep on the couch. It's not comfortable, trust me. I decide to just sleep next to her. I know I will control myself and not disrespect her. It was actually one of the best nights of sleep I've ever had. Cora cuddled against my body, it's one of the best feelings.*

In the morning, she shakes me awake. "Hey, sleepy head." She says once I stir.

"Good morning beautiful." I say with a smile.

"Sorry I fell asleep." She replies.

"Don't worry about it, you had a big day yesterday." I tell her.

She thinks for a minute. "I have to go to work soon, so I'll need a ride to my car, please." She informs me, "Have you seen my phone?" She asks.

"It died, so I plugged it in for you, over there." I say while pointing to the nightstand.

Cora goes to her phone and is turning it back on. Suddenly, the phone is buzzing nonstop for at least a minute and a half. She quickly places a phone call.

After about twenty seconds, she says, "I'm ok, Megan. Sorry, I forgot to text you. I fell asleep at Jett's house on accident." She must have had many calls and texts from Megan. She then blushes, and looks at me, I am getting dressed while she talks on the phone. I don't want to intrude on her conversation. "It's not like that, I'll be home in a bit. I just didn't want to worry you anymore." She says to her friend. "Bye." And she hangs up the phone.

"You want any coffee or breakfast before I take you to your car?" I ask her.

"No thanks, I have to hurry home and get ready." She tells me.

"Ok, let's go if you're ready then." I say.

She grabs her phone and swim bag, then follows me into the garage. She tells me how to get to her parents and I nod to show I understand. *I already know where her parents live but I don't want her to know I stalked her a little bit.*

"I know I don't really have to say this, but just in case. Do not summon your fin in front of anyone except your dad and me, for now. And don't tell anyone about you being a mermaid, even jokingly. We don't know who is behind these disappearances yet, so you have to be careful around everyone, understand?" I explain and ask.

"Yes, I understand." She says with a head nod.

I smile and she smiles back. *I am falling for this girl and I can't be with her. I wish things could be different. I wonder if the council would change the rules for me. They do like me, but it would be wrong of me to ask. Especially since I believe she is the granddaughter to one of its members.* Suddenly, she frowns. "What's wrong?" I ask, with a frown myself.

"Nothing" is her response. *Sure doesn't seem like nothing.* I pull up to her parents' house, and put my car in park. I turn to face her, and touch her cheek with my hand lightly.

"Seriously, what's wrong? You look so sad and I don't like it." I ask again.

The sexual tension between us is getting stronger. "It's just not fair, I found someone that I actually like and nothing can come out of it." She tells me, just letting her heart open for me, it makes a rip in my heart.

I give her sad eyes now. "Oh, Cora, I'm sorry. I feel the same way. It's killing me, not being able to touch you, kiss you...make you come." I say with a hungry look in my eye. She sucks in a bit of air, *she is making me so hard right now.* She bites her lip. *God, that drives me crazy.* "I've been dreaming of it, every night since I've met you." I say.

"Actually, I have too." She tells me while squirming in her seat. *I can see what I'm doing to her, I bet her panties are soaked right now. I wish I could see for myself.*

We have gravitated towards each other, getting closer by the second, staring into each other's eyes. *I want this so badly. I want to kiss her* and before I get the chance, she pounces at me. Smacking her lips against mine. We kiss passionately, swirling my tongue against hers. *She tastes amazing.*

Then, she breaks the kiss. "I'm sorry." She says.

"Get back here." I tell her while grabbing the nape of her neck and bringing her to my lips again. She's sucking and nibbling at my lips, her hands rubbing my muscles over my shirt and in my hair. *We shouldn't be doing this, it will get me into trouble, but I don't really care. I want her too badly.* We kiss until we are out of breath. We both pull apart and breathe heavily.

"Fuck Cora!" I say while tugging her hair a bit.

"Yes please." She whispers, I suck in a breath and exhale slowly. *This girl will be my demise. I can't seem to control myself like I thought. I have to distract myself, and she needs to go to work or she'll be late.*

I unlock the doors, "You better go before you're late for work." I sigh.

"Yea, you're right. When will I see you next?" She asks.

This puts a smile on my face. *We are friends, after all, if nothing else. Plus being her guardian, I should be around her at all times. I will let her go to work on her own though, for the time being.* "When is your shift over tonight?" I ask her.

"Seven." She says.

"Want to come over after work? I can make you dinner and we can watch more of 'the office', that was a really good show." I say.

"Sounds like a plan." She replies, "Bye Jett!"

"Bye, beautiful." She shuts the door and heads to her car and backs out of the driveway. I am wondering what I'm going to do with this wonderful woman. I run my hand into my hair in frustration, while staring off into space. Then, I notice Cora has driven off so I drive back to my house.

What am I going to do with myself for the next eight hours? I told Cora that I would cook her dinner. I don't know much about cooking, but I can try. We don't cook in the ocean. Raw fish and fruit and veggies are our main food sources. I will have to go to the grocery store. I go to my computer and pull up google. I search for easy recipes. I don't get to eat cow a lot so I look for beef recipes. I see a picture of spaghetti. *That looks amazing, and not hard to make it seems.* I pull out my phone and text Cora.

'Hey beautiful, do you like spaghetti?' Send.

I don't receive a text back right away so I keep researching recipes that she might like. I make a grocery list, and grab my keys. I walk to my car in the garage and drive to the store. The parking lot is pretty empty. *Lunch time is a good time to go to the grocery store, I guess. Only old people and 'milfs' in here.* I pack my cart full of almost everything, *this is going to be expensive.* I have a bank account on land, thanks to the tribe.

While in the aisle looking for spaghetti sauce, an old lady says to me, "if you're making spaghetti, be sure to get garlic bread!"

That's a good idea, never had that before. "Thanks for the tip, ma'am." I tell her with a smile. I get some get some frozen french fries, and pizzas, and garlic bread. I didn't get any fish because I'm on land and would like to broaden my horizons. Once I pay for all the groceries, I pack up my car and head home.

Once I'm home, I put all the food away. I check my phone, and still no text from Cora. I decide to work out in the gym room of the house. There is a treadmill, weight machine with various weights, and an exercise bike. I pick the weight machine first and work on my legs. They don't have as much power as my arms because I don't usually train with my legs, I have my fin. I continue this for about thirty minutes and switch to my arms. Again, I do thirty minutes intervals then switch to the treadmill. I run on the treadmill for thirty minutes then I switch to the exercise bike. I do a thirty minute stretch. I call it quits once I'm done. I've been working out for two hours and have a nice sweat going. I check myself out in the mirror and I'm liking what I'm seeing. *I've got it going on, if I do say so myself.* I check my phone again and I finally have a text back from Cora.

'Hi, yes I love spaghetti. You need to stop calling me beautiful. It's not fair if we can only be friends. Going back to work and won't have my phone on me.'

I know I shouldn't flirt with her, it's not fair to either of us. But I really can't help myself. She's different than anyone else I've ever met. I've met women in the sea and on land, but she is just different. I feel a connection to her. I can be myself around her. I text her back.

'I can't help but flirt with you. I'm sorry, I know it's not fair. I will try harder to be professional from now on. See you at dinner.'

I will try for her sake. I don't know if I can do it, but I will try. I have a couple hours before Cora gets off work. I take a nice long shower, and shave my face. By the time I get out the bathroom, I've got about two hours before seven. I would like to get everything ready before she gets here, except the garlic bread. I want that to be fresh, for her and myself, since it's the first time I'm eating it. I decide to watch a few episodes of 'the office' before I start cooking.

I watch two, and see it's six now. I better start on dinner. I pull the big pot out of the cabinet and fill it with water. Then, I wait for it to boil. While I wait, I brown up the meat and drain it. The water is boiling so I throw the noodles in. I stir the sauce in with the meat and cook it on low. Once the noodles are done, I drain them and stir them into the spaghetti sauce. I turn all the burners off on the stove, when I hear a car pull up. *Cora must be here.* Suddenly, my front door bursts open and Cora runs in and slams the door. She slides down the door and sits on the floor. I look at her bewildered until I see her face. Her eyes are wide and full of panic, fear etched into the lines on her forehead. Then I look at her in concern, fear dripping from my mind.

"What happened?" I ask.

"Someone just grabbed me from behind and covered my mouth and was dragging me away from my car while I was leaving work. I got free and jabbed my keys into his face, then drove off as fast as I could." She says in between deep breaths.

I get serious while she said all of that, and grab her face, lightly on the cheeks. "Are you all right?" I ask while looking her over.

"Yea, I'm fine, just shaken up. Will you hold me for a minute?" she asks me.

I grab her into a big hug, wrapping my arms around her body. We stay like this for a while. *I could touch her forever and never get tired of it. I am smelling her hair, it smells of strawberries and cream. We really do fit together nicely.*

She pulls away first, "Should I go to the police?" She asks me.

"Honestly, I wouldn't because it could be another tribe. They might have found you too. I'm just really lucky I found you first. From now on, I go where you go." I tell her.

"What like twenty four seven? You have to go to the bathroom with me too?" She rolls her eyes at me.

"Please, Cora. This isn't a joke, do not fight me on this. I will not get in your way but I will do my job." I say.

"Fine." She says with a little pout. *I really don't care if she doesn't like it, it's my job to protect her.* "So, is dinner ready? I think all this adrenaline made me starving." She says.

"Yea, everything but the garlic bread, I waited to make that so it's fresh for you." I exclaim.

"Why thank you, good sir." She says with a little curtsy. I chuckle.

We walk into the kitchen together. She sits on one of the stools in the kitchen while I pull the bread out of the freezer. I pop it into the oven, should only take a few minutes.

"So, guess what happened today." She says.

"Something else happened? Eventful day, huh?" I ask.

"You have no idea. First, my ex comes in with his kid. Then, remember that guy Jake from the bar?" She asks me.

"Yes." I say with a head nod.

She continues, "He also came into the aquarium. Megan was telling me this morning that he came into her work and was asking her all these questions about me. What my parents did, and about my swimming habits. It really creeped her out. He gave me a bad vibe while he was there so I hid in the back room till he left." She explains.

I think for a minute then say, "What if he was the one who attacked you? What if he is from an enemy tribe? It would make sense, why you got that vibe, your powers must be developing."

"Wait, what? Powers? Like 'Spidey sense'?" She asks.

I smile a big smile. "Well, I don't know what 'Spidey sense' is but, yes powers. You are one, if not the only one, who has them. As a Lunafriya, your DNA possesses the perfect balance so you develop powers. You should have known about them ages ago, but I understand why your father did what he did." I state.

"How do you know I'm a Lunafriya? How can you be so sure?" She asks me.

Beeeeeeeeeeeeeeeep. The timer goes off and the bread is ready. Dinner is ready. I am busy finishing the last touches of dinner and forget her question. *Everything smells delicious. I can't wait to eat.* I fix us both some plates and set hers down in front of her. We sit at the kitchen island and eat. *Wow! This food is amazing.* I can't help but shovel it into my mouth.

"It's not a race, you know." She says with a small lip twist.

I smile, "It's just so good. First time I've ever had spaghetti." I say.

"Really? It's one of my staples." She tells me.

"What would you like to do after dinner?" I ask Cora.

She thinks about it for a minute. "Can we go to the lake?" She asks me.

I give her a wary look, "I don't know if we should. Since you were attacked tonight, some other tribe has to know who you are. They could be watching all the bodies of water around here. I just don't want anyone to find you." I say.

She gives me a pitiful look. "I understand. I just thought the water might help me. I guess you want to watch a movie?" She is so sad and defeated.

I think about it for a minute while staring into her eyes. *I will do anything to make her happy. Her eyes are an icy blue, almost gray. I could stare into them for hours.* "Ok, let's swim but only for a little while, then we'll watch a movie, your pick." I say.

She lights up with happiness, bouncing up and down in her seat. "Ok, can we go now?" She asks excitedly.

I laugh a big belly laugh, "Let's finish our dinners first." I tell her.

She immediately starts shoveling her spaghetti into her mouth. This makes me laugh even more, harder this time. *I like hanging out with this girl, even if we can only be friends, I'd rather be friends than nothing at all.* I'm almost done with my plate. Only a couple more huge bites and she finishes her plate as well.

We walk to the beach together. *I figured she'd want to stop at her car to get her suit but she just walked right past it. I didn't get my suit because I knew I wouldn't need it, I have my fin.* I look at Cora out the corner of my eye. She is smirking.

"I didn't bring my suit." She says.

I smirk at her too, "Neither did I, but we aren't going to need them, we have tails remember."

She looks surprised and then she smiles at me. "Easy for you to say, you don't need a shirt." She whips off her shirt and slowly takes her pants off.

She is in just her panties and bra. *How am I supposed to not get a hard-on right now? I want her now. I want to rip off those panties with my teeth.* I am staring at her with hunger in my eyes. She smiles a knowing smile at me. I shake my head and try to focus on something else.

"This is hard." I say.

"What is?" She says with an eyebrow raised up and a cocky smile.

I shake my head and laugh, "Are you always this sarcastic?" I ask her.

"No, not always, just most of the time." She says with a chuckle.

I can't help but smile at her. *She seriously is my dream girl.* "Let's swim." I tell her, *Maybe that will help my sexual frustrations.*

We walk to the shore together after putting our clothes on the picnic table under the willow tree. We get into the water and we both immediately sigh in relief. I look over at Cora, *she has her eyes closed and looks so fucking sexy. She looks to be enjoying this very much. I wonder if that is her 'O' face.*

I will my fin, I see that she is getting faster at willing her own. *Her fin is beautiful. All purple and green swirls. Mine is more of a striped pattern while hers is swirls, just like Master Zale's. Mine is mostly orange and green with some black.* She starts swimming around, just playing. I follow her every move while also keeping an eye out for anyone else. She puts her head under the water and I join her. There are many fish out tonight. She is watching the fish with intense focus.

Suddenly, the fish start to swim around me in circles. *What the hell?* I have a surprised look on my face and look back at Cora.

She smiles a gigantic smile and says, "So, I think I found one of my powers. I told the fish to do that. The fish at the aquarium always have done what I wanted them to do." I smile the biggest smile. *Yes! I was right! I knew I found the right girl!* I am so ecstatic right now.

"I knew it! I fucking knew it!" I say while swimming fast to Cora. I scoop her up in my arms and we spin around and around, laughing while we spin. I let her go, remembering I promised to be more professional. "I can't wait till your other powers develop. We need to go to Halcyon and see the council." I tell her.

"Wait, Halcyon? What is that? And how many powers will I get? Do you know what they are?" She bombards me with questions.

I knew she'd have a bunch of questions. I smile and chuckle a bit, "Halcyon is my city and also my tribe name. It's where all Halcyons live. The city is my home. I don't know how many powers you will get but the stories have listed a few. You should be able to have will over sea-life, your 'Spidey sense', as you called it, and the power of electricity." I explain to her.

She gets an excited look on her face. "Oh, and I'm pretty sure your grandfather is on the tribe council. He said his son's name was Ray. That's your dad's name. Just makes sense." I add.

Her jaw drops. She is totally floored right now. "WOW!" is all she manages to say.

"I know this is a lot to take. I'm sorry, to have to tell you all this. You really should have a talk with your dad. I will join you if you want." I tell her.

"No, that's ok. I want to talk to him alone." She tells me. She swims around lazily. *She has to be taking all of this new information in. I can see the wheels in her head turning round and round.*

"So, can we do something to take my mind off of all this crazy stuff happening? I need to chill the fuck out." She says.

"Let's fish." I tell her with a crooked smile.

I know she would like to because of her dream she was telling me about yesterday, and it's something I also enjoy. She follows behind me. I look and see a small school of fish near a rock pile. I try to cut off their escape path but it doesn't work, the fish get away. *I used to catch fish like this with my sister, Meri, it brings back good memories.*

Suddenly, a fish swims right into my hand and lays down, if a fish can lay down. I bust out laughing. "You know, you're a lot better at fishing than I am. You could tell these fish to get into a net and they would do it no problem. It's a very helpful skill when your main food source is fish." I say with a chuckle.

"Yea, I guess that would be useful." She says with a smile. She looks around and thinks for a few seconds. "I think I just realized another power." She says.

"Oh yeah? What's that?" I ask.

"This is my dream I've had since I was a toddler. Us, catching fish together, the fish swimming right into your hand, all of this, I have dreamt, for many, many nights. I think I can see the future in my dreams, sometimes." She explains to me.

"I thought of that yesterday, when you mentioned that. We should take your dreams seriously from now on, just in case." I say.

She smiles. *I love it when she smiles. She looks so happy and carefree. I am glad I get a lot of smiles from Cora.*

"What are you smiling about?" I ask with a smile of my own.

"Just remembering my dream from last night, I sure hope that one comes true." She says with a wicked grin.

"What happened in your dream last night?" I ask again while getting closer to her. *I have a feeling I know what she is going to say. Her eyes are all glossy. She is begging me to fuck her with those bedroom eyes. I am searching to see if she really wants me as much as I want her.*

She licks her lips and says, "We happened."

That was all it took, I pounce at her and grab her by the nape of her neck and kiss her deeply. She is moaning into my mouth. Our tongues are twirling together. *She tastes so good.* She is rubbing my arms and back while we make out. My one hand is in her hair, the other is on her hip bone rubbing her skin and fin. *I wish we were on land for this. I need my cock to fully give her what she wants.* She pulls away. My lips are tender from our deep kissing. We are taking deep breathes.

"Sorry." I say. *We shouldn't be doing this but if she dreamed about it, then it's going to happen either way.*

"No, I'm sorry. I don't want to get you into trouble." She tells me.

"Doesn't really matter now, I think, it is bound to happen, you dreamed of it. We both really want it, might as well go for it." I say while pulling her into another kiss.

We kiss and dry hump for a few minutes. Then, she pulls away. "Can we go to your house?" She asks. *Yes! This is what I want as well.*

I smile wickedly at her, "Yes, let's go home." We swim quickly to the shore, and will our legs back. I scan the area to make sure no one is around and we get our stuff from the table. I brought two towels down for us earlier and we quickly dry off and head back to my house.

She doesn't bother putting her clothes back on. *It is such a turn on, watching her walk around the beach and surrounding woods in her underwear. I could see every booty shake and titty jiggle while walking. I'm already hard as a rock.* As soon as we get inside, I pick her up and back her against the wall. I passionately kiss her neck and lips. I can feel how wet she is from her panties, they are soaked. I shove my hard-on against her hip to let her know how much I want her. She reaches down and strokes my cock. I groan into her neck. *Fuck that feels good. I haven't slept with anyone in a long while.* Every touch she is giving me is sending tingles down my spine. I give her little nips and she squeals. *She fucking loves it.*

I rub her clit on the outside of her panties. She squirms at my touch. I start to carry her into the bedroom and throw her lightly onto the bed. I jump on top of her and kiss her again. We are both still in our wet underwear but I am rubbing my dick against her mound. She squirms more and moans loudly. *I missed this feeling.* She pulls my boxers off of me with her feet while I am unclasping her bra in the back. *I want to see those glorious tits..* Once I get the bra off, her breasts flop out. *They are huge and I want a taste.* I suck on her nipples, she moans again. I lift her hips up and pull her panties off. I rub my cock against her clit again while sucking her nipples. It feels even better this time with skin to skin contact. We are both moaning. I am about to stick my dick inside of her when she starts to talk.

"Do you have protection?" She asks me.

I stop immediately and feel defeated. *I forgot about condoms, but I shouldn't have had a need for them.* "No, actually I don't. I'm not supposed to be having sex on this trip to land." I say. I start to back away from her.

She smiles, "Don't worry about it, I'm on birth control." She says while guiding my cock to her opening.

I gently put the tip in and she gasps. *Fuck, she feels amazing.* I slowly start to go deeper. She starts to moan louder. Soon, I am pumping fast and she is groaning. I grab her breast and squeeze while flicking a thumb over her nipple. She is getting tighter and tighter. It feels like she is about to come. She is moaning loud and fast, her breath short. I am moaning into her ear a bit. Her moans are turning me on and spurring me on faster. I feel close to coming myself but I don't want to stop so soon. She moans loudly and comes, her pussy is wrapping my cock so tightly. I slow my pace and let her catch her breath.

Then, I stop to flip her around. *I want to see her glorious ass.* She gets on all fours and sticks her ass up for me. I lick my fingers and rub her opening, making sure she is properly wet. She groans and moves slightly at my touch. I position myself behind her and shove my whole cock inside her in one quick motion. She gasps, not expecting me to do that and I start pumping fast. Her ass is bouncing with every thrust. I grab a hold and squeeze her ass cheeks. She is rubbing her clit and touching my balls while I pound her from behind. This is all it takes for me to come. I start to moan loudly and I come inside of her. I lay my head on her back while breathing heavily. Soon, I pull out of her and cuddle with her. We both fall asleep fast, cuddled in each other's arms. *We probably shouldn't have done that but I'm so happy that we did.*

Chapter 7

Cora's perspective

Well, that was a crazy night! I wake up in Jett's bed again this morning. Cuddled, just like we were yesterday morning, except this time, we're both naked. *He must be a cuddler.* I look for my phone. It's sitting next to me on the night stand. I grab it and check the time. *Good, it's only seven thirty. I have plenty of time to get home and take a shower and get ready for work.* I look over at Jett. He is sleeping so peacefully. *I can't believe we had sex last night!* My heart pounds. His eyes start to flutter open.

"Good morning, beautiful." He says with a sexy smile.

"Good morning, handsome." I tell him right back.

"What time is it? And what time do you work today?" He asks.

"It's seven thirty right now. Today is my late day, I don't start till one." I tell him with a yawn.

"Well, in that case, I think I'll have some breakfast." He says while ducking under the blankets.

That's a weird way to get out of bed, but he doesn't get out of bed. He makes his way between my thighs and starts to lick my clit. "Holy Fuck, Jett!" I say while grabbing his hair under the blankets. *He is going down on me and it feels so amazing. My ex, Kevin, didn't like oral. He said it was disgusting. I won't say I've never done it but oral is usually something you don't do with one night stands.*

Jett is circling his tongue around my clit and inside me. I moan loudly. He reaches up and sticks his fingers into my mouth. I suck hard on his fingers, twirling my tongue around them. All the while, he is still licking me. He pulls his finger out of my mouth and brings them down to my opening. He puts two fingers at my opening and teases me.

I groan, "Please." I beg to him. He shoves his fingers inside of me and continues his licking torture. He fucks me with his fingers and his mouth. Soon, I get over the edge and explode with sensations. I come hard around his fingers.

He stops and lifts the blanket back over his head. "That was some delicious breakfast." He says with a smile, wiping his mouth on the back of his hand.

I laugh. *This is the best feeling in the world.* "Wow" is all I can say between breathes. He smiles still. After I catch my breath, I say, "Well, I'm hungry and want some breakfast too!" I pull him back up to the head of the bed, with his help. *His cock is pretty big. I've never had this big of a cock before.* I lick my lips. His dick is already hard and standing at attention. I grab his cock in my hands and give it a little squeeze. He gasps a little. I give the tip of his cock a little lick and he moans. *I love that sound.* I lick the under ridge of the tip and suck, while rubbing the length of his cock.

I can taste his saltiness and I like it. I shove his dick deeper into my mouth. He is groaning with pleasure. I work my hands up and down on the parts my mouth can't reach and suck as deep as I can go. Twirling my tongue around as much as I can. I grab his balls a little and that sets him off.

"Cora, I'm going to come." He says. I stay where I am and let him come in my mouth as he did for me. He moans fast and loud, squirting into my throat. I gag a little but shallow his seed. After I finish, I wipe my mouth on the back of my hand.

"Delicious." I say with a smirk.

"You are amazing, Cora." He tells me.

My heart flutters, "So are you." I state.

I can't help but get a little bummed out though. *We shouldn't be doing this he said, he said it was against his oath.* I must have a frown because Jett asks, "What's wrong?"

"Oh nothing." I sigh.

Jett looks at me with suspicious eyes. "Don't give me that shit, I know something is wrong. What is it, beautiful?" He says.

I look into his eyes. *I might as well just tell him what is running through my mind.* "Well, you said we couldn't do this. That it was against your oath. Everything about this relationship is just doomed for us. Why are you all of a sudden ok with it?" I say with a deep breath.

"Technically, yes we shouldn't be doing this. I took an oath to not get involved with my subjects. I have upheld my oath, until you. It's not like I am the only person to break this oath, actually your grandfather broke his oath to be with your grandmother. Things turned out all right for him. He's now an elder in the council." *Woah, my grandpa is an elder of the council?* He continues while looking deeply into my eyes, "Your father broke his oath, and nothing bad happened to him. I am okay with us being in a relationship because I want you. I want your heart and your soul." He's rubbing his hands up my sides towards my breasts, "And your body." *He makes me feel so good.* Jett's hands get to my breasts and he squeezes. "These are amazing, you know that?" He says.

I chuckle. "Yea, I know." I roll my eyes while saying this. He laughs. "I should start heading home so I can shower and get ready for work." I tell him.

He's still squeezing my breasts, and teasing my nipples. They are hard at his touch and he puts his mouth on one of them and licks. In between sucks, he says, "Take a shower here, with me."

He is majorly turning me on, and shower sex would be fantastic right now. "Ok, but I still need to go home to get new clothes to wear for the day. I am doing the feeding lesson on the manta rays today, and I have to look good." I tell him with a smirk.

He picks me up off the bed and carries me into the bathroom with him. I squeal and kick my legs, laughing. He sets me down on the floor and starts the water in the shower.

"Ladies first." He says while opening the glass shower door and directing me inside. He already has another hard-on. I climb inside the tub and Jett follows. I put my head under the fall of water. *It is very refreshing.* Jett puts his body on my back. I can feel his cock on my ass.

"Do you have shampoo and conditioner?" I ask him.

"Yea, let me get that for you." His body leaves mine and it makes my back side cold. I shudder a bit. Jett puts the bath products on the ledge where I can see it. Once my hair is completely wet, I wash it, and then condition. Jett grabs the body wash and puts a large dab on his hands. He then proceeds to wash my body for me. *It feels great, I love any touches he gives me.* I grab the shampoo and wash his hair for him. It is short, so it doesn't take a long time to wash. He rinses his hair and I grab the body wash for him too. Once we are both sudsed up, he moves closer to me till we have skin to skin contact. He rubs my back and butt and I do the same to him. We are under the shower head and rinsing the soap off each other.

His body is so sculpted. Every line of muscle is defined. Jett then starts to rub me lower and hitting my clit. I gasp. He slides his finger inside of me. I clench down on his finger, enjoying the full sensation. *He makes me feel so good.* He looks down at me and I smile and grab his cock. His finger still inside of me and his thumb on my clit, he vibrates his hand. I moan and squeeze his cock a little tighter. Jett nibbles on my ear.

"You like that, baby?" He asks in a throaty whisper.

"Yes." I pant out. The water is making lubrication against us, making to easier to play with him. He is moaning into my ear. *I love that sound.* Eventually, Jett lifts my one leg up and props it against the shower door. Then, he slides his cock inside of me. I gasp at the fullness then moan at the pleasure. He takes it slow, pumping in and out. Letting us both fully enjoy each other.

The water is starting to get cold, but I really don't care. It doesn't seem to be bothering Jett either. My hands are like prunes. I feel like I'm close. I start to touch myself while Jett pumps faster. Soon, I explode and I hear Jett moaning like he is coming too. Once we are done, we clean up and he turns the water off. I step out of the shower and grab a towel.

I dry off and say, "I still have to go home, I need clean clothes to wear for work."

He smiles at me. "That's not a problem, we can go after I make us something to eat."

I am pretty hungry. "Ok" is all I say.

Jett tosses me a t-shirt of his. I put on my underwear and bra then his shirt. *It is really long on me, Jett is much bigger than I am, but who isn't. I'm on the short side.* Jett went into the kitchen while I got dressed. I follow once I'm done. He is busy, preparing breakfast.

"What's for breakfast?" I ask.

"Oral was for breakfast." He smirks at me, I roll my eyes with a smile. "Pancakes are for brunch." He says.

"Woohoo! Pancakes!" I yell. *I really like pancakes.* This surprises Jett and he actually jumps a little. I laugh. "Sorry, pancakes are my weakness."

He laughs too, "That is good to know."

The delicious smell is intoxicating. I walk up behind Jett and give him a backwards hug, laying my head in his back, while breathing in the pancake smell.

"Almost ready, why don't you go sit at the island, and I'll get your plate." He says.

I go immediately to the kitchen island, *don't have to tell me twice when pancakes are involved.* Jett gives me a plate for four pancakes. He has maple syrup, and butter on the countertop already so I start loading up my cakes and eating. Jett is still finishing up cooking his batch of pancakes, it doesn't take long and he sits next to me. We eat in silence, just both of us content with our brunch. I look at the time and it is around eleven already. I have two hours till I have to be at work.

"After we finish, I want to go home and change." I tell him. Jett nods at me. He looks to be deep in thought. "What's on your mind?" I ask him.

"It's nothing, I was just thinking about taking you to my city. I think you will really enjoy it." He tells me.

I wonder what an underwater city looks like. Is this the place I should have grown up in? I would really like to go. "When are we going to go?" I ask.

"We have to wait until you develop the rest of your powers. Once you do, I promise we will go. You have to meet my baby sister. She is dying to meet you." He tells me.

Oh, he has a sister. That's cool. I'm an only child, I always wanted a sister. "How old is she? What's her name?" I ask him even more questions.

"Meri and she's twenty. She's a real big fan of the Lunafriya's." He replies.

"Are there others like me?" I ask again.

"Well, we don't really know. They were thought to have been extinct for one hundred and fifty years. But I'm sure there are others."

We finish our pancakes and I go put my pants on from yesterday. "I'm going to go home now." I tell him while he's cleaning the plates.

"Wait, I was serious when I said I go where you go. Let me finish this then I will drive you home." He says.

"I have my own car, I can drive myself. It's not like you can go to work with me anyways." I explain to him.

"You can drive your own car if you would like but yes I am going to work with you. You could quit if you like. You will have to eventually, if you plan to live in Halcyon." He says.

This actually makes me mad. *I love my job, I will never quit. And what makes him think I want to live in Halcyon?* My teeth are clenched. "I'm not quitting and you are not coming to my work, you can do one loop of the aquarium, and watch my lesson on the rays. Then, you have to leave. I don't care if you wait in the car, but I am not getting fired from my favorite place." I say to him.

"Ok, that sounds reasonable." He responds.

I roll my eyes. *I hope the rest of my powers develop soon, so I don't need him as a guardian anymore, and can just have him as a boyfriend.* I head to my car while Jett goes to his. I start mine up and drive to my house, with Jett following behind. Once, I get home, I see that Megan is not home, she did say she worked a double today. We both pull up into the driveway.

"Welcome to my home." I say to Jett.

"Very nice! Is it just you and Megan here?" He asks.

"Yup" is all I say while unlocking the door. I show Jett around the house ending at my bedroom. "And this is my room." I say.

He picks me up and throws me on my bed. I squeal with excitement and surprise. He has a sexy panther look to him. He jumps on top of me and we make out for a few minutes. I eventually pull away from him.

"I really have to get ready for work." I tell him.

"Ok." He says while giving me a pouty face and sliding off of me.

I get up and go to my closet. *I want to look nice today.* I pick out my khaki pants, my black tank top, and my baggy work shirt with the aquarium logo on it. I tie it in a knot at my waist. Once I'm done dressing, I look in my full length mirror. I like the way I look. These pants accentuate my butt nicely and the knot hides my tummy. I want to do my hair and make-up so I leave my closet and see Jett is still in my room. He is looking at my swimming trophies.

"I will be in my bathroom, if you need me." I tell him.

I do my make-up first, just simple eyeliner and mascara. With my hair, I decide to do two french braids. It takes me a while to do the braids myself, usually Megan does them for me. I had to undo them a couple times because they didn't look right to me. Finally, I got them looking as good as I can. I check my phone for the time and it is a little after noon. I will have to leave soon to get to work a little early. I walk into the bedroom and Jett is now looking at all of my photos.

"We need a picture of us on here." He says. I have a photo collage in my room of me and all my friends. It used to be filled with pictures of Kevin and me but I tore those down and burned those two years ago. I pick up my digital camera.

"Come here." I say to him while rolling my finger towards me. He comes over to me and looks deeply into my eyes. I snap a picture of us like that. Then I make him look at the camera and tell him to smile, I take another selfie of us. Just for the hell of it, I take another with us kissing.

Once we are done, I say, "Now we have three pictures of us. I will print them after work. By the way, I need to leave like now, for work."

He smiles at me, "Ok, let's go. I'll drive you in my car." He tells me.

"Ok, fine." I pout at him. "Let me just text Megan and tell her, so she doesn't freak out when she sees my car but I'm nowhere around." I pull out my phone and text her quickly. We walk to his car together after I lock the house back up.

The drive to work is pleasant. Just us, enjoying each other's company. *My cheeks hurt from smiling so much. Jett has been smiling just as much as me. I love his laugh, it does strange things to my body.* We get to the aquarium and I tell him to park in the back. We arrived fifteen minutes before I have to clock in.

"I have to go in, but you can join me at one. I will be doing the manta ray lesson." I tell him.

He gives me a deep kiss. "See you in there, beautiful." He says.

My heart flutters. "Bye." I say giving him another peck on the lips before leaving the car. I walk into the back door. Steve is in the back, checking the tanks and all their levels.

"Morning Steve!" I say happily to him.

He chuckles, "Afternoon, Cora." He replies.

"Am I still doing the lesson today?" I ask him.

"Yea, Jean is feeling better so she's in the touch pool area today." He says. *Yes! I would have been disappointed if I didn't get to do the lesson again today.* I set my stuff down in my locker and walk up front to Jenny.

"Morning, Jenny!" I sing to her. She laughs as well.

"Hello, Cora. Someone woke up on the right side of the bed this morning, huh?" She says with a smirk and a wink.

"Yea, actually." I say with a huge smile. "I wanted to tell you that my new boyfriend is coming in to check the place out." As soon as I finish telling her this, Jett walks in the door. "Speak of the devil, here he is now." I say.

Jenny's eyes get huge. "Oh my god, Cora, he is fine!" She says with an emphasis on the word fine. I smile. *Yes, he is, and all mine!*

"Hi, baby." Jett tells me once he gets up to the front desk. I smile again. *I swear, my cheeks are going to fall off. They hurt from smiling way too much. But that's a good thing, right?*

"Hi, Jett." I roll my eyes at him for always calling me pet names. "This is my boss, Jenny." I direct his focus to her.

"Nice to meet you, Jenny." Jett says while placing a kiss on her hand.

Jenny giggles, like actually full on giggles, like a school girl. I roll my eyes again. "Nice to meet you too, Jett. You can go into the aquarium for free, friends and family discount." She says.

Wow, that's real nice of her, even my parents had to pay last time they came in. I raise my eyebrows at him, and shrug. "I will show Jett around, then head to the rays, ok?" I ask Jenny. *We might be friends, but she's still my boss.*

"That's fine, honey." She says while waving us off.

The first room we walk into is the touch pool. I walk over to one of the tanks with him. Jett reaches in and touches a starfish. I use my powers to make it crawl on his hand. He laughs. "Did you do that?" He whispers.

"Yes." I respond. I make the starfish get off of him and back on the rock. "Want to see the other areas? This one is more for the kids." I ask him.

"Sure, lead the way." He says. I take him to the next room. This one is the electric fish. The room is pitch black except for the black lights. It makes the luminescent skin of the fish glow. "Wow." Jett remarks. I laugh. *It is pretty cool but he gets to see all of this in real life, every day in the ocean.*

I follow the path and lead him into the next room. It's the seahorse tank. *I love the seahorses. I wish they were bigger so I could actually ride them.* That's a silly thought, I chuckle.

"What's so funny?" Jett asks.

"Oh, it's nothing. Just thought it'd be cool if the seahorses were big enough to ride."

He laughs, "You sure do have a weird mind."

I mockingly scoff, "I take pride in my weirdness." I say. He shakes his head with a smile. The next room is the ray room. "You get a good spot up front, I have to do the lesson in about five minutes, at one thirty." I tell Jett.

People have already started gathering at the tank. The manta rays are swimming around the circular open-top tank. Guests can see them at all angles. I go to the feeding station and grab the microphone headset from the top of the mini fridge. I set the microphone to the P/A system.

"Good afternoon, North Creek aquarium guests, the ray feeding will begin in about five minutes. Join us in the ray room to enjoy watching these magnificent creatures."

I turn the microphone off, and change the mode to the ray room. I check to make sure the mini fridge has the plankton. *Steve must have put it in a bucket for me in preparation. I mentally note to thank him later*. I pull the bucket out of the fridge, and set it on top. My area is blocked off, so no one can get too close to me. I look around for Jett. He is straight across the tank from me, watching the rays. More people are filing in to watch. I wait till no more people are coming in the door and turn my mic back on.

"Hello everyone! Welcome to the ray room! Today, we will be feeding the rays and learning a bit about them as well. Now, as you can see their mouths are on the bottom of their bodies. They swim around the bottom of the tank and pick the plankton up with their mouths. They don't actually have teeth but little plates that suck up the food."

I toss in the plankton by the handful, making sure to get everywhere in the tank. The rays swim around, happily eating. Once they have gotten their full. I decide to try and play a little. I continue with my lesson.

"Manta rays are graceful swimmers. They swim by moving their pectoral fins up and down which propels their bodies through the water. Their short tails allow the manta rays to be more acrobatic with its movements, and they have even been seen leaping out of the water."

I use my powers while saying this and will a ray to jump out of the water at the perfect time. The crowd oohs and aahs. I smile, and focus on Jett. He is shaking his head but is laughing so I don't think he's mad at me for that.

I continue, "Manta rays eat tiny marine organisms including plankton, small fish and crustaceans. Today, they just had some plankton grub." I make the rays swim around the sides of the tank, so you can see their bellies. "Here, you can see a close up on their mouths. Some of them look to be smiling."

The kids always get a kick out of that, yelling, "Yea!" I let the fish do what they wish. Most of them go back to finding food, some continue to circle the sides of the tank.

"Now, although the manta ray is not considered to be a species that is in danger of extinction in the wild, their population numbers have been declining more quickly in recent years. Manta rays are particularly susceptible to water pollution and are quickly affected by overfishing in certain areas, and therefore lack of food. So, let's try to help all fish, by cleaning up the oceans and beaches, and not using as much plastic. Thank you for your time." I finish with a bow.

Everyone claps. I turn off my mic, and set it back down on the fridge. I turn around and Jett is there.

He is smiling. "That was cool and informative. Those things will still fuck you up in the ocean." He whispers.

I laugh, "Yes, I know. That's how Steve Irwin died." I tell him.

"Who's Steve Irwin?" he asks.

I bust out laughing. "Oh, my sweet summer child." I say referencing Game of Thrones.

"What the fuck are you talking about?' He laughs at me.

I shake my head. "Sorry, I'm not used to someone who doesn't get pop culture. Most of my language is movie quotes and TV shows." I laugh. "Would you like to see the big tank?" I ask.

"Sure." He says. I lead him to the next room. This room is the big tank. The whole wall is glass, then it leads to an underwater tunnel into the next room where the sharks are. This is where all the sea turtles and salt water fish are.

"This is one of my other favorite places. I like to come in here after closing and talk to the fish. I didn't know at the time that they could actually listen." I tell him. "I like cleaning the tank and swimming with the turtles."

"I can't wait to take you to the ocean, you will love it." He tells me. *I can't wait either. I hope the rest of my powers develop soon.* I smile at him. I lead him under the tunnel to the sharks. None are very big, but we have seven sharks, the largest reaching at about four feet.

"Now these things are deadly, I got lucky with my run-in, and only got this small scar." He says while showing me his scar on his upper arm.

"You sure did get lucky, they can tear you up." I say. After the shark room is the octopus room. He's a sneaky bugger. Always hiding and trying to escape. "This is my buddy Frank, he's a mischievous one." I tell Jett. He chuckles.

The next room isn't really a room but a hallway filled with tanks. They are all local fish. This hallway leads to the gift shop and out to the front lobby. "Well, you've seen the whole aquarium. I have to get back to work, what will you do for the next five hours?" I ask.

"I think I will stay in the car and watch out for anything suspicious." He says.

I roll my eyes. "Really? You don't have to do that. Just go home and pick me up at seven." I tell him.

"I go where you go," is all he says.

I sigh. "Fine. See you in five hours." I give him a quick kiss and turn around and walk to Jenny at the front desk. Jett left the building.

"What would you like me to do now, Jenny?" I ask.

"Could you cover the touch pool while Jean takes her lunch?" She says.

"Not a problem." I walk over to Jean. "Hey, you can take your lunch now, I'll cover you." I say to Jean.

"Oh ok, good thing too, I'm starving. Who was that hot guy you were with earlier?" She asks.

"That was my boyfriend, Jett." I say with a smile. *I like the sound of that.*

She smiles too, "Girl he was smokin!" She giggles.

"Yes, I know." I say with an eye roll. Jean takes her leave and I have fun with the kids at the touch pool, showing them my tricks with the starfish and crabs. Most of the kids freaked out, but some were fascinated. I see Steve watching me from the back room. Once he notices that I saw him watching, he walks up to me.

"How do you get them to do that? And the rays? I have fed them almost every day for the last twenty years, and they have never jumped out of the tank like that." Steve asks and looks at me wondering.

Shit, what am I supposed to say now? I shrug at him. "I honestly don't know, I guess the fish just like me, and the ray jumped out on its own, I've never seen it do that before." I say to him.

"Huh, interesting, maybe I have to put a top on the tank so they don't jump out, don't want any of my rays getting hurt." Steve mumbles while walking away. *Well, I guess that worked. I have to use my powers more carefully next time.*

I continue to watch over the touch pool area until Jean comes back from lunch. She comes back a little late and she looks to have been crying, her eyes are red and puffy.

"What happened?" I ask her with concern.

"Oh, it's nothing. I just got into a fight with my boyfriend over the phone. I always cry when we get into fights, I'm too emotional." She says with tears still running down her face but trying to smile.

"Oh honey, go into the bathroom and splash cold water on your face. I can cover for you, take as much time as you need." *I know Jean and her boyfriend aren't doing that well, they are constantly fighting, I feel bad for her.*

"Thank you," she says quietly and runs off. After about another twenty minutes, Jean finally comes back. "Girl, I'm sorry. I ended up getting sick while I was in there." She states.

"It's ok." I say with a smile.

She looks around to make sure no one is listening to us. "I haven't told anyone yet, but the reason I've been sick and emotional lately is that I'm pregnant." She whispers to me.

My eyes get big. "Oh wow! Congrats Jean!" I say a little too loudly for her liking.

"Shh, we don't want too many people to know just yet." She tells me.

"I'm sorry, how did Billy take the news?" I ask her.

She frowns a little. "He wasn't happy at first, but now he seems to be dealing with it. Honestly, I don't know if we are going to make it together this whole pregnancy. I already want to break up with him because of all the fighting." She whimpers.

That sucks, "I'm sorry, but you do what you have to do. Things will get better either way you choose." I tell her while giving her a hug.

"Thanks, Cora." She says.

"No problem, and remember I'm here for you if you need to vent or anything." I tell her again.

"I'll remember that, thanks again. You best go see Jenny and cover her lunch before she yells at us." Jean says with a smile.

"I'll do that, you hang in there Jean." I say while walking to the front desk.

Jenny is ringing up customers trying to enter the aquarium. She notices me and once the customers are gone she lays into me. "What was taking so long? Jean was supposed to be back half an hour ago." *She has a bit of an attitude but I know she doesn't mean it, just trying to be the boss.*

"Jean had a fight with Billy again, she was crying so I covered her while she calmed down, everything is ok now." I tell her.

She shakes her head, "Those kids. Will you cover me now for lunch?" She asks.

"Of course," I say. She nods and signs out of the register. I input my code on the register and greet the new guests coming in. "Hello and welcome to North Creek Aquarium!" I bellow out. *I really do love my job, everything about it. I love the people I work with, I love the fish, and I love the smell. There is no way I can quit this job, but if I'm in the ocean, I wouldn't be able to work here, would I? I guess I have a lot of decisions to make.*

We actually have a steady number of guests coming in for being a small town. People do travel from out of town to come here though. It's not the biggest aquarium in Michigan, but it is still pretty cool and cheaper than the bigger aquariums we have in Michigan. Plus, we have the cute small town charm here. We do get a bit of tourists.

Jenny comes back, "Wow! We are pretty busy today." She says.

"Yup, it's Saturday. What would you like me to do for the next three hours?" I ask her.

"Umm, How about you just walk around, and tell the guests some facts, answer questions. You know, stuff like that." She tells me.

"Ok, will do!" I give her an army salute. I walk off, and start to entertain the guests with fish facts. I see a few adults looking at the starfish, I go up to them and say, "Did you know that starfish have no brains? Kind of like my ex." And that gets them laughing.

I smile and walk away towards the next room. The room is pitch black except for the purple lights. Many groups of people are watching the giant schools of neon tetras swim around together. There isn't much to say about the tetras so I continue to walk to the seahorse room. *I love these creatures, they are so elegant.* I walk up to a group that are watching a seahorse give birth. *It's fascinating to watch.*

A little girl, about six years old, yells to her mother. "Look the mommy seahorse is having babies!"

I turn to the whole group, "Actually that is the daddy seahorse. The male is who holds the eggs until they hatch and births them." I tell them.

"Oh wow, that's interesting, isn't it?" The mom says.

"Didn't know that." Another person says.

"Yup, it's true. And they can have up to one thousand five hundred eggs at a time." We watch the seahorse give birth and I make a mental note to tell Steve about it when I see him next. He will want to remove the bigger seahorses to another tank till the babies get bigger. I walk to the back room to find Steve. He's not back there. I continue my roam around the aquarium to find him. Next is the ray room. Steve is in there cleaning the tank after the feeding, *don't want the uneaten plankton to gunk up the filters.*

"Hey Steve, a seahorse just gave birth, might want to move the adults so they don't eat the young." I tell him.

He smiles, "Ah yes, I was wondering when that would happen. I knew it should have been soon, I have a tank already set up, thanks for letting me know." He says.

"No prob, bob." I state and go to the next room, the big tank. This room is packed with people. The turtles are swimming around in circles around the tunnels.

I walk by people and tell them turtle facts. "Sea turtles can live over one hundred years, depending on the species." I say to on group. "Different species of sea turtles depend on different diets, one will eat jellyfish, the next will eat crabs, and some eat plant life." I tell another group.

Everyone looks to be happy and enjoying watching all the fish swim about. I make my way to the next room, the sharks. A few boys are watching the sharks with joy in their eyes. *I always liked the sharks we have. They are really not aggressive, at least not to me. I can clean the tank without them bugging me.*

I tell the boys, "Did you know, that sharks have ten thousand times better sense of smell than humans, and they can detect an animal's heartbeat through the water."

The boys are interested, yelling out, "Cool!"

I continue since they are enjoying me telling them facts. "Sharks have about forty to forty five teeth, but lose them frequently. They can have used over thirty thousand teeth in their lifetime."

After that, they seem to lose interest and want to see other things. I shrug and walk to the next room, Frank's room. *My mischievous octopi friend.* People are having a hard time finding him. *He must be camouflaged.* I go to the tank and look for him myself. I can't even see hm. I try to will him to change to his normal orange coloring. I hear people gasping and saying they found him. *He must have listened to me.* That makes me smile. I look myself and see that Frank has indeed changed to orange and is climbing over to the side of the tank that I am at. He sticks to the side of the glass and looks me in the eye, or at least, it feels like he does. His tentacle also seems to wave at me. I wave back to him. *"Hiya Frank, nice to see you!"* I tell him with my mind. He goes back into his corner and changes his coloring back to brown to not be seen. I shake my head.

Just then, the P/A system turns on, "Attention guests, the aquarium will close in fifteen minutes, please make your way through to the gift shop to exit, thank you and have a great night." *Jenny wants people out today, she usually only makes an announcement five minutes before closing.* I help people find the exit. Once I think no one else is coming though, I make my way to the front and do another sweep of the whole building. There was a few stragglers in the beginning but every other area was clear.

We help ring up the last customer at the gift shop. I do another sweep, just to make sure every room is clear. I help Jean cover the touch pool tanks. Jenny says that we can leave. We walk to the back room together and grab our stuff from the lockers. I tell Jean bye and good luck, we hug and walk through the back door, out to the parking lot. Jett pulls up to the door as soon as we get out.

"Oh wow! Curb service." Jean jokes.

"Yup." I laugh, but I know he did that because of what happened yesterday. I step into the car.

"Hello, beautiful." Jett says while giving me a kiss.

His lips are soft and delicious. "Hi. Were you bored all day?" I ask him.

"No, this is my job. My mind kept me company, but I do have to admit I kept counting down the minutes till I got to see you again." He says, this makes me smile.

"I was too." I tell him truthfully. My stomach growls at me, I'm hungry. I haven't eaten since brunch. "Can we hang out at my place tonight? Also, let's stop at a fast food joint, I'm starving." I say to him.

"Of course, where would you like to go?" He asks. *He's always so considerate. Seriously, like the perfect guy for me.*

"Well, is there a place you've never been and would like to try?" I ask him.

"I haven't been to many except the McDonald's and it was only okay. I'm sure I will like where ever you pick." He says to me.

We are still in the parking lot, I pick a place quickly. "Well, let's go to Taco Bell. It's cheap and filling." I tell him.

He nods and starts to drive. I tell him the way to the restaurant. We order our food and drive to my house. Megan's car is still not home, but she shouldn't be home till late, and that's if she doesn't go out afterwards, might be even later. Jett parks his car behind mine in the driveway. He follows me inside the house and into my bedroom. I plop down on my bed.

"Have you ever played any video games?" I ask him while he sits next to me.

"No, not really, just board games." He says. *I am shocked. I mean, I get it, he's a merman. They live in the water, can't have TVs or electrical systems in water. But he lives on land for now. You would think he would have at least played one video game.* I must have a funny look on my face because Jett busts out laughing.

"What is so funny? I am the one who should be laughing at you, never playing a video game." I give him a mock scoff.

I separate our food and start eating, *I'm fucking starving.* "Well, at the cabin, I know there are video games in the game room but I really haven't checked it out yet." He says before taking a bite of his burrito. His eyes get all huge. "These are amazing!" He shouts a little bit.

I laugh. "So, you're telling me, that your house has a theater, and a game room?" I ask incredulously.

"Yea, and a library. Now the library, I have checked out, extensively." He states. I feel like I'm going to pass out.

"Seriously?" I ask again, flabbergasted.

He chuckles. "Yes, seriously. I will show it to you next time we are there."

I do want a thorough look into both those rooms. "Ok, I'll hold you on that. Swimming, video games, and reading are my favorite hobbies."

He smiles, "working out, fishing, and trident training are my favorite hobbies." He says.

I like that we are learning things about each other. "Well, I was going to say, let's play some Mario Kart but since you've never played a video game before, it wouldn't be fair. I'd kick your ass so bad in that game." We both laugh. We enjoy each other's company while finishing our food.

"I've been thinking about some exercises that might help you develop all of your powers." Jett states while staring off into space.

He said he doesn't know exactly all the powers I might get but we know I can control marine life, and I can dream of the future. We have to wait till I develop my electricity power till I can see the council. I wonder if I will get any more powers than that.

"What kind of exercises?" I ask kind of scared.

"I read about them in this book." He says while taking a book out of his back pocket and handing it to me.

The book is titled Lunafriya Lore. I get excited because I might learn about what I am. I skim through the book.

"We will have to start training very soon. What are you doing tomorrow?" He asks.

"I'm off work, the aquarium is closed but I promised Megan I'd have girl's day with her." I tell him.

"Ok, Monday then." He says.

I nod my head. I set the book down on my nightstand to read later. "Just so you know, a girl's day means no boys allowed." I tell him with a smirk.

"I go where you go." He says and I start to protest. "I will stay out of sight, you won't even know I'm there, but if any trouble happens, know I'm there." He says with a serious face.

I study his face. I didn't even notice we got so close, our legs are now touching. I reach out and caress his cheek and look into his eyes. *I am falling for this man. He is willing to protect me with his life and let me have some alone time.* I give him a little kiss.

"Thank you, really. I need s girl's day and so does Megan." I tell him.

Jett rubs my lower back, going under the shirt to get skin contact. *It feels amazing*. My hand goes to his shoulder. "Not a problem, baby." He whispers in my ear.

His hands get lower and lower towards my ass with each circular rub on my back. I put my hand on his thigh and he jumps a little bit. I can hear his smile in my ear. I start to rub his thigh getting close to his cock but not touching it, just teasing him. I see his cock get hard for me in his jeans. I smile and bite my lip. I pull back enough so that I can reach his lips and give him a deep, passionate kiss. His hands are now squeezing my ass and picking me up to put on his lap. We are making out, tongues twirling, hands are rubbing everywhere, grinding on his cock. I moan into his mouth.

He takes my shirt off and throws it across the room. I grab his and pull it off for him. We can't get enough of each other. He is unhooking my bra while we kiss. He gets it unclasped so I shrug the bra off to reveal my breasts. His hand and mouth immediately go for them. I moan again. I unbutton his jeans and then my own. I step off of him and shimmy out of my pants. I am standing before him in just my panties. I feel slightly uncomfortable, because I'm not a stick thin model. I have curves and a belly.

He looks at me and whistles, "Baby, you are sexy as hell." He says. I blush and smile. He takes his pants off and reaches his hand out for me. He pulls me on his lap again. Our skin touches and feels like fire, but in a good way. His cock is so hard, it presses on my bud through my thin panties.

"I am so wet right now." I whisper in his ear. He moans and presses his dick against me harder. That makes me gasp. He moves my underwear off to the side to expose my sex. I pull his dick out of the hole in his boxers. He makes sure I am wet enough by licking his hand and dragging it down my clit to my vagina. He slides a finger in smoothly. I moan and he removes his hand. I jump up and slide down his dick slowly.

We both gasp and moan. I move up and down riding his cock. He lays his head down and grabs my waist, helping me move. *I never really had the confidence to be on top, but I am really enjoying myself.* Jett starts to thrust his hips up when I go down, making him penetrate me deeper. I moan loudly. We keep this pace for a while until Jett grabs my back and flips me so I'm lying on my back now. He then proceeds to fuck me hard. My legs are up and above my head. I feel close to climaxing so I rub my clit while he drills me. It feels so amazingly good. His breathing is getting ragged so I believe he is close to finishing as well.

This makes me explode with climax. I'm moaning so loudly that I can barely hearing him coming as well. He slows to a stop. He puts my legs down and I try to catch my breath, with him still inside me.

Jett kisses my forehead, "That...was...amazing." He says between breathes.

"Yes, it was." I smile. Jett slides out of me and I jump up to go to my bathroom, he follows. I give Jett a towel to clean himself up and I use the toilet then clean myself too. Once I leave the bathroom, I see that Jett is dressed again. I am still naked so I go to my dresser and put my pajamas on, my sexy pajamas, of course.

"So, what would you like to do now?" I ask him. He smiles and shrugs his shoulders. I roll my eyes. I check the time on my phone. It's little after ten at night. I see that I have a text message from Megan.

"Hey bitch. I'm home. Having wild sex, huh? You're so loud!" She also put some emoji's. I gasp and then laugh.

Jett looks at me, "What?" he asks with a smile.

"Megan is home, and she heard us having sex." I laugh again. Jett joins me. "Oh well, not like I've never heard her loud mouth before." I say. I shoot her a text back, "Oops, sorry." And an emoji winking face. I set my phone down and set up my laptop. I have a ton of movies stored on there.

Just then a knock raps on my bedroom door. "You guys decent?" Megan yells.

I shake my head, "Yea, come on in." She opens the door and walks in.

"Hey, hi Jett." She says. We both greet her back. "So, you still up for girl's day tomorrow?" She asks.

"Of course I am! What are we doing first? A run?" I ask her.

"Yes, I would like to do a run. Let's set the alarm for seven." She says.

I roll my eyes and sigh, "Ok, but you have to make my coffee before waking me up." I tell her.

"Ok, bitch, I will. You guys have a good night, I'm hitting the hay." She yawns and walks out.

"Goodnight Megs." I call out.

"Good night Megan." Jett says. We are alone once more. I set up the laptop so that we can lay down on my bed and watch. I pick the episode of The Office that we left off on. I push play and we get comfortable. I love cuddling with him. We just fit so well together, like we were made to be. Slowly I drift off to sleep after the first episode, wrapped in Jett's arms.

I had a dream that night. In the dream, Jett and I were training at the lake. I can see everything so clearly. Jett is encouraging me to try and summon my electric powers. And I eventually succeed. I smile in my sleep.

Chapter 8

Jett's perspective

Last night was amazing. Cora and I finally had sex! I start to stir awake. I flutter my eyes open and she is cuddled in my arms.

"Good morning, beautiful." I say with a smile.

"Good morning, handsome" She tells me right back.

"What time is it? And what time do you work today?" I ask.

"It's seven thirty right now. Today is my late day, I don't start till one." She says with a yawn.

"Well, in that case, I think I'll have some breakfast." I say while ducking under the blankets. I make my way between her legs and start to lick her clit.

"Holy fuck, Jett!" She yells while grabbing my hair under the blankets. *She tastes so fucking good. I could do this all day.* I circle my tongue around her bud and inside her. She moans loudly. I reach up and stick two fingers into her mouth. She sucks hard on my fingers, twirling her tongue around them. This makes me hard and I continue licking her. I pull my fingers out of her mouth and bring them down to her pussy. I put two fingers at her opening and tease her.

She groans, "Please." She begs me. *I love the sound of her begging.* I shove my fingers inside of her and continue to lick her clit. I fuck her with my fingers and mouth. Soon, she goes over the edge and climaxes hard on my face. I wipe my face and look up at her from beneath the blankets and smile.

"That was some delicious breakfast." I say with a smile.

She laughs while catching her breath. "Wow" is all she says. I keep smiling, knowing that I am the one who made her feel so great. After she catches her breath, she says, "Well, I want some breakfast too!"

She pulls me back up to the head of the bed, with my help. My cock is already standing at attention. She licks her lips while staring at my cock. It looks like she likes what she sees. She grabs my cock in her hands and gives it a little squeeze. *Fuck, that feels good.* I gasp a little. She gives the tip of my dick a little lick and I moan. She licks the under ridge of my tip and sucks, while rubbing the length of my cock. *She really knows what she's doing, it feels fucking amazing.* She shoves my dick deeper into her mouth and gags a little. I am groaning with pleasure. She works her hands up and down on the parts her mouth can't reach and sucks as deep as she can go. Twirling her tongue around as much as she can. She grabs my balls a little and that sets me off.

"Cora, I'm going to come." I tell her. She stays where she is and lets me come in her mouth. I moan fast and loud, squirting into her throat. She gags a little but shallows my seed. *Fuck, that was hot!* After I finish, she wipes her mouth on the back of her hand.

"Delicious." She says with a smirk.

"You are amazing, Cora." I tell her.

"So are you." She states. We both just had amazing oral, but Cora is frowning.

"What's wrong?" I ask her concerned.

"Oh, nothing." She sighs.

I look at her with suspicious eyes. "Don't give me that shit, I know something is wrong. What is it, beautiful?" I ask again.

She looks into my eyes and takes a deep breath. "Well, you said we couldn't do this. That it was against your oath. Everything about this relationship is just doomed for us. Why are you all of a sudden ok with it?" She asks with a deep breath again.

"Technically, yes, we shouldn't be doing this. I took an oath to not get involved with my subjects. I have upheld my oath, until you. It's not like I am the only person to break his oath, actually your grandfather broke his oath to be with your grandmother. Things turned out alright for him. He's now an elder on the council." I continue while looking deeply into her eyes. "Your father broke his oath, and nothing bad happened to him. I am ok with us being in a relationship because I want you. I want your heart, your soul." I run my hands up her sides towards her tits,

"And your body." My hands get to her breasts and I squeeze. "These are amazing, you know

that?" I say.

She chuckles. "Yea, I know." She rolls her eyes while saying that. I laugh. "I should start

heading home so I can shower and get ready for work." She tells me.

I'm still squeezing her tits and teasing her nipples. They are hard and I put my mouth on

one of them and suck. *I want her again so badly, even though I just had her last night.* In

between sucks, I say, "Take a shower here, with me."

She moans and grinds on my cock a bit. "Ok, but I still need to go home to get new

clothes to wear for the day. I am doing the feeding lesson on the rays today, and I have to look

good." She tells me with a smirk.

I pick her up off the bed and carry her into the bathroom with me. She squeals and kicks

her legs, laughing. I chuckle and set her down on the floor and start the water in the shower.

"Ladies first." I say while opening the glass shower door and directing her inside. I

already have another hard-on. She climbs inside the tub and I follow. She puts her head under the

fall of water. *She looks so unbelievably sexy.* I put my body against her back.

"Do you have shampoo and conditioner?" She asks me.

"Yea, let me get that for you." My body leaves hers and it makes me a little cold. She

shudders a bit. She must have gotten cold too. I put the bath products on the ledge where she can

see it. Cora starts to wash her hair then condition. I grab the body wash and put a large dab on

my hands. I then proceed to wash her body for her.

Her body is perfection. Just the right amount of cushion, curves so deep, I could swim in

them. She grabs the shampoo and washes my hair for me. It is short, so it doesn't take a long time to wash. I rinse my hair and she grabs the body wash for me too. Once we are both sudsed up, I move closer to her till we have skin to skin contact. I rub her back and ass and she does the same to me. We are under the shower head and rinsing the soap off each other.

I then start to rub lower and hitting her clit. She gasps. I slide my finger inside of her. She clenches down on my finger. *She wants me inside of her.* I look down at her and she smiles and grabs my cock. My finger still inside of her and my thumb on her clit, I vibrate my hand fast. She moans and squeezes my cock tighter.

I nibble on her ear, "You like that, baby?" I ask in a throaty whisper.

"Yes." She pants out. The water is making lubrication against us, making it easier to play with each other. I am moaning into her ear. *I need to be inside of her, now.* I lift her one leg up and prop it against the shower door. Then, I slide my cock inside of her. She gasps at the fullness then moans at the pleasure. I take it slow, pumping in and out. Letting us both fully enjoy each other.

The water is starting to get cold, but I really don't care. It doesn't seem to be bothering Cora either. I feel like I'm close but I want her to come first. She starts to touch herself, so I fuck her harder. Soon, she explodes and grips my cock with her pussy. This sets me off and I come hard inside of her. Once we are done, we clean up and I turn the water off. She steps out of the shower and grabs a towel.

We dry off and she says, "I still have to go home, I need clean clothes to wear for work."

I smile at her, "That's not a problem. We can go after I make us something to eat." I tell her.

"Ok" is all she says.

I toss her an old t-shirt of mine. *Something about women in nothing but your shirt is just sexy as hell.* She puts it on and it is really long on her, I am much bigger than her, but she is pretty short. I need to go to the kitchen or we will just end up having sex again. She eventually follows me out into the kitchen. I am busy, preparing our food.

"What's for breakfast?" She asks.

"Oral was for breakfast." I smirk at her, she rolls her eyes with a smile. "Pancakes are for brunch." I say.

"Woohoo! Pancakes!" She yells. This surprises me since I didn't know she was going to yell and I jump a bit. She laughs, "Sorry, pancakes are my weakness."

I laugh too, "That is good to know." I tell her.

She walks up behind me and gives me a backwards hug, laying her head on my back. It feels really nice. I've never had feelings for anyone like this before.

"Almost ready, why don't you go sit at the island and I'll get your plate." I tell her.

She goes immediately to the kitchen island. I give her a plate of four pancakes. I have set maple syrup and butter in the countertop already so she starts loading up her pancakes and eating. I am still finishing up cooking my batch of pancakes, it doesn't take long and we sit next to each other. We eat in silence, just both of us content with our brunch.

"After we finish, I want to go home and change." She tells me. I nod at her, mouth full of pancakes, deep in thought about taking her to my city. *I need to introduce her to Meri, my sister would flip out if she knew about the truth of Cora and me though.* "What's on your mind?" She asks me.

"It's nothing, I was just thinking about taking you to my city. I think you will really enjoy it." I tell her.

She gets an excited look on her face, "When are we going to go?" She asks.

"We have to wait until you develop the rest of your powers. Once you do, I promise we will go. You have to meet my baby sister. She is dying to meet you." I reply.

"How old is she? What's her name?" She asks me.

"Meri, and she's twenty. She's a real big fan of the Lunafriya's." I answer her.

"Are there others like me?" She asks again, just full of questions.

"Well, we don't really know. They were thought to have been extinct for one hundred and fifty years, but I'm sure there are others." I tell her.

We finish our pancakes and I clean up our plates. Cora leaves the room for a few minutes. She comes back with her pants on and says, "I'm going home now."

I stop what I'm doing. "Wait. I was serious when I said I go where you go. Let me finish this then I will drive you home." I tell her.

"I have my own car, I can drive myself, it's not like you can go to work with me anyways." She explains to me.

"You can drive your own car if you would like but yes, I am going to work with you. You could quit if you like, you will have to eventually if you plan to live in Halcyon." I respond to her. *How does she not get how much danger she is in, last of her kind, as far as we know?*

She gets angry. "I am not quitting and you are not coming to my work. You can do one loop of the aquarium, and watch my lesson on the rays, then you have to leave. I don't care if you wait in the car. I am not getting fired from my favorite place." She says with clenched teeth.

I have to calm her down. "Ok, that sounds reasonable." I respond. She rolls her eyes. She sure does that a lot. But at least she doesn't seem mad anymore. I smile my lady killer smile at her. She smiles back and I think, we're good.

She heads to her car while I go to mine. We start our cars and she pulls out of the driveway first and heads to her house. I follow behind her, even though I know the way, she doesn't need to know that. It would make me look like a creepy stalker, which is only kind of true, but it's part of the job. We both pull up into her driveway.

"Welcome to my home." She says to me.

"Very nice! Is it just you and Megan here?" I ask.

"Yup" is all she says while unlocking the door. She shows me around the house ending at her bedroom. "And this is my room." She says.

I pick her up and throw her on her bed. She squeals with excitement and surprise. She has 'fuck me' eyes, so I jump on top of her and we make out for a few minutes. I'm in a playful mood. Eventually, she pulls away from me.

"I really have to get ready for work." She tells me.

"Ok." I say while giving her a pouty face and sliding off of her. She gets up and goes to the closet and shuts the door. I look around her room, everything is neat and tidy. She has a lot of trophies. I stand up and look at them closer. All of them are for swimming, and all in first place. *How did her father not know she was a mermaid? It makes no sense.*

Cora steps out of her closet fully dressed in her work uniform. It actually looks sexy as hell. "I will be in my bathroom if you need me." She tells me and walks out of the room.

I see she has a whole board filled with pictures. They are all of her and other people. I recognize the ones with Megan in them, but there are a few people that I don't know. I'm just glad she has no pictures of her ex up there. She comes back into the room, looking all kinds of fine. She did her make-up and her hair in braids. *I really like it, and want to hold on to those while fucking her from behind.* I get a smirk and change the subject or she will be late to work because I'll make my fantasies a reality.

"We need a picture of us on here." I say.

"Come here." She says to me while rolling her finger towards her.

I go to her and look deeply into her beautiful blue eyes. She snaps a picture of us like that. Then, she makes me look at the camera and tells me to smile, she takes another picture of us. She then kisses me and takes a picture while we kiss.

Once we are done, she says, "Now we have three pictures of us. I will print them after work. By the way, I need to leave like now for work."

I smile at her, "Ok, let's go. I'll drive you in my car." I tell her.

"Ok, fine." She pouts. "Let me just text Megan and tell her, so she doesn't freak out when she sees my car but I'm nowhere around." She pulls out her cell and texts quickly. We walk to my car together after she locks the house up.

Spending time with her has been amazing. It doesn't feel like I'm on a job right now. The drive to her workplace is nice. Just us, enjoying each other's company. My cheeks hurt from smiling so much. Cora has been smiling just as much as me.

I love the sound of her laugh and her beautiful face. We get to the aquarium and she tells me to park in the back. We arrived fifteen minutes before she has to clock in.

"I have to go in but you can join me at one. I will be doing the ray lesson." She tells me.

I give her a deep kiss. "See you in there, beautiful." I tell her.

"Bye." She says while giving me another peck on the lips before leaving the car. I watch her walk towards the back door. *Her ass is plump and looking great in those pants.* The door closes and I have about fifteen minutes to kill before I can go in.

I pull out the book I found in my library at home. It's titled _Lunafriya Lore._ I figured we might learn something about her or how to get her to develop all of her powers. I skim through the book. I check the time and it's about time I head in. I walk to the front of the aquarium and open the door. Cora is at the front desk with an older woman. They both look at me.

I smile and walk towards her. "Hi, baby." I say once I get up to the front desk. She smiles.

"Hi Jett. This is my boss Jenny." She directs my attention to her.

"Nice to meet you Jenny." I say while placing a kiss on her hand. Jenny giggles. I see Cora roll her eyes again.

"Nice to meet you too, Jett. You can go into the aquarium for free, friends and family discount." Jenny says.

Cora raises her eyebrows at me, and shrugs. "I will show Jett around and then head to the ray room, ok?" She asks Jenny.

"That's fine, honey." She says while waving us off.

The first room we walk into is the touch pool area. I follow her to one of the tanks and reach in and touch a starfish, it crawls on my hand. I laugh.

"Did you do that?" I whisper even though I already know the answer.

"Yes." She responds with a smile. She makes the starfish get off me and back on the rock. "Want to see the other areas? This one is more for the kids." She asks me.

"Sure, lead the way." I say.

She takes me to the next room. This one is the electric fish. The room is pitch black except for the black lights, it makes the luminescent skin of the fish glow. "Wow!" I remark. She laughs, _I wonder what she's laughing at._

She follows the path and leads me into the next room. It's the seahorse tanks. *I've always liked these guys.* She chuckles again.

"What's so funny?" I ask her bemused.

"Oh, it's nothing, just thought it'd be cool if the seahorses were big enough to ride." She giggles.

I laugh at that, "You sure do have a weird mind." I tell her.

She mockingly scoffs, "I take pride in my weirdness." She says. I shake my head with a smile. The next room is the ray room. "You get a good spot up front. I have to do the lesson in about five minutes, at one thirty." She tells me.

People have already started gathering at the tank. The rays are swimming around the circular open top tank. I pick a spot that is directly in front of Cora. *I came here to see her, not really the fish.* She is setting up her station. I watch as she puts a headset on.

All of a sudden, I hear her voice over the speaker system. "Good afternoon, North Creek Aquarium guests. The mantra ray feeding will begin in about five minutes. Join us in the ray room to enjoy watching these magnificent creatures." She says. *She must really love this job and all of these animals.* She looks around for me and we lock eyes. She smiles, I smile right back. More people are filing in to watch.

She starts her lesson. "Hello everyone! Welcome to the ray room! Today, we will be feeding the rays and learning a bit about them as well. Now as you can see, their mouths are on the bottom of their bodies. They swim around the bottom of the tank and pick the plankton up with their mouths. They don't actually have teeth but little plates that suck up the food."

She tosses in the plankton by the handful, making sure to get everywhere in the tank. The rays swim around, happily eating. I don't take my eyes off of Cora. *She really is the most beautiful woman I have ever met, I'm glad to call her mine.* She continues with her lesson.

"Manta rays are graceful swimmers. They swim by moving their pectoral fins up and down which propels their bodies through the water. Their short tails allow the rays to be more acrobatic with its movement, and they have even been seen leaping out of the water."

Once she says this, a ray jumps out of the water making a splash and soaking some guests. The crowd oohs and aahs. She smiles, and looks at me. I shake my head and laugh. *I know she just used her power. She also needs to be more careful, I note to talk to her about that later.*

She continues, "Manta rays eat tiny marine organisms including plankton, small fish, and crustaceans. Today, they had some plankton grub." The rays swim around the sides of the tank. "Here, you can see a close up on their mouths. Some of them look to be smiling."

She is in her element right now. You can just tell how much she loves these creatures. "Now, although the manta ray is not considered to be a species that is in danger of extinction in the wild, their population numbers have been declining more quickly in recent years. They are particularly susceptible to pollution in the water and are quickly affected by overfishing in certain areas, and therefore a lack of food. So, let's try to help all fish, by cleaning up the oceans and beaches and not using as much plastic. Thank you for your time." She finishes with a bow.

Everyone claps. Some people leave the room and others stay to watch the rays some more. I walk up to Cora.

"That was cool and informative. Those things will still fuck you up in the ocean." I whisper.

She laughs, "Yes, I know. That's how Steve Irwin died." She tells me.

"Who's Steve Irwin?" I ask.

She busts out laughing. "Oh, my sweet summer child." She says referencing something, I have no idea what.

"What the fuck are you talking about?" I laugh at her.

She shakes her head. "Sorry, I'm not used to someone who doesn't get pop culture. Most of my language is movie quotes and TV shows." She laughs. "Would you like to see the big tank?" She asks me.

"Sure." I say.

She leads me to the next room. The whole wall is glass, then it leads to an underwater tunnel into the next room. This is where all the sea turtles and salt water fish are. *This reminds me of home.*

"This is one of my other favorite places. I like to come in here after closing and talk to the fish. I didn't know at the time that they could actually listen." She tells me. "I like cleaning the tank and swimming with the sea turtles." She says.

"I can't wait to take you to the ocean, you will love it." I tell her.

She smiles at me. She leads me under the tunnel to the sharks. None are very big, but I've had my own run-ins with these fuckers. I hate sharks.

"Now these things are deadly, I got lucky with my run-in, and only got this small scar." I tell her while showing her my scar on my upper arm.

"You sure did get lucky, they can tear you up." She says. After the shark room is the octopus room. "This is my buddy, Frank. He's a mischievous one." She tells me.

I chuckle. The next room isn't really a room but a long hallway filled with tanks. They are all local fish. This hallway leads to the gift shop and out to the front lobby.

"Well, you've seen the whole aquarium, I have to get back to work. What will you do for the next five hours?" She asks.

"I think I will stay in the car and watch out for anything suspicious." I say.

She rolls her eyes again, "Really? You don't have to do that. Just go home and pick me up at seven." She tells me.

"I go where you go," is all I say.

She sighs, "Fine. See you in five hours." She gives me a quick kiss and turns around and walks to Jenny at the front desk. I wave to Jenny and walk out of the building.

I go around to the back of the building, where my car is. I check the parking lot for signs of the struggle that Cora had last night. I look around on the ground and actually see drips of blood. *Good job Cora, she certainly can take care of herself.*

I go to my car and sit. I am glad I brought the book with me or I wouldn't have anything to do for the next five hours. I keep watch while reading, looking for anything suspicious. I move the car from where I parked earlier, I need to be able to see both front and back doors of the building. I pick up the book and start at the beginning.

It starts with the Lunafriya history. Something I already know, things they teach in school. That the Lunafriyas were an elite group of warrior women who had powers. Power to control marine animals, and electricity, with other powers that changed from woman to woman. *Cora can dream of the future, and has the will over marine animals. We have to wait till she develops her lightning strikes before I present her to the council.* I look through the book to see anything about training that we can do to help her get her powers.

There actually is a whole chapter on their training techniques. Some things that we can try are, of course, being in the water. First, we can just try to have her focus and think about sending the current running in her body out through her hands. If that doesn't work then we have to step it up a notch and find some electric eels. The book also states that the Lunafriyas were a sisterhood. They rely on each other and their powers for strength. As far as we know, there are no others for her to rely on. This will be tough for her but I will help every step of the way.

I've been reading for so long that my eyes hurt. I am constantly keeping an eye out for anything as well. I look at the time and it's ten minutes before seven. *Good, I will be happy to see Cora. It's been only five hours since I've seen her but it feels longer. I miss her lips and her body against mine. I literally can't get her out of my mind.* I'm being extra cautious and when I see Cora open the back door, I drive and pick her up at the door. I'm not taking any chances.

"Hello, beautiful." I say while giving her a kiss. Her lips are soft.

"Hi, were you bored all day?" She asks me.

"No, this is my job. My mind kept me company, but I do have to admit I kept counting down the minutes till I got to see you again." I say, this makes her smile.

"I was too." She tells me. I love her smile. "Can we hang out at my place tonight? Also, let's stop at a fast food joint, I'm starving." She says to me.

"Of course, where would you like to go?" I ask.

"Well, is there a place you've never been and would like to try?" She asks.

"I haven't been to many except the McDonald's and it was only ok. I'm sure I will like where ever you pick." I tell her.

We are still in the parking lot, she picks a place quickly, "Well, let's go to Taco Bell. It's cheap and filling." She states.

I nod and start to drive. She tells me the way to the restaurant, I had no idea. We order our food, I just got what she gets, since I've never been there and I drive back to her house. I park the car behind hers in the driveway. I follow her inside the house and into her bedroom.

She plops down on her bed, "Have you ever played any video games?" She asks me. I sit down next to her.

"No, not really, just board games." Her mouth is agape, and she looks at me shocked. It makes me laugh really loud, *she must not be used to a man that doesn't play video games.*

"What's so funny? I am the one who should be laughing at you, never playing a video game." She gives me a mock scoff. She separates our food and starts eating.

"Well, at the cabin, I know there are video games in the game room but I really haven't checked it out yet." I tell her before taking a bite of my burrito. My eyes get all big, "These things are amazing!" I shout a bit.

She laughs, "So, you're telling me, that your house has a theater, and a game room?" She asks incredulously.

"Yea, and a library. Now the library, I have checked out, extensively." I state. There she goes again, with the shocked expression.

"Seriously?" She asks again, flabbergasted. I chuckle.

"Yes, seriously. I will show it to you next time we are there." I tell her.

"Ok, I'll hold you on that. Swimming, video games, and reading are my favorite hobbies." She says. I smile.

"Working out, fishing, and trident training are my favorite hobbies." I say. *I like that we are learning things about each other.*

"Well, I was going to say, let's play some Mario Kart but since you've never played a video game before, it wouldn't be fair. I'd kick your ass so bad in that game." We both laugh. We are enjoying each other's company while finishing our food.

I've been thinking a lot about what the book said, I need go tell her about the training that I found. "I've been thinking about some exercises that might help you develop all of your powers." I state while staring off into space. *I really hope these exercises will help her.*

"What kind of exercises?" She asks kind of scared looking. *I don't want to scare her. I'll just let her read about them herself.*

"I read about them in this book." I say while taking the book out of my back pocket and handing it to her. "We will have to start training very soon. What are you doing tomorrow?" I ask.

"I'm off work, the aquarium is closed but I promised Megan I'd have a girl's day with her." She tells me.

"Ok, Monday then." I say. She nods her head. She sets the book down on her nightstand.

"Just so you know, a girl's day means no boys allowed." She tells me with a smirk.

"I go where you go." I say and she starts to protest. "I will stay out of sight, you won't even know I'm there, but if any trouble happens, know I'm there." I say with a serious face.

She studies my face. I didn't notice that we got so close to each other, our legs are now touching. She reaches out and caresses my cheek and looks into my eyes. *I am falling for this woman. Her beauty, and sarcastic wit are to die for.* She gives me a little kiss.

"Thank you, really. I need a girl's day and so does Megan." She says. I rub her back, going under her shirt to get skin contact. Her hand goes to my shoulder and squeezes.

"Not a problem, baby." I whisper in her ear. My hands are getting lower and lower towards her ass with each circular rub on her back. *I love that juicy ass.* She puts her hand on my thigh and it makes me jump a bit. This makes me smile. She starts to rub my thigh getting close to my cock but not touching it, just teasing me. I guess I'm teasing her right now too. It makes me hard. She smiles and bites her lip.

She gives me a deep passionate kiss. While we make out, I squeeze her ass cheeks in my hands and then pick her up to put on my lap. We are making out hard, tongues twirling, hands are rubbing everywhere. She's grinding on my cock. She moans into my mouth. I take her shirt off and throw it across the room. She grabs mine and pulls it off too. We can't get enough of each other. I am unhooking her bra while we kiss. *I need those tits in my face.* I unclasp it so she shrugs the bra off to reveal her huge tits.

I immediately grab them and put one in my mouth. She moans loudly again. She unbuttons my jeans and then her own. She steps off of me and shimmies out of her pants. She is standing before me in just her panties. I drink in every inch of her with my eyes. *She is breath-taking. Her curves are perfect, her ass and tits are glorious.* It makes me wolf whistle.

"Baby, you are sexy as hell." I tell her.

She blushes and smiles. I take my pants off as well and reach out for her. I pull her down on top of me again. Our skin touches and I feel a slight shock of electricity. It hurts in a good way. My cock is so hard, it presses on her clit through her thin panties.

"I am so wet right now." She whispers in my ear.

Oh Poseidon, that's fucking hot. I moan and press my dick against her harder. *I need her, right now, this very instant.* She gasps when I move her underwear off to the side to expose her sex. She pulls my dick out of the hole in my boxers. I make sure she is wet enough by licking my hand and dragging it down her clit to her opening. I slide a finger in smoothly. She moans and I remove my hand. She jumps up and slides down my dick slowly.

We both gasp and moan. She moves up and down, riding my cock. I lay my head back and grab her waist, helping her move. She looks to be enjoying herself up there but I need more of her. I start to thrust my hips up when she goes down, making me penetrate her deeper. She moans very loudly. We keep this pace for a while until I want to be on top, and give her a break.

I grab her back and flip her so she is laying down now. I then proceed to fuck her hard. Her legs are up and near my head. She starts to rub her clit while I drill her. *It feels so amazingly good.* Her breathing is getting ragged as well as mine so I believe she is close to finishing as well. I wait till she comes.

Her loud, almost screaming moaning sets me over the edge and I come too. I slow to a stop. She puts her legs down and tries to catch her breath. I kiss her forehead.

"That...was...amazing!" I say between breathes.

"Yes, it was." She says, her smile huge. I slide out of her and she jumps up and goes to her bathroom. I follow.

Cora gives me a towel to clean myself up. She sits on the toilet and I take that as my leave and go to her room to get dressed. She leaves the bathroom, still naked except for her panties so she goes to her closet and puts some pajamas on. *The pajamas don't really help much, I still want her, even though we just got done having amazing sex.*

"So, what would you like to do now?" She asks. I smile and check out her body and shrug my shoulders. She rolls her eyes and picks up her phone. She gasps and then laughs.

I look at her puzzled, "What?" I ask with a smile.

"Megan is home, and she heard us having sex." She laughs again. I join her. *It's her own fault, she was the loud one.* "Oh well, not like I've never heard her loud mouth before." She says. She types something on her phone and sets it down. She finds her laptop and sets it up on the bed.

Just then, we hear a knock on the door. "You guys decent?" Megan yells.

Cora shakes her head, "Yea, come on in."

Megan opens the door and walks in. "Hey Cora, hi Jett." She says. We both greet her back. "So, you still up for girl's day tomorrow?" She asks Cora.

"Of course I am, what are we doing first? A run?" She asks her.

"Yes, I would like to do a run. Let's set the alarm for seven." Megan says.

Cora rolls her eyes and sighs, "Ok, but you have to make my coffee before waking me up." She tells her. *I'm thinking Cora is not a morning person.*

"Ok, bitch, I will. You guys have a good night, I'm hitting the hay." She yawns and walks out.

"Goodnight Megs." Cora calls out.

"Good night, Megan." I say.

We are alone once more. She sets up the laptop so that we can lay down on her bed and watch. She puts on the episode of The Office that we left off on. She pushes play and we get comfortable. *I love cuddling with her. We just fit so well together, like we were made to be.* We watch about an episode and a half before she falls asleep on my chest. I pause the show and shut the laptop, then put it on the nightstand, all without trying to wake her. I let her sleep on me for a couple hours before I fall into a light sleep myself.

I wake before six in the morning and slip out of her bed. *I don't want to be here when she wakes up. I want her to have a girl's day with her friend. I will be close but she won't see me unless something happens.* I kiss her forehead before I leave her house through the window.

Chapter 9

Cora's perspective

The stupid alarm goes off at seven. I turn it off and want to throw it across the room, but I don't. I just lay back down and try to fall back asleep. I notice Jett is gone. *I wonder where he went, he said he would be close, but he is close enough to hear us? I don't want him to hear our girlfriend talk.*

Megan knocks on my door. "Housekeeping, you want towel?" She says in her Tommy Boy voice.

"No, thank you, sleeping." I yell out.

Megan opens the door anyways. "Come on, Cora, get up. I have your cappuccino right here." She says.

I sit up, ready for my coffee. "Thank you." I tell her before taking a sip.

"No problem, now hurry up and get dressed. We have a lot of stuff to do today!" She sings out while walking out of my room.

I roll my eyes. *I wonder what she has planned for today, hopefully nothing too god awful.* I finish my coffee, and set the cup down. Now I have to pick out what I want to wear today. I go in my closet and get my comfy leggings and a hoodie. I just throw those on quickly before Megan barges in my room again. I walk out of my room after quickly brushing my hair in a messy bun and brushing my teeth. I go grab my tennis shoes from the front door.

"Almost ready!" I yell out, I don't know where Megan currently is.

She walks around the corner and says "FINALLY!" while leaning on the wall, stretching. I roll my eyes.

"So, what's the plan for today?" I ask while doing my own stretches. She's the one who always plans our girl's days. Mainly because she got sick of always swimming in the lake when I picked, but she actually plans some really fun times.

"First, of course, we go for a quick run, then come back and get ready for the day. Then, glow in the dark putt-putt and the arcade, lunch at Antonio's, then we come back for a pajama marathon of....Jurassic Park!" She explains with emphasis.

I smile. "Sounds like a perfect day! Let's go!" I say. *Never thought I'd be excited to go running, but I really want to get the fun stuff started already.* I open up the front door and walk out, with Megan following.

I wait on the porch while she is locking up the house. I look around to see if I can see Jett anywhere, but I don't. Megan sees what I'm doing and looks at me puzzled.

"Just looking around, can't be too careful." I say with a shrug.

"Good idea." She responds with a head nod.

We start our run down our street then turn left to go deeper into the neighborhood. We like to go this way because the landscapes are beautiful. We tend to look around and get ideas for our own garden and yard. Every yard is covered in a light blanket of snow, but not the sidewalks or streets.

Megan goes a light pace so that I can keep up with her. She knows that I really don't like to talk while we run, so she gives me my silence, and I really appreciate it. It gives me time to think about topics that I can talk to her about. *Jett is a safe topic, except the part where he is a mer-man and his real job. Work is ok, except the part where I got attacked by her one night stand, Jake. I can tell her a bit about mine and Jett's relationship, just not the part where we shouldn't be together and he wants to take me away from land.* I've been thinking so much that I didn't realize we made it home already.

"Wow! That seemed fast." I say once we stop at our house.

"We could go again." Megan responds with a smirk.

I roll my eyes, "No, thanks." I tell her while walking up the porch steps.

She follows and grabs her keys to unlock the door. I see something out of the corner of my eye and swing my head around. It was Jett, I'm sure of it but I don't see anything anymore. I follow Megan inside the house and walk to my bedroom.

"I'm going to take a shower!" She yells down to me.

"Ok, I'll take one after you." I yell back.

I open the door to my room and my window is open. I look at it for a second before looking around and see Jett sitting on my bed. I smile. "What are you doing here?" I shake my head, "Its girl's day, if Megan saw you here, she'd flip." I scold him.

He walks over to me and gives me a big hug. "Sorry, I just wanted to see you, she is in the shower and won't know I'm here, I promise." He says then gives me a kiss. I happily kiss him back. He pulls away first this time. "We have to stop or I won't be able to help myself and rip those clothes off of you." He says with a smirk.

I flutter my eyes. *I want him to rip my clothes off.* I hear the shower turn off. "Ok, Megan is getting out of the shower now, you need to leave. Come over tonight after she goes to sleep." I tell him.

"Good bye, beautiful." He says with another kiss before I shove him out the window.

"Good bye." I tell him before he leaves. I watch as he runs to his car which is down the block. I shut the window and lock it.

Just then, Megan pounds on my door, "All done, jump on in!" She yells.

"Ok!" I yell back. *That was a close one.* I go into my personal bathroom and take a quick shower.

Once I'm done, I run into my closet and look for an outfit. Something that I can move around comfortably in but also a little sexy since I know Jett will be watching me all day.

Suddenly I get an epiphany, and I know exactly what I want to wear. My mouth curves into an ironic smirk. I find my colorful mermaid scale leggings and my small black tank top with my huge grey over-tank that says 'Mermaid hair, Don't care' on it. It makes me laugh even more now that I know that I am an actual mermaid! I put my clothes on and then go into the bathroom to put make-up on and do my hair.

I already know that Megan will put a ton of make-up on, she's probably doing a video for YouTube as we speak. I only do the bare minimum on make-up. Eye liner, eye shadow, and mascara, that's it. I let my hair air dry but fluff it so it's got some waves and volume to it. My hair is quite long. I usually only put it in a ponytail or bun, it's refreshing to have it down. Once I finish, I look at myself in the full length mirror, *it will do*. I walk out to the living room and wait for Megan.

Megan comes down the hallway about ten minutes later, looking amazing. She was sensible and wore jeans and tennis shoes with a flowy top. Her make-up is done to the nines.

"Ready, bitch?" She asks me. I roll my eyes.

"Yup, who's driving?" I grab my phone and chuck it in my purse.

"I will, I just filled my tank." She says.

I follow her out the door. I look around again and notice Jett's car. I can't see him inside because he's too far away and the tinted windows but I give him a nod anyways. Megan locks the door and we get into her car. Right when she starts the car, she has to turn down her blaring radio.

"Sorry." She says with a laugh.

I shrug, "No prob, bob." I remark.

"So, how are things going with Jett?" She asks with a smirk. She pulls out of the driveway and drives to Zap Zone.

I get a huge smile on my face, "Everything is amazing. He is so prefect for me." I tell her. I look out the side mirror, and see him following us but from afar.

"It sounded pretty amazing." She replies.

I roll my eyes, and laugh. "Like I've never heard you before." I say back.

"You know I'm just teasing you. I'm happy that you are happy and that you are finally getting laid!" She laughs out.

I roll my eyes again and laugh. She is the sister I chose, we like to rag on each other. In no time, we arrive at Zap Zone. They have everything from an arcade, to putt-putt, go-karts, and laser tag. Today is Sunday, so the morning is not too busy but after lunch, it will be packed with families.

"What would you like to do first?" I ask her.

"Umm, let's go right for the putt-putt and do everything else later." She says.

I nod and follow her to the back booth. We rent a locker to throw our stuff in and pay for the putt-putt. We go inside with our sticks and balls. The light is dark and black-lighted. Everything glows neon. Megan wore her black-light make-up so her face glows. It makes me laugh hysterically. She is taking pictures of herself. Once she's done, we start the game. We hit all eighteen holes without anyone around, *I wonder if Jett is here. I hope not because we talked a lot about him.* I win, of course, but it's fun.

We return our clubs and head for the go-karts. It's Sunday, so there are a few people here but mostly everyone in town is in church right now. Once it's after noon, this place will be packed. Might as well head to the go-karts now before the line gets huge. It's just Megan and I on the track. Again, I win. I have a bit of a competitive streak.

We hit the change machines and play arcade games. I get a butt-load of tickets while Megan gets some but way less than me. Ski-ball is my game of choice, Megan likes Dance Dance Revolution. Once I spend my whole forty dollars' worth of quarters, we head to the ticket counter and exchange our tickets. Megan got a whistle and a sticky hand with her tickets. I got the stuffed animal shark with mine. Today has been great so far. We are both laughing and enjoying our girl's day.

"Are you hungry yet?" Megan asks me.

"Yea, actually, I'm starving." I say with a belly growl at the same time. We both laugh.

We head to her car and to our favorite restaurant, Antonio's. The bread basket here is amazing! On occasion, we have ordered just the bread for carryout. Today, we are greeted by our favorite hostess, she sits us in our favorite booth. Luckily, it wasn't occupied. We know the waiter well enough, we come here often. Ian is his name. He knows exactly what we want, so he brings the bread basket out before taking our drink order. We both decide to get an alcoholic drink with our lunch. I just order a large house salad, and Megan gets the penne pasta. Once Ian leaves with our orders, Megan starts in on me.

"Cora, I know you are happy right now, but don't rush into anything with Jett, take things slow." She advices me.

I roll my eyes at her. "Hey, I'm not the one who sleeps with guys and never sees them again, you know I take things slow, usually." I tell her. "There is just something about him, Megan, I can't explain it but I think I found my dream guy." *Seriously, quite literally my dream guy, since I've actually dreamed of him so often throughout my life.* "The one I'm supposed to be with. Everything just goes smoothly with him. I can be myself, and not force anything. Only time will tell, I guess." I end with a flat tone and shrug.

Megan has a huge smile. "I'm really happy for you, I will have to hang out with him more, get his vibe." She says. I can't help it, I smile too. I love hanging out with my best friend.

Ian, the waiter, who is so hot by the way, but not interested in women,-trust Megan to try to sleep with the hot waiter,-brings out our meals. We thank him and dig in. My salad is huge but looks delicious, I pour the dressing all over and take a huge unladylike bite. It makes Megan laugh and repeat with her pasta. I'm glad to have found a friend who gets me.

We finish our lunch and bring most of it back home, it will probably be our dinner as well. We walk back to her car, I look around the parking lot and notice Jett's car. I give another nonchalant nod to the car, I hope he noticed. Before we head home, Megan stops at the local party store. We pick up some snacks and two bottles of wine.

We head back to our house, I can see Jett's car following us in the distance from the rearview mirror. Megan doesn't pay any attention to it. She pulls the car into the driveway and unlocks the door to the house.

"I'm going to change into house clothes, meet you on the couch." She says.

"Ok, want some popcorn?" I ask. We always have a stash of popcorn at the house.

"You know it, bitch!" She says while walking away to her room.

I roll my eyes and shake my head laughing while heading into the kitchen. I grab the popcorn and throw it into the microwave. I find our popcorn bowl and wait for the delicious treat. Once it's done, I pour the popcorn into the bowl and head into the living room. I set the bowl down and return to the kitchen for the wine. I grab two glasses down and pour us both some. I return to the living room and Megan is there getting the movies out of the bookshelf DVD case. She pops the first Jurassic Park movie in.

"You know, I was thinking, you can invite Jett over if you want, I have to get to know him, right? Might as well be over a movie marathon with wine." She says while grabbing her glass and winking at me.

"Really? I don't have too. It's supposed to be girl's day." I tell her.

"It would make me happy, to see you happy." She smiles. *Ok, if she really wants me too, I will call and invite him over.*

"Ok, if you really want me to call him I will, just don't start the movie yet. I bet any money he hasn't seen them yet." I tell her.

Her eyes get wide, "Are you fucking kidding me? Hasn't see Jurassic Park?" She shouts. I laugh at her.

"He hasn't seen much TV or movies, he was sheltered." I state with laughter.

She shakes her head, "Now he definitely needs to come over and watch with us!" She declares and whips my phone off the couch into her hands and dials Jett's number. I try to grab my phone from her but she was too quick and pushes me away.

Jett answers quickly, I can hear him over the phone. "Hey, beautiful." He states.

"Oh, thanks Jett, but this is Megan." She says.

"What's wrong? What happened to Cora?" I hear panic in his voice.

I roll my eyes at Megan and finally grab my phone from her. "Hey, sorry. Megan grabbed my phone so quick." I give her an evil glare. She laughs at me. I can hear Jett relax over the phone with his breathing. "So, Megan wanted me to invite you to watch a movie marathon with us, since I mentioned that you've probably never seen the Jurassic Park movies before." I babble out quickly.

I can hear his smile. It makes me smile too. "I'll be there in a few minutes, baby." He says while hanging up.

"He'll be here soon." I tell Megan while play slapping her on the leg. "Don't take my phone like that please, you freaked him out." I finish.

"Sorry, love. Didn't mean to upset you guys, just being friendly." She says.

I smile at her. "Thanks for being my best friend." I say while giving her a hug.

"Thank you too, bitch." She says. We both have to wipe a tear away, *stupid hormones.*

In about ten minutes, there is a knock at the door, I know it's Jett, and so I run to the front door. I open the door and Jett is standing there, all sexy in his black pants and orange t-shirt. *It reminds me of his fin.*

"Hi baby." He says.

It make me blush, "Hi." I reply with a small wave. *Why am I so nervous?* He scoops me up in his arms and gives me a big kiss. I kiss him back but once we break apart, I have to stop us before we get ahead of ourselves. "Megan is in the living room, waiting for us." I tell him with my eyebrows raised.

He nods and sweeps his arm in the 'after you' sense. I lead the way. Megan is sitting on the couch, with now three wine glasses on the table. She must have got him a glass when I answered the door.

"Hiya Jett!" Megan beams.

"Hello." He says and waves to her before sitting next to me on the couch. "How was your girl's day? Frankly, I was surprised to hear from you." He addresses to both of us.

"It was great, exactly what I needed. Now I can't wait to watch these movies and get wine wasted." I say with a smirk.

"Yes, first, we went to glow in the dark putt-putt." Megan is describing our whole day to Jett. I roll my eyes to him, smile and give a little shoulder shrug. He will have to get used to Megan. I sip my wine, it's good, but I prefer a white wine, this one is Megan's favorite and it's a red.

"Ready for the movie?" I ask as soon as Megan stopped talking. She nods and pushes play on the remote. I can see Jett watching me out the corner of my eye. I turn and nod to the TV and my wine glass. He gets the hint and picks up his glass and takes a sip. I can see the disgusted look on his face from the wine. It makes me laugh but he powers through it anyways and takes a large gulp.

The movie finally starts. I am curled up next to Jett, his hand is on my thigh, his thumb rubbing back and forth, caressing me. *It's driving me wild.* His touch sends electric currents down my leg, I shiver. He stops but I see a small smile form on his lips out the corner of my eye. Megan is already done with her glass of wine and the movie just started. She pours herself another and tops our glasses off.

I sip mine slowly, I'm not much of a drinker. Jett is keeping pace with me. I know he doesn't like the wine, he make a disgusted face with every sip. The first movie is over now. We have all been dutifully watching and drinking. Now the one bottle of wine is gone, thanks mostly to Megan. She steps out of the living room to the kitchen to get the other bottle we bought before putting in the second movie.

I let out a groan. "Ugh, I hate the second one. It's just not done as well as the rest." I sigh out.

"Pffft. Well, we would skip it but since Jett has never seen it, we have to watch it." Megan says slurring her words a bit, she is the one who drank most of that first bottle. She jumps on the couch next to us. "So, Jett, what do you do for a living?" Megan asks him.

"I'm a fisherman." Jett responds politely, giving me a little wink that she didn't notice.

She laughs, "And you make a living off that?" When Megan drinks, she tends to get a little rude. I think, it's because she is a waitress and puts on a fake persona at work. She needs to let her true self out more, and her true self can be a bitch sometimes.

Luckily, she has me to call her out. "Megan! Don't be rude." I chastise her.

She actually looks guilty, total puppy dog eyes, "Sorry. The wine must have gone to my head." She apologizes to Jett.

He laughs a bit, not a care in the world. "It's ok, but to answer your question, yes, I make a living off of fishing. I'm quite good, not as good as Cora here though." I look back at him. He winks at me again, with a sexy grin on his face. I shake my head at him and smile.

"Wait? Cora, you went fishing?" She asks me shocked.

I look at her now, "Well, I did once recently with Jett, it was really fun!" I tell her. *I'm not going into the details with her of how we went fishing. That would get us both into trouble.*

The second movie starts and we all watch while sipping our wine. Megan goes slower on this bottle, I think it's because it's the last on we bought. Before the movie is even over, Megan passes out on the couch. Jett looks over at her and then smiles at me. That smile makes my heart skip a beat.

"How long will she be asleep for? Think she's out for the night?" He asks with his eyebrow arched. I look over at Megan, curled up on the couch, into a tight little ball. I roll my eyes and look back at Jett.

"She's down for a while. She'll probably wake up real late and stay up all night, then hate herself tomorrow for it." I tell him. I check the clock and it's only five in the afternoon. I'm actually getting quite hungry and the movie is almost over. "Once the movie is over, shall I make us some dinner?" I ask him.

He smiles again, "That sounds great!" He says.

While he watches the movie, I think about what to make for dinner. *Nothing that will take forever to make, something simple, that shows him I can cook. I decide to make a shepherd's pie. It's simple and doesn't take too long.* Soon the credits roll, and I shut the TV off. I get up and cover Megan with a blanket and then I grab Jett's hand and lead him into the kitchen with me.

"Have you ever had shepherd's pie before?" I ask him.

He shakes his head, "No, what's that?" He answers with a question of his own.

"It's beef with veggies and mashed potatoes on top, I also put cheese on top of the potatoes but I don't have too if you prefer not." I explain.

"However you make it is fine, can't wait to try it!" He smiles at me again before sitting on a chair in the kitchen.

I nod and start grabbing what I need. I brown up the meat in a pan and just grab a can of corn. I boil the potatoes and then mash them. All the while, Jett is staring at me, just watching my every move. I give him extra look worthy poses, like bending over when I don't really need to, and shaking my ass to a song in my head. It makes me smile and wet, just looking at him, his dark eyes hooded with lust. I have to squeeze my thighs together to relieve the pressure.

I layer all the ingredients and throw it in the oven. I walk over to Jett and sit in his lap. He grabs my ass and pulls me closer to him.

"Did you wear this outfit on purpose?" He asks with a smile.

"Why, yes I did! I thought it would be a little funny and ironic, since I've had this outfit before I knew I was in fact, a mermaid." I say practically beaming. My hands on his shoulder blades, I rub his back. He squeezes my ass a little tighter.

"It's fucking sexy, but I can't wait to take you out of it." He exclaims.

I gasp, *it's exactly what I want right now. We have about twenty minutes before dinner will be ready. We have time for a quickie.* "Let's do it, right here, right now. A quickie before dinner is done." I whisper in his ear.

He groans, "Take your pants off before I rip them off." He says with authority.

I stand up and peel my leggings off slowly, trying my best to do a strip tease. Jett bites his lip. He whips out his dick and starts to stroke himself. He's already rock hard. I climb back onto his lap and slowly glide onto his dick. He fills me up deliciously.

I try to keep quiet, just in case Megan does wake up. This isn't something I want her to see. I slowly lift myself up and down on his cock, both of us moaning into each other's ear. He slides his hand between us and rubs a finger on my clit while I ride him, I am so close to orgasming. I scream out, "Oh yes, fuck! Don't stop!" It isn't long before we are both coming together, trying to catch our breath and the timer dings. I laugh.

"Perfect timing!" I say, he laughs too.

I go clean myself up and hurry into the kitchen to grab the dinner out of the oven but Jett beat me too it. He is pulling the pie out of the oven when I walk into the room. I thank him and put the cheese on it and put it right back into the oven for about five more minutes. Jett goes into the bathroom. I can't help to smile. *I found a great man, that just so happens to have been assigned to me. I wonder what will happen when we get to the sea. Will we still act like boyfriend and girlfriend? Or will we have to hide our love from everyone?* I plan to ask him these questions later. I pull dinner out again once the cheese has browned a bit. Jett joins me at the kitchen table. I make us both a plate and we dig in once it's cooled down a bit.

Jett's face is priceless. I almost spit out my food with laughter. He obviously loves the food. He shoves it down his throat without chewing it seems.

"Like it?" I ask with a smirk.

His eyes get big, "This is the best thing I have ever eaten." He says with a passion.

"Well good, that makes me happy." I reply.

"You make me happy." He replies back.

I roll my eyes, "So, how's it going to be when we get to the sea?" I ask, *might as well get it over with.*

"What do you mean?" He asks me.

"I mean, like are we going to keep our relationship a secret? Or let people know?" I respond.

He thinks about it for a few minutes, "I don't think we would be able to keep this a secret for long, but at first, maybe we should." He replies. I nod my head, it sounds logical. "So, I know we planned to train tomorrow but if you wanted, we could start tonight, since your girl's day got cut short." Jett comments.

I think about it for about thirty seconds. *Megan will probably be asleep till around ten at night and then who knows what she would want to do then. I know I would want to sleep, I have to work in the morning, so I will not be going anywhere that late.*

"Yea, that sounds good. I've been excited about training since my dream last night." I tell him.

He looks at me with curiosity, "What was your dream?" He asks.

I smile, "We were training and after a few tries, I used my lightning power." I explain my dream to him.

Jett smiles, "Let's go then." He says while grabbing my hand and pulling me up from the chair.

"Ok, but let me get my suit and text Megan to let her know." I tell him. I walk to my bedroom while Jett waits in the hallway for me. I can't help but smile. *My cheeks have been hurting every day since I've met him, that's how much he's made me smile. I'm just so fucking happy right now. I never thought I'd be this happy after what happened with Kevin. I thought he was the love of my life, we were together for six years. We were high school sweethearts, I thought we was about to propose and then I learned about his infidelity once his son born. I ended it as soon as I found out.*

But now I realize that I wasn't actually happy with Kevin. Being with Jett has been so enormously different than when I was with Kevin. I actually know what happiness feels like now and it's only been about a week since I've known Jett.

I shake my head and clear my thoughts. I grab one of my swim suits, the two piece, and put it on under my clothes. Then I walk down the hallway to Jett. I grab my phone and text Megan quickly, telling her where we went, so she doesn't worry if she wakes up. I look up at Jett, he's so fucking gorgeous, and his smile is perfection.

"Ready!" I tell him. He nods and reaches for my hand.

We walk, hand in hand, to his car. We drive to the lake by his house, my favorite lake. It's not quite dark yet but we head down to the beach anyways, it's deserted. We make it to the picnic table under the willow tree and I undress and look up at Jett. He stares at me with hunger in his eyes again. I smile and blush then look down at my feet. He walks up to me and directs my face up with his with finger to look at him.

Staring into my eyes, he says, "You are amazingly beautiful, did you know that?" That makes me smile and blush even more. I've never felt more loved by anyone else. I lean up to plant a kiss on his lips.

"Thank you." I tell him.

"For what?" He asks.

"Just for being the sweetest guy I've ever met, I can't believe it's only been a week since we've met, feels like I've known you my whole life." I reply. *Technically, he is my dream guy, I've been dreaming about him since I was a young girl.* He continues to stare into my eyes.

"Yea, same here. It feels like we were meant for each other, I was meant to be your guardian, and I was meant to break my oath." He tells me. My smile falls a little once he mentions his damn oath, I just feel so shitty about that. "Hey." He says while picking my head back up to look at his face. "Don't worry about that, I will get through anything the council throws at me." He states.

I kiss him passionately; the things he is prepared to go through for our love, it just astonishes me. He breaks the kiss this time.

"We have to stop or I will drag you back to my house and fuck you, then we won't get any training done." He says.

I blow out a deep breath. "Ok." I nod and we walk to the water together, hand in hand.

Once we are deep enough in the water, I summon my fin and swim under the water, Jett follows.

"So, how do we do this?" I ask.

"Well, first let's have you focus on something and see if you can summon your power, just like your fin." He says.

I swim around for a few minutes and look around. I spot a huge piece of a tree branch, and focus on that. I stretch my hand out in front of me and try to will my power out of my hands. Nothing happens. I know with summoning my fin, I had to think of my dream, it was the only way it worked for me. I decide to try my dream from last night. I focus on the branch again, stretching my hand out and think of how I felt in the dream. Nothing happens again. I feel a little frustrated. I shake my head and clear my thoughts. I try again, this time I close my eyes and focus hard on my hands.

My hand stretched out in front of me, I start to feel a burning sensation in my palm. It hurts so bad that I scream out in pain and open my eyes. There is a long string of lightning coming out of my hand hitting the tree branch. My face lights up, totally forgetting about the pain. *I did it! I really fucking did it! I am a Lunafriya after all!* I look over at Jett, and he is beaming a smile so bright, it looks like his cheeks hurt. I turn off my power and he swims over to me so fast. He grabs me by the waist and spins us around laughing.

"I knew it! I fucking knew I was right! You are a Lunafriya warrior!" He says.

I try shooting the branch again with my lightning and it works the first time. It even hurts my hand less this time. "So, does that mean we can go to Halcyon now?" I ask him.

"Yes, we need to go as soon as you can. Tomorrow would be ideal." He replies

"But I work tomorrow." I tell him. He stares at me, I can see the wheels turning in his head. "What?" I ask.

"I don't know how to say this without you getting angry. But you are going to have to quit eventually. We need you in the sea, not on land. You have a job and it's to be a warrior, not work in an aquarium. You should quit and not go into work tomorrow." He responds.

I actually am a little angry. I make a large groan and push out of his arms. I ball my hands into fists, they are burning. I look down and they are sparking. I'm absorbing the lightning into my own hands.

"Hey! Hey." Jett says while grabbing my upper arms and rubbing them, "Calm down baby, it's ok. We can wait and go whenever you want."

I take a couple of deep breaths, steadying myself. *I understand that I will eventually have to quit my job, I really do. I understand that I am the first Lunafriya in one hundred and fifty years, just look at what I can do! I'm told that I am needed in the sea. But for what? I'm just not ready to leave my life on land. I love my job, and my friend Megan. I love my parents and I don't want to leave any of that behind. My dad left the sea and didn't want this life for me. I guess that this life was chosen for me though. I think I need to make a decision. I technically don't have to go to the sea at all, if I don't want.* "I need to see my dad." I say, Jett nods his head.

"Ok, baby." He replies while kissing the top of my head.

My powers have stopped and I wiggle my fingers. "Can we leave now? I'm drained." I tell him. I feel like I've been running a marathon or something.

"Sure." He says while swimming with me back to shore. He has to help me because I'm so exhausted. I summon my legs, it took a lot of effort though. Jett carries me back to his car and drives me home. It's only around eight in the afternoon but as soon as I get into my bed, I pass out. It was a tiring day. I plan to call my dad tomorrow and have a long talk with him.

Chapter 10

Jett's perspective

I left Cora's house at five in the morning. The house is quiet and both women are sleeping still. I crawled out the window just in case Megan was awake, I don't want to scare anyone. I'm still tired so I decide to head to the nearest open coffee shop for a quick coffee and muffin.

I head back to my car and wait outside of Cora's house. I wait for about two hours until I see the women leave the house. Cora is just in an oversized hoodie and pants, and her friend Megan is wearing some exercise gear. I get out of my car and hide. I told her that she wouldn't see me today unless there is trouble. I don't want to disrupt her girl's day. I see Cora looking around, probably trying to see me, but I've hidden myself well.

The women start their run. I keep a close eye but far enough that they can't see me. I'm hiding behind bushes and trees. Hopefully, no one call the cops because they see a man following some women. That would be kind of hard to explain. The women hold a steady pace for about forty five minutes before they arrive back to their house. I hide behind my car which is parked down the street from their house. I see Cora look back at me and smile, not sure if she saw me or not, but she probably did.

She looks so fucking sexy, I need to see her real quick. My body just gravitates toward hers. Once they enter the house, I run over to Cora's bedroom window, and open it. I sneak inside her room and lay down on her bed, waiting for her. I hear them talking about who gets to take a shower first, sounds like Megan will first. Cora opens her door and closes it fast. She stares at her open window for a few seconds before she notices me.

She gasps, "What are you doing here?" She shakes her head. "It's girl's day, if Megan saw you here, she'd flip." She scolds me.

I walk over to her and give her a big hug. "Sorry, I just wanted to see you, she is in the shower and won't know I'm here, I promise." I say then give her a kiss. She happily kisses me back. We make out for a few minutes until I pull away. "We have to stop or I won't be able to help myself and rip those clothes off of you." I say with a smirk.

She flutters her eyes and gasps. I hear the shower turn off. "Ok, Megan is getting out of the shower now, you need to leave. Come over tonight after she goes to sleep." Cora tells me.

"Goodbye beautiful." I say with another kiss before she shoves me back out the window.

"Goodbye." She tells me before she closes and locks her window. I run back to my car to wait for them.

It's about another hour and a half before the ladies step out of the house. I see Cora looking fine as hell. She is wearing some mermaid looking scale pants and a shirt that says 'Mermaid Hair Don't Care'. It actually makes me laugh out loud. I see her look over my way and nod her head. They jump into Megan's car and drive away. I follow them but not too closely. They pull into a place with a huge sign that says 'Zap Zone'.

They get out of the car and head into the building. I decide to just wait in my car. I don't want to intrude on their day. It gives me more time to read the history book about the Lunafriya warriors. Their history is fascinating. An elite group of women warriors who have powers to protect oceans. It has been told that it was the Damone tribe that killed off all of the Lunafriya's. For their own personal gain of power. The Damone tribe is the big bad tribe that you have to worry about. They are known killers and who started every war.

It takes three hours before I see the women step outside the building. They both look super happy and that they enjoyed themselves. They jump into Megan's car and drive to a restaurant. I decide that I am also hungry so while they are in the restaurant I head to the fast food joint across the street. I go through the drive-thru and get a couple of burgers. I park in the restaurant parking lot and wait for them while I scarf down my burgers. I see them leave with some carry out boxes. I see Cora give me another nod before she heads into the car. I follow behind again.

They stop at a party store before heading back home. I park my car a few houses down the block and wait. Twenty minutes after they arrive home, I get a phone call from Cora.

I answer on the first ring. "Hey, beautiful." I state.

"Oh thanks Jett, but this is Megan." She says.

"What's wrong? What happened to Cora?" I panic. My heart is beating super hard in my chest. Then, Cora gets on the phone.

"Hey, sorry. Megan grabbed my phone so quick." I hear a laugh. I breathe a sigh of relief. That actually scared me. "So, Megan wanted me to invite you to watch a movie marathon with us, since I mentioned you've probably never seen the Jurassic Park movies before." She babbles out quickly. I smile. *I guess I'm invited to girl's day after all.*

"I'll be there in a few minutes, baby." I say while hanging up. I'm already at her house but I have to wait a little while before going over. I decide to head home and change my clothes, so I'm not wearing what I wore yesterday. I pick my black pants and orange t-shirt. I picked this to match my fin, since Cora is wearing a mermaid outfit. I race back to her house and knock on the door. Cora answers the door, "Hi, baby." I say. It makes her blush.

"Hi," she replies with a small wave. I scoop her up in my arms and give her a big kiss. She kisses me back but once we break apart, she has to stop us before we get ahead of ourselves. "Megan is in the living room, waiting for us." She tells me with her eyebrows raised. I nod and sweep my arms ahead, in the 'after you' sense. She leads the way. Megan is sitting on the couch, with three full wine glasses on the table.

"Hiya Jett!" Megan beams.

"Hello." I say and wave to her before sitting next to Cora on the couch. "How was your girl's day? Frankly I was surprised to hear from you." I address them both.

"It was great, exactly what I needed, now I can't wait to watch these movies and get wine wasted." Cora says with a smirk.

"Yes, first, we went to glow in the dark putt-putt." Megan is describing their whole day to me. Cora rolls her eyes, smiles, and gives a little shoulder shrug. I listen to Megan babble on but eventually tune her out. Cora sips her wine. She is adorable.

Once Megan finally stops talking, Cora asks, "Ready for the movie?"

Megan nods and pushes play on the remote. I watch Cora instead of the TV. I can't help myself. She must have noticed me because she turns and nods to the TV and to her wine glass. I get the hint and pick up my glass and take a sip. I've never had wine before, more of a beer guy myself. It is disgusting but I choke the gulp down and finish as much as I can. I must have made a face because Cora laughs a bit.

The movie finally starts. Cora is curled up next to me, my hand is on her thigh, my thumb rubbing back and forth, caressing her. I can't help myself, I just need to touch her any way I can. I can tell my touch is doing things to her, she shivers. I stop but a small smile forms on my lips. Megan is already done with her glass of wine and the movie just started. She pours herself another and tops our glasses off.

Ugh, it's gross but I don't want to seem like a pussy so I drink mine when Cora drinks hers. The first movie is over now. It was a really good movie, I enjoyed myself. We have all been dutifully watching and drinking. Now the one bottle of wine is gone. Megan steps out of the living room to the kitchen to get the other bottle they bought before putting in the second movie.

Cora lets out a groan, "Ugh, I hate the second one. It's just not done as well as the rest." She sighs out.

"Pffft. Well, we would skip it but since Jett has never seen it, we have to watch it." Megan says slurring her words a bit. She is the one who drank most of that bottle of wine. She jumps on the couch next to us. "So, Jett, what do you do for a living?" Megan asks me.

"I'm a fisherman." I respond politely, giving Cora a little wink that Megan didn't notice.

Megan laughs, "And you make a living off that?" She asks kind of bitchy like. I raise my one eyebrow at Cora.

"Megan! Don't be rude." She chastises her. Megan actually looks guilty.

"Sorry, the wine must have gone to my head." She apologizes to me.

I laugh a bit, not really caring at all. "It's ok, but to answer your question. Yes, I make a living off of fishing. I'm quite good, not as good as Cora here though." I say.

Cora looks back at me. I wink at her again, with a grin on my face. She shakes her head at me and gives me a sexy smile.

"Wait? Cora, you went fishing?" Megan asks her.

She looks over at her now. "Well, I did once with Jett recently. It was really fun!" She tells her and shakes her head at me.

The second movie starts and we all watch while sipping our wine. Megan goes slower on this bottle. Before the movie is even over, Megan passes out on the couch. I look over at Cora and then smile at her. She smiles back, that smile makes my heart skip a beat.

I take a steadying breath, "How long will she be asleep for? Think she's out for the night?" I ask with my eyebrows arched.

She looks over at Megan, curled up on the couch, into a tight little ball. She rolls her eyes and looks back at me.

"She's down for a while, she'll probably wake up real late and stay up all night, then hate herself tomorrow for it." She checks the clock and it's only five in the afternoon. "Once the movie is over, shall I make us some dinner?" She asks me.

I smile again, actually pretty hungry, "That sounds great!" I say.

We finish the movie together. Soon the credits roll, and she shuts the TV off. She also gets up and covers Megan with a blanket. She is the sweetest person I've ever met. She then grabs my hand and leads me into the kitchen with her.

"Have you ever had shepherd's pie before?" She asks me.

I shake my head, "No, what's that?" I answer with a question of my own.

"It's beef with veggies and mashed potatoes on top, I also put cheese on top of the potatoes but I don't have to if you prefer not." She explains.

"However you make it is fine, can't wait to try it!" I smile at her again before sitting on a chair in the kitchen.

She nods and starts grabbing what she needs. She starts to cook dinner. I watch her every move. She dances around the kitchen, shaking her ass and bending over in front of me. She is driving me wild. *I just want to grab that ass and squeeze, hard. I want to stick my dick into her and pound that ass.* She throws the food into the oven. She walks over to me and sits on my lap. I grab that ass and pull her closer to me, so my dick rubs against her pants.

"Did you wear this outfit on purpose?" I ask with a smile.

"Why, yes I did! I thought it would be a little funny and ironic, since I've had this outfit before I knew I was, in fact, a mermaid." She says practically beaming.

Her hands on my shoulders, she rubs my back. I squeeze her ass a little tighter. "It's fucking sexy, but I can't wait to take you out of it." I exclaim.

She gasps, "Let's do it, right here, right now. A quickie before dinner is done." She whispers in my ear.

I groan, "Take your pants off before I rip them off." I say with authority. She stands and peels her pants off slowly, trying her best to do a strip tease. It's really fucking sexy. My dick is already rock hard. I bite my lip.

I whip out my dick and start to stroke myself. She climbs back onto my lap and slowly glides onto my dick. I fill her up completely. She tries to keep quiet, but it's not working that well, she's a moaner. She slowly lifts herself up and down on my cock, both of us moaning into each other's ear. I grab her ass to help her rise up and down better. I slide my hand between us and rub a finger on her clit while she rides me.

She is so close to orgasming, she is tightening her pussy, then screams out, "Oh yes. Fuck. Don't stop!" It isn't long before we are both coming together, trying to catch our breath and the timer dings.

She laughs, "Perfect timing!" She says, I laugh too. She goes to clean herself up and hurries to grab dinner out of the oven, but I beat her to it. After washing my hands in the kitchen sink, of course. She puts the cheese on it and puts it right back into the oven.

I go into the bathroom to clean myself up more. I can't help to smile. *I found my subject, and she, just so happens to be the most amazing women I've ever met. I feel myself falling in love with her, but I can't yet right? We have only known each other a week.*

I go back into the kitchen. She pulls dinner out again once the cheese has browned a bit. I join her at the kitchen table. She makes us both a plate and we dig in once it's cooled down. *Oh my Poseidon! This meal is amazing!* I shove it down my throat without chewing.

She laughs and almost chokes, "Like it?" She asks with a smirk.

My eyes get big, "This is the best thing that I have ever eaten." I say with passion.

"Well good, that makes me happy." She replies.

"You make me happy." I reply back, acting like a love sick puppy dog.

She rolls her eyes and smiles, then frowns a bit. "So, how's it going to be when we get to the sea?" She asks, wonderment in her eyes.

"What do you mean?" I ask her.

"I mean, like are we going to keep our relationship a secret? Or let people know?" She responds.

I think about it for a few minutes. "I don't think we would be able to keep this a secret for long, but at first, maybe we should." I reply. She nods her head. "So, I know we planned to train tomorrow but if you wanted, we could start tonight, since your girl's day got cut short." I comment.

She thinks about it for thirty seconds. "Yea, that sounds good, I've been excited about training since my dream last night." She tells me. I look at her with curiosity. *She never mentioned any dream, I will have to ask her about her dreams more often.*

"What was your dream?" I ask.

She smiles, we were training and after a few tries, I used my lightning power." She explains the dream a bit.

I smile, "Let's go then." I say while grabbing her hand and pulling her up from the chair.

"Ok, but let me get my suit and text Megan to let her know." She tells me. She walks to her bedroom while I wait in the hallway for her. I'm glad I wore my suit under my pants today, just in case.

She finally walks into the hallway. She grabs her phone and messes with it for a few minutes. She looks up at me. She's so fucking gorgeous, that smile is perfection.

"Ready!" She tells me. I nod and reach for her hand.

We walk hand in hand to my car. We drive to the lake by my house. It's not quite dark yet but we head down to the beach anyways, no one is around. We make it to the picnic table under the willow tree and she un-dresses and looks up at me. I stare at her with hunger in my eyes. She smiles and blushes then looks down at her feet. I come up to her and direct her face up with my finger to look at me. Staring into her eyes, *I want to tell her I love her, but it's too soon.* I actually say, "You are amazingly beautiful, did you know that?"

That makes her smile and blush even more. She leans up to plant a kiss in my lips.

"Thank you." She tells me.

"For what?" I ask with a smile.

"Just for being the sweetest guy I've ever met, I can't believe it's only been a week since we've met, it feels like I've known you my whole life." She replies.

I can see the love in her eyes. I know it, she loves me too. I stare into her eyes. "Yea, same here. It feels like we were meant for each other. I was meant to be your guardian, and I was meant to break my oath." I tell her. Her face falls a little once I mention my oath. "Hey." I say while picking her head back up to look in my eyes, "Don't worry about that, I will get through anything the council throws at me." I state.

She kisses me passionately. I am willing to go through anything for this women. Nothing can break us apart, I will even die for her. I have to break the kiss this time.

"We have to stop or I will drag you back to my house and fuck you, then we won't get any training done." I say.

She blows out a deep breath. "Ok." She nods and we walk to the water together, hand in hand. Once we are deep enough in the water, we summon our fins and swim around under the water. "So, how do we do this?" She asks.

"Well, first, let's have you focus on something and see if you can summon your power, just like your fin." I tell her.

She looks around. I watch her every move and keep an eye out for anything suspicious. She spots a huge piece of a tree branch, and focuses on that. She stretches her hand out in front of her and tries to will her power out. Nothing happens. She tries again, harder this time. Still nothing happens.

She looks a little frustrated. She shakes her head and tries again, this time she closes her eyes and focuses hard. Her hand out stretched in front of her. I watch while her hand starts to light up. She starts to scream and a bolt of lightning shoots out to the tree branch. *YES! I fucking knew it!* She looks over at me. I am beaming a smile so bright, my cheeks hurt. She turns her power off and I swim over to her so fast. I grab her by the waist and spin us around laughing.

"I knew it! I fucking knew I was right! You are a Lunafriya warrior!" I say just so elated. She tries shooting the branch again with her lightning and it works the first time.

"So, does that mean we can go to Halcyon now?" She asks me.

"Yes, we need to go as soon as you can. Tomorrow would be ideal." I reply.

"But I work tomorrow." She tells me. I stare at her. *How does she not get that she has to quit her job? She needs to come to the sea and protect the city, and stop this war.* "What?" She asks me.

"I don't know how to say this without you getting angry, but you are going to have to quit eventually. We need you in the sea, not on land. You have a job and it's to be a warrior, not work in an aquarium. You should just quit and not go into work tomorrow." I respond.

She starts to shake. Cora makes a large groan and pushes out of my arms. She balls her hands into fists. I look down and they are sparking. She is really upset.

"Hey! Hey." I say while grabbing her upper arms and rubbing them. "Calm down baby, it's ok. We can wait and go whenever you want."

She takes a couple deep breaths, steadying herself. It takes about ten minutes before she speaks another word. All the while, her powers have stopped.

"I need to see my dad." She says.

I nod my head. "Ok, baby." I reply.

She wiggles her fingers, "Can we leave now? I'm drained." She tells me.

"Sure." I say while swimming with her back to the shore. I have to help her, she's so weak right now. She needs to train more before she will be of any use in the war.

We summon back our legs, it took a lot of effort for her though. I carry her back to my car and drive her home. It was a silent drive back to her house. It's only around eight at night but as soon as I get her into her bed, she passes out. It was a tiring day for her. I lay next to her for a few minutes, cuddling her hard.

Hopefully I didn't scare her, I don't know if she's ready to leave the land yet. I'm going to go to Halcyon while she sleeps, she should be safe at home with Megan. I need to talk to the council.

I cover Cora up and make sure all of her windows in her room are locked. I don't like leaving her especially since she is the one all the tribes are searching for, but I have too. I head down the hallway passing by the living room, to leave by the front door. Megan is stirring awake.

"Good morning or should I say night?" I say to her.

She laughs, "Where's Cora?" She asks rubbing her eyes.

"She is asleep in bed, I'm about to leave, will you let her know I left and I'll call her tomorrow? Actually, can I have your phone number? In case anything happens?" I ask her.

"Sure. Is something supposed to happen?" She asks back.

"Well, with all the disappearances lately, I just want you ladies to be safe. It's better to be safe than sorry." I tell her.

She holds out her hand, I'm guessing for my phone. I grab my phone out my pocket and hand it to her. She inputs her number.

"Thank you, I'm going to leave now. Please lock up behind me." I say.

"Yea yea, ok dad!" She comments sarcastically.

I chuckle and walk out the door. I hear her lock the door behind me. I go to my car and drive to my house. *I hate to leave Cora, but this needs to be done. I was told to report back as soon as I found anything out. Well, I found something out alright, I found the fucking Lunafriya!*

I park in my driveway and go into my house. I set my phone down and strip into just my suit. I leave the house and set out to the lake. It's pitch black outside and no one is around. I walk into the water and summon my fin once my legs are fully under. I swim to the portal to the sea.

Once I'm through the portal, I look around. I can see the lights of Halcyon city. The guards are standing watch. I swim up to the front gate and state my name.

"Jett, of the Halcyon tribe, to see the council" I state.

The guards nod and let me through. I swim straight to town hall. Caol is guarding the council chamber again.

"Hey bud, any news?" He asks.

I beam at him. Caol has been my best friend since we were little guppies, I tell him the good news. "I fucking found her, Caol! I found a Lunafriya!" I whisper so no one can overhear.

He gasps, "No way! Are you serious?" He asks.

"As serious as I'll ever be, I need to tell the council." I tell him.

He smiles back. "The council members are in their bed chambers, I will alert them that you have news to share. Wait in the council chambers for them, please." He replies and swims off.

I open the door and wait. It doesn't take long for the council masters, Zale, Kae, and Yarrow to arrive.

"So, young Jett, we heard you have news for us. It better be good news to wake us from our slumbers so late." Master Kae comments grimly. *I have an urge to roll my eyes, it's only nine in the afternoon.*

"Sirs." I take a bow. "The woman I was talking about the other day, she has developed her powers, she is a Lunafriya." I state.

They gasp in unison. Master Yarrow speaks first. "What kind of powers has she developed?" He asks.

I nod, "She has control over sea-life, has dreams of the future, and has lightning bolts come out of her hands." I answer him.

Master Zale asks, "And what of her lineage? Have you found out her parents?"

I smile at him, Master Zale has always been my favorite. "Her father is Ray, she is your granddaughter, Sir." I respond.

He gets the biggest smile I've ever seen. "Good work, young Jett!" Master Zale responds.

"When are you going to bring her to the council?" Master Kae asks. I look at them each in turn.

"She is having second thoughts about leaving the land. I'm trying to convince her to quit her job but she is fighting me. She wants to speak with her father first." I state.

Each of the masters look at each other. "We need her here, convince her to join us. I would love to meet my granddaughter, and if you could, try to convince that son of mine to join her." Master Zale speaks. I nod my head and bow.

"You are dismissed, let the water flow freely." Master Kae waves me away.

"Let the water flow freely." I chant back. The masters leave the council chambers out the back door. I leave through the front. Caol is still standing guard.

"What's the mission now?" He asks.

"I have to convince her to join us in the sea. It's proving to be a difficult task, she doesn't want to leave land yet." I tell him.

"If anyone can convince her, it's you. Just show her that magic cock of yours, she'll be hooked." He laughs out, I join him. *If only he knew that I already did, if only he knew that I broke my oath and am actually falling in love with her.* I change the subject.

"Well, since I'm here, I might as well say hi to Meri before I leave again. Next time you see me, I'll have the Lunafriya in tow." I tell him and he salutes me, I salute him back.

I swim to my house, my sea house. The lights are off except one, Meri's room. I make my way into the house and be loud so Meri can hear me, I don't want to scare her like last time.

"Meri! It's Jett!" I yell out once I turn the lights on.

Meri swims out of her room. "Jett! Any news?" She asks. I knew she'd be extra excited. I smile at my baby sister.

"Yes! Cora is a Lunafriya! She developed her lightning power today." I tell her. Her eyes get huge, her mouth hangs open in disbelief.

"Oh my Poseidon, really? Can I meet her?" She asks.

"Of course, but I did something bad." I say. She looks at me wary. "I broke my oath." I state, she gasps. "But I'm in love with her, we couldn't help it." She thinks about this for a minute.

"Everything should be fine, other people have broken their oaths, and nothing bad happened." She says.

"Yea, but not with a Lunafriya." I respond and shake my head.

"When is she coming to the sea?" Meri asks.

I shrug, "As soon as I can convince her to join us. She is stubborn." I say.

"Can I join you on land?" Maybe I can help you." She asks.

I look at her with brows furrowed. "You need permission from the council to come to land." I reply.

She scoffs, "Like they can stop me, I've never been to land and I've been studying the Lunafriya warriors my whole life. Don't ruin this for me." She is a feisty one, my sister. There is no way I can stop her once she's made up her mind. Cora and Meri will get along great. I roll my eyes.

"We are a bunch of rule breakers in this house." I say and shake my head.

"I blame the person who raised me." Meri says while nudging my side. She pleads with me with her eyes.

I give in, "Oh, alright. Hurry before anyone notices I'm taking you with me." I finish.

She squeals and hugs me. "Oh thank you, thank you Jett! You are the best big brother ever." She screams out.

She turns off all the lights and we head out of town, telling the guards at the front gate that we are going hunting. They will notice that she is gone tomorrow, but she will have to deal with the consequences. It was her decision to leave.

We head to the portal and swim through. Meri is so excited, she won't stop smiling. Once we are in the lake and pop through the water, I teach her how to summon her legs. It takes a while for her to do but she finally summons them. We swim back to shore, it's funny to see her walk on legs, she's like a baby deer, and her legs are wobbly.

"Stop laughing at me." She says. I calm my laughter and hold her up.

"The house is this way, there are clothes for you there." I tell her. We walk back to my house and she looks around.

"This is so cool!" She states. I smile, I'm happy to see my sister happy.

"Let's sleep now, you can meet Cora tomorrow." I tell her. I lead her into the spare room and tell her good night. I go check my phone, nothing there, so I text Cora. 'I went home after you fell asleep. My sister is with me, she wants to meet you tomorrow. Call me when you wake, beautiful.' I head to my room and fall asleep as soon as I hit my pillow. Today was a long day.

Chapter 11

Cora's perspective

I wake up in a fright. My heart is pounding so fast and I'm covered in a cold sweat. I just had the craziest dream. In the dream, I was with Jett and two other people, a male and a female that I don't know. We were trying to find Megan, I don't know where she was but I remember feeling scared for her. I calm down my breathing and check my phone, it's nine in the morning. I have a text from Jett.

'I went home after you fell asleep. My sister is with me, she wants to meet you tomorrow. Call me when you wake beautiful.'

My heart swells, *I love this man. He makes me feel things that I've never felt before. And his sister is with him? So does that mean he went to his real home? His sea home? I can't wait to meet her.* I decide to drink some coffee before I call him, I need to wake up more. I crawl out of bed and head into the kitchen. Megan is no longer on the couch, she must have woke up and moved to her room. I start up the Keurig, find my favorite cappuccino capsule, and pop it in. It doesn't take long to make and soon I am sipping my coffee on the couch. I dial Jett's number. He answers on the second ring.

"Good morning beautiful!" He says happily.

"Hiya handsome!" I chuckle back.

"Did you sleep well? Any dreams?" He asks.

"Well, I slept good but my dream was kind of scary." I tell him.

"Oh yea? How so?" He asks again. I can hear the change in his voice, he's serious now.

"All I can remember is that I was with you and two other people, a male and a female and we were looking for Megan. I remember feeling scared out of my mind. You don't think anything bad will happen to her, do you?" I explain the dream and ask.

He breathes into the phone for a bit. "We should take your dreams seriously from now on. Is Megan home right now?" He asks.

"I don't know yet, hold on." I say. I check for her car, it's in the driveway. I go to her room and knock. No one answers. I get a little freaked out so I open the door. She is sleeping on her bed. I breathe a sigh of relief. I shut the door quietly and get back on the phone. "She is sleeping in her bed." I tell him. He lets out a deep breath.

"What time do you work today?" He asks me.

"Umm, well I am supposed to work at eleven but I think I might call off so I can see my dad." I say. *I need to get this talk over with. Jett says I'm needed in the sea. I want to know what my dad thinks. Plus I've never called off work before, one time should be absolutely fine.*

"You do what you want, baby. Call me after you're done so you can meet Meri." He replies.

"Ok, will do." I respond.

"And beautiful?" He says.

"Yea?" I ask.

"I know we've only known each other for about a week but I just wanted to tell you…that I think…I love you." He blurts out.

I stop what I'm doing. My breath catches in my throat. *It's too soon to be saying this but I think I love him too.*

"You still there?" He asks.

I clear my throat, "Ah hum, yea, I am. Sorry, that caught me off guard but I feel the same way. I know it's too soon but…I love you too." I can tell he is smiling, I can hear it in his voice. I am smiling too. This man loves me!

"Ok baby, call me later, bye." He says.

"Bye" I choke out and hang up.

I decide I better get this call over with, I call my boss Jenny. She answers after a while. "Hey Cora, what's up?" She says.

"Hi Jenny, I'm sorry but I'm going to have to call off today. I'm having a personal emergency." I state right away.

She sighs, "Ok dear, don't worry about it. I don't think you've ever called off before." She says.

"Thanks Jenny." I say before hanging up, that was quick. Might as well call my dad while I'm at it. I dial his number.

He answers with a "Hiya, baby seal!" His nickname for me since I was little.

"Hi dad, what are you doing today? I need to talk to you." I tell him.

"I don't have any plans. Honey, are you ok?" He asks.

"Yea, I'm fine, I just need your opinion on things. Do you think you could meet me at Prism Lake in about an hour?" I ask.

"I'll be there, honey." He says.

"See you there, love you." I say before hanging up.

I jump quickly in the shower, I feel sticky from the sweat I woke up in. While in the shower, I think about my dream. *I swear if anything happens to Megan, I don't know what I'd do, but I know it wouldn't be pretty.* I scrub up and wash my hair.

Once I'm done, I towel dry and go to my closet to pick my outfit. I know I'm going to wear a swim suit underneath but I want to make a good first impression with Meri. I'm an only child, I've always wanted a sister. I pick my black safari style shorts and a pretty yellow flowery top. I grab a one piece swim suit and put on all my clothes. I just let my hair air-dry, and decide to forgo any make-up, it will just wash off at the lake anyways.

I step into the living room and hear Megan in the kitchen.

"Good morning sunshine!" I say once I get into the kitchen.

"Mornin'." She croaks out with sleep still in her eyes.

"So, I had a crazy bad dream about you. Please be careful, call me if anything happens. Jett and I will be there so quickly." I tell her.

She scoffs and laughs, "Ok, mom, it was just a dream. Don't you have work today?" She asks.

I nod, "Yea, but I called off. My dad needs me for something." I explain.

She gasps. "What? Miss Cora, calling off? Have you ever done that?" She asks again.

"Nope, that's why it's not a big deal. Dad needs me, Jenny said it was fine." I respond. *I wish I could tell her the truth, I've never lied to my best friend before. The thing is, I would actually really like to talk to her and get her opinion on everything. Maybe if I bend the truth a little.* "Hey, so I have a question, I need your opinion." I state.

"What's up?" She asks.

"Jett has asked me to move in with him. What should I do? On one hand, I love him and want to be with him always. On the other, I don't really want to move away from my friends, family, and job." I tell her. *So it's not a flat out lie, just omitting the fact that I would be moving to the sea.* She thinks about it for a few minutes.

"Hon, you have to do what you want. Follow your heart, if you love him and want to be with him, then do it. If everything doesn't work out, you could always move back in with me. I would miss you dearly but we could always talk on the phone." She explains, *but we couldn't actually talk on the phone, I'd be in the sea, where electronics won't work.*

"Well, we'd be on a fishing boat with no cell service." I tell her just another little lie.

She gasps, "Why would you ever want to live like that?" She jokingly asks. It makes me smile. "I actually think it would be good for you, think of all the fishy research you would get done." She smiles and wags her eyebrows.

"Thanks, Megs. I might just do it." I give her a hug, "Now, off to meet dad. Again, please be careful." I grab my phone and purse and head out the front door.

The drive to the lake is a slow one, morning traffic sucks. I pull into the lake parking lot, dad's car is already here. I park next to him, but he's not in his car. I crane my neck to look for him on the beach. Of course, he's at the willow tree table, waiting for me. I walk down to the table.

"Hiya, dad!" I yell while halfway there, he waves to me. Once I make it to the table, we hug.

"What's up sweetheart?" Dad asks.

"Can we go for a swim first? Then we'll talk?" I ask him.

He nods and removes his shirt, he's already wearing his suit. I take my clothes off too, and we walk to the water. I look around to make sure no one else is at the lake today, I see no one. The water sends an electric current up my body, stronger than before. As soon as my legs are covered fully in water, I summon my fin, and so does dad. We stay under the water, and don't go near the surface.

"Dad, I have something to show you." I tell him once we had a little bit of swimming fun with our fins. First, I decide to show him my control over sea-life. I spot a school of fish and make them swim around my dad in circles. He looks surprised at first, then looks at me understandingly with astonishment. "That's not all." I say and lift up my hand and focus on a large rock. My lightning spurts out of my hand in a long but strong line. It hits the rock and the rock breaks into two. Dad is just staring at me, not saying anything. "I'm a Lunafriya warrior, dad." I simply state.

He shakes his head, "I'm sorry" is all he says.

I get confused, "Why are your sorry, dad?" I ask. He lays his palms out, and shrugs his shoulders.

"This shouldn't have happened to you. It's all my fault." He squeaks out.

I give him a serious look, "Dad, I don't blame you for anything. I think my powers are amazing. I'm proud to be the first Lunafriya in one hundred and fifty years. I remember most of the stories that you told me as a kid, I can't believe I'm one of them!" I tell him.

"You don't get it, sweetheart. You now have a permanent bull's eye on your back. Some of the tribes will kill you, just for being what you are." He says while looking sadly into my eyes.

"Well, that's why I have Jett, my guardian, right?" I ask him.

"Yes, that will help, where is he?" He asks. "He should be around you at all times now." He finishes and looks around.

"He's at his house, which is right at the lake, he's nearby." I tell him. "That's what I wanted to talk about. Should I leave the land for the sea? Should I fulfill my destiny and leave everything I've ever known behind? Or just live a life on land and forget the sea, like you did?" I bombard him with questions and look at him pleadingly.

"That's only something you can answer for yourself." He states. "I made the decision to leave the sea because I fell in love with your mother, while on a mission. I broke my oath to protect the sea with my life, and to never leave. It was the best decision I've ever made because of you. On one hand, I am proud to have a Lunafriya for a daughter. On the other, I'm scared for your life. The Damone tribe wiped out all the Lunafriya's to gain control of the sea, they might try it again, if you fight them." He finishes his statement with worry written all over his face.

This gives me a lot to think about. "Thanks for the talk, dad, but I'm no closer to making my decision now. I love Jett, but I don't want to die, or leave my family and friends, everything I've ever known." I say while sweeping my arms.

"Wait, did you say you love Jett?" He asks.

Shit! I wasn't supposed to tell him that, and I'm a terrible liar to him, he knows when I lie. "Uh, yea. We fell in love, we tried not to. I didn't want him to break his oath, but things just happened. There was no fighting it, we were made for each other." I deadpan, hoping I don't get a lecture. He actually smiles though, I am surprised.

He shakes his head with a little smile still on his lips, "This family is just a bunch of rule breakers and hopeless romantics, every generation." He says.

I smile too. I know, I was told my grandfather broke his oath for my grandmother, and my dad broke his for my mom, I didn't take an oath but Jett broke his for me.

"I know this decision is hard, but it's something you have to do for yourself. Look deep in your heart, and find your answer. Don't make a hasty decision." He says while hugging me. "Now, let's just swim and forget everything, clear your head. But first, any other powers I should know about?" He asks.

I smile, "Yea, I dream of the future sometimes. Like sometimes, my dreams come true. But I'm hoping my dream last night doesn't." I tell him.

He looks at me curiously, "What happened in the dream?" He asks. I explain the dream to him in as much detail as I can remember. "I think maybe you should keep a close eye on Megan, just in case." He says.

We drop the conversation and just swim around for a few hours. I'm having fun with my dad, racing and fishing with him. *This is how it should have been my entire life. I should have known that I was a mermaid, my dad should have known. He was just too stubborn to see it. This is one of the best days of my life. If life is like this every day in the sea, then I might just pick the sea, and be able to be with Jett, my entire life.*

Dad is looking tired, "Had enough for the day?" I ask him.

He nods, "I'm not as young as I used to be." He replies. We swim back to shore and summon our legs. We sit at the picnic table. "My suggestion," dad says, "is to just visit Halcyon city. It's my birthplace and your grandfather is on the council. Then make your decision."

I nod my head, taking his thoughts into consideration. I would really like to visit the city. Everything Jett's told me about it, just sounds amazing. Dad gives me one last hug before leaving me on the beach to think. I watch as he walks to his car and drives away.

I sit there and just think for a few hours. I decide to finally call Jett.

"Hey, beautiful." He answers on the first ring.

"Hi, I'm at the lake." I tell him.

"I'll be there in a minute." He says and hangs up. I grip my knees to my chest and wait.

Suddenly, I see someone come out of the lake. No one was here earlier. I thought it might have been Jett but I was just on the phone with him. My heart jumps into my throat. The person is walking towards me. I scream out "JETT!" And let my lightning power go towards the mystery man. The man dodges my powers and hides behind a tree. I see Jett running towards me from the bushes.

I run to him, out of breathe, "Someone...came...out of...the lake. He's behind...that tree." I point. "I shot...at him...with my powers, I was scared." I tell him.

Jett drags me behind his body, while we walk to the tree. "Show yourself!" Jett yells. My heart is pounding so fast.

"Jett? That you?" The man asks from behind the tree, poking his head out. Jett looks confused.

"Caol? What are you doing here?" he asks.

The man named Caol, comes out from behind the tree. "Don't shoot!" He yells with a smile. Jett smiles at him and grabs my arm to push it down. I look at him confused.

"He's a friend." Jett tells me. We walk towards Caol, and the men hug, slapping each other on the back. "What are you doing here?" Jett asks him.

"Your sister, she's missing." He says solemnly.

Jett shakes his head, "No, she's at the house. I couldn't stop her from coming with me last night." Jett tells him.

Caol lets out a long breath, "I was worried." Caol explains. Then he looks at me and smiles. "So, here is the Lunafriya." He exclaims.

I smile and wave. "Hi, sorry about shooting at you, I'm Cora." I apologize.

He takes my hand and kneels, "Caol, at your service. I offer you my guardian services until the day I die." He says with his head bowed.

"Um, thank you." I say.

"Let's go to the house, we've made too much of a commotion already." Jett states. I follow him back to the house with Caol behind me. Jett opens the door, I see a woman in the kitchen, guessing that's Meri. As soon as Caol see her, he runs to her.

"Meri!" He exclaims while they hug. Jett looks at them quizzically. "Don't ever do that to me again, you hear me. I was scared out of my mind." Caol scolds Meri.

"Sorry, sweetie, but I just had to meet the Lunafriya." She says, then they kiss.

"Woah, woah, woah! What the fuck! That's my baby sister!" Jett yells. They both look at us like they just remembered that we were here too. Meri looks a little sheepish while Caol has the biggest smile on his face, and wraps his arms around Meri's shoulder.

"And my girlfriend." Caol says.

Jett's face turns a dark shade of red. His fists ball up tight. I place my hand on his arm and give him a little tiny jolt of lightning.

"Ouch!" He looks at me, "what was that for?" He asks. His face turns back to his normal color.

"To calm you down, remember, you can't help who you fall in love with." I plead at him with my eyes. His eyes soften and he grabs my face in his hands.

Now it's Caol's time to look confused. He gasps, "You broke your oath?" He asks Jett. Jett nods his head. Caol gets a big smile again, "You sly seal!" He says while punching Jett's arm.

"So, how long has this been going on?" Jett says while pointing between the two of them, Caol and Meri.

Meri shrugs, "a couple months." She answers.

Jett shakes his head. "Well, I can't stop you. But know this Caol, you hurt her, I will kill you. Or maybe I'll get my girlfriend to do it for me." He says. I smile, *this is the first time he's called me his girlfriend!*

Meri looks at me with wide eyes. "Hi, I'm Meri, Jett's sister." She tells me.

"Hello, name's Cora." I respond.

"She shot at me." Caol tells her with a large grin.

Now it's my turn to look sheepish. She looks at me again. "Sorry, I didn't know he was a friend." I explain.

Meri waves me off, "Don't worry about it, you have got to protect yourself, right?" She says. I nod. "Can I see your powers?" She asks. I was about to respond when Jett answers for me.

"Later, we don't want any other tribe to know about her yet and she already might have been seen." I get angry at myself. *I shouldn't have used my powers on land. How stupid could I be?* "Let's eat some food, I'm starving." Jett says.

"I already made a late lunch, some sandwiches and coleslaw." Meri tells him.

I just now realize how hungry I am. We all look at the sandwiches and make plates, family style, sitting at the kitchen island. The whole time is laughter and stories about when they were younger. I just sit and listen while eating. They don't want to hear my boring stories about living on land, I'm sure of it. The only thing I liked about my childhood was going to the lake.

We all decide to wait everything out in the house, and watch a movie. I get to pick because none of them watched movies much before. I go over to the movie wall. Ghostbusters catches my eye. I smile and grab it. I start singing the theme song. "If there's something strange…in the neighborhood…who you gonna call? GHOSTBUSTERS!" I finish with a twist

and show them the movie I picked. They all laugh at me. "It's one of my favorites." I tell them.
Jett pops it in the DVD player and we all sit and watch. By the end of the movie, everyone is
dancing to the theme song.

"Well, I should probably head back to the city, Krill is covering for me." Caol says after
the movie is finished.

Meri gives him puppy dog eyes, "I'm not leaving. I'll join you when Jett and Cora go."
She tells him.

He shakes his head, "Alright, not like I can stop you anyways." He says while giving her
a kiss on the lips.

Jett looks away, can't say I blame him. If my sister and best friend were hooking up, I'd
be happy but also not want to see it happening.

"It's almost dark, let's all go swimming and Cora can show you guys her powers before
you leave." Jett suggests. I would love to go swimming again. Everyone agrees and we head
down to the lake.

Jett grabs my hand and holds it while we walk to the picnic table under the willow tree. It
makes my heart swoon. Meri and Caol are following behind us. Once we reach the table,
everyone strips out of their clothes and we all just have our suits on. Jett winks at me and we
walk to the water. As soon as my toes touch the water, the electric current flows up my body, it
relaxes all of my muscles. I blow out a deep breath. Jett grabs my hand again and we go deeper
into the water. I summon my fin and the rest follow suit.

We swim around each other, playing in the water. I see some fish and make them swim
around the others in a figure eight pattern. Jett smiles at me. Meri and Caol laugh and reach out
for the fish. I make one lay in each of their hands. Meri stares at the fish, then at me, wide eyed

with fascination and awe. I let the fish swim away. She swims up to me, her fin is almost exactly like Jett's but with more green than his has. Caol's fin is a deep royal blue.

"It's been my life's work to study the Lunafriya warriors." She tells me.

I smile, "Good, glad to have met you, then. Maybe you know more than Jett does." I respond.

Jett looks at us with mock pain and scoffs. "Everything she knows, she learned from me." He says while jerking his thumb towards his sister. Meri rolls her eyes as the same time as I do. "Ok. Now that's just weird." Jett says after seeing us do that.

We all laugh. I know Caol has already seen my lightning power but Meri hasn't. I see the huge tree branch from earlier.

"Watch this!" I exclaim to Meri, she watches me intently, never blinking. I focus on the branch and lift my arm up. I feel the familiar burning sensation in my palm and watch as a long string of electricity flows from it and hits the branch.

Meri's eyes light up with glee, "Poseidon's Trident! That's wicked!" She yells excitedly. It makes me beam with joy, my cheeks hurt again from smiling. "Have you tried to make balls instead of the long string?" She asks.

I think about that. "No, I just developed this power last night, how would I even try that?" I ask.

She thinks on this for a minute. The men are just watching us a little distance away. They are talking but I can't make out what they are saying.

"Try cupping your hands together like this while shooting the power out, and do only quick small bursts." She shows me what she means with her hands. I try it out and to my surprise, I have a little lightning ball in my hand. Meri smiles, "Now toss it." She says.

I throw it over to the branch, once it hits, the ball flattens and electrocutes a small area around it, killing a poor defenseless fish. I look over shocked and race to the fish. It is already floating to the surface. My heart is breaking over this fish. I didn't want to hurt any sea-life. It's been my life's work to save it.

Without thinking, I grab the fish, and place two fingers over its side, where the heart is. I think about the fish, swimming around, laying eggs, doing what fish do. I try to will it back to life. Nothing happens. My chest feels like a weight is pushing down hard, I can't breathe. I try again, willing the fish to live, focusing even harder. I'm sobbing, pleading with the fish.

Jett swims up beside me and grabs my shoulders, "Cora. Hey, it's ok. It's just a fish. You didn't mean for it to be a causality, but things happen sometimes."

I shake my head, I won't take that for an answer. I'm focusing hard, I tune out Jett and I feel I might pop a brain vessel, and sobs are wracking my body. My hands feel warm, not the stinging like they do when I use my lightning power, but more of a pulsing warmness.

Suddenly, the fish twitches, its eyes change back to black from a milky white, and it swims out of my hands. I stare straight ahead, processing. Jett squeezes my shoulders tightly. I look over at him. His face is surprised, and shocked, his eyes wide.

"Cora? Did you just do what I think you just did?" He asks.

I smile, "If you saw me bringing that fish back to life, then yes!" I exclaim. Jett looks over at Meri and Caol who are also shell-shocked. He begins to laugh, and I join him.

They swim over to us, "What just happened?" Caol asks. Jett looks over and smiles at him, arm still around my shoulder.

"She just brought something back from the dead, no big deal." He jokes. *Glad my sarcastic nature is rubbing off on him*, I smile.

Meri's jaw drops, "But...but that's never been done before..." She deadpans. We all smile, but suddenly I feel very tired and I need to sit down. Jett notices my body language, and directs everyone back to shore. We all summon our legs and Jett carries me back to the table and sits me down. I take some long deep breaths. Jett rubs my back. Meri and Caol sit across the table from us.

My phone rings, I have no strength right now so Jett checks it. "It's Megan." He says.

I lay my hand out and he sets the phone in my hand. I push the green answer button, "Hey, Megs." I croak out.

"Hello, Cora. Long time no SEE." It's not Megan, it's a man's voice. I know that voice, it sounds familiar. I immediately sit up, no longer tired, my body coursing with adrenaline.

"Who is this? Where is Megan?" I demand. The voice laughs, a sickly, cold, evil laugh. Everyone is looking at me with concern. I stare at Jett. My eyes wide, tears forming. I hear screaming in the background.

"Shut up bitch!" The voice yells, "If you want to see your pretty friend alive again, then come to the North Creek Pier at midnight, and come alone." Then the phone clicks off.

I gasp for air, "NOOOOO!" I yell out. Jett is pleading with me to tell him what happened. I look over at him, tears flowing down my cheeks, "My dream came true."

Chapter 12

Jett's perspective

I wake early the next morning, around six. I don't want to miss Cora's call and Meri has never been on land before. I need to make sure her legs are strong enough before I let her walk on her own. I walk into the kitchen and grab some eggs out of the fridge. I fry them up and pop some bread in the toaster. Only takes a few minutes and my egg sandwich is done. I sit quietly at the kitchen island, and eat.

Before I'm done eating, I hear a voice, "Can you make me one too?" I look up and Meri is walking to me, just a little wobbly.

I smile, "Sure, how's your legs feeling?" I ask her.

She smiles back, "They feel a little like jellyfish but I'm getting used to them." She says. She sits on a stool. I finish my sandwich really quickly and start to make another one for Meri. "That smells good!" Meri comments.

I chuckle at her, "Just wait till you try it!" I tell her.

I wait to see her reaction to the food. In the sea, you don't get much choice with food. Its fish or plants, water chestnuts, seaweed, and some fruits. On land, there are many more flavors. Meri takes her first bite. Her eyes get huge! She devours the sandwich in four bites.

"That was the greatest thing I've ever eaten!" She says while wiping her mouth.

I smile, "You're going to be saying that after every meal. Food here actually has flavor!" I tell her.

She smiles and rubs her leg muscles. "I want to strengthen them up, any tips?" She asks.

I nod, "Yea, I know a few exercises you can try." I lead her to the exercise room and put her on the stationary bike. "Pedal this one for a while, then switch to this machine." I tell her while patting the treadmill. I set the timer on the bike for her for ten minutes and showed her how to change the difficulty. I decide that I'll work out too while I wait for Cora to call. I run on the treadmill first then we switch machines. I do some pull-ups on the bar, then some push-ups.

Meri is "done exercising forever" and goes into the kitchen "to find more delicious food." She says.

She is walking steady now. I switch to the weight bench. Once my arms and legs are starting to burn, I stop and jump in the shower. I can't help but worry about Cora. *I really should be with her at all times now. I couldn't forgive myself if anything happens to her while I'm away.* I quickly get out of the shower and change into clean clothes. My suit and just a plain green t-shirt. I check my phone and no calls or texts from Cora. It's now almost nine in the morning. I go to find what Meri is getting into. She is in the kitchen. The counter is filled with food and bowls.

She looks up, "I found a cookbook in the drawer, so I started to whip up some recipes I want to try." She says.

"Well, I can't wait to eat whatever you make." I smirk at her. She is currently making coleslaw. "Why coleslaw?" I ask, looking at her confused.

"It's easy to make and you had all the ingredients, you need to go to the store." She says. *She's right, I do need to go to the store.* I shrug at her and nod.

My phone starts to ring. I check and it's Cora, I answer it on the second ring. "Good morning, beautiful!" I say happily. My heart does a flip and relaxes once I know she's ok.

"Hiya, handsome!" She says back. It makes me smile and Meri looks at me amused.

I turn away from her, "Did you sleep well? Any dreams?" I ask.

"Well, I slept good, but my dream was kind of scary." She tells me.

"Oh yea? How so?" I ask again. My tone changes, we have to take her dreams seriously from now on.

"All I remember is that I was with you and two other people, a male and a female and we were looking for Megan, I remember feeling scared out of my mind. You don't think anything bad will happen to her, do you?" She explains the dream and asks.

I breathe into the phone for a bit, thinking. "We should take your dreams seriously from now on, is Megan home right now" I ask.

"I don't know yet, hold on." She says. She doesn't speak for a good five minutes. I'm holding my breath, fearing the worst. "She is sleeping in her bed." She finally says. I let out a deep long breath.

"What time do you work today?" I ask her.

"Umm, well, I am supposed to work at eleven but I think I might call off so I can see my dad." She replies.

Well, that's surprising. Yesterday, she was so angry when I mentioned that she needed to quit. I won't push the issue. "You do what you want, baby. Call me after you're done so you can meet Meri." I reply.

"Ok, will do." She responds.

"And beautiful?" I say. I walk away from Meri and her eavesdropping and go to my room.

"Yea?" She asks.

"I know we've only known each other for about a week but I just wanted to tell you…that I think…I love you." I just blurt it out. *What the hell am I doing? I feel like a fucking idiot but I just had to tell her how I really felt.* All I hear is silence. "You still there?" I ask. *Shit! I fucked everything up!*

She clears her throat, "Ah hum, yea, I am. Sorry, that caught me off guard but…I feel the same way. I know it's too soon but…I love you too." My lips break out into the hugest grin I've ever had. *I got the love of a fucking Lunafriya! The most beautiful woman I've ever met.* I can tell she's smiling too.

"Ok baby, call me later, bye." I tell her.

"Bye." She chokes out and hangs up.

I walk back into the kitchen. Meri is now eating some frozen waffles straight out of the freezer. "You have to cook those." I laugh at her.

"I wondered why it was so hard." She laughs back.

"Just pop them in the toaster." I tell her, and she does. A few minutes goes by, and the waffles pop out of the toaster. "Now, grab a plate and put some syrup on them, trust me." I say.

She takes a bite. Her eyes go wide again. "Oh my Poseidon! These are amazing!" She says. I laugh and shake my head at her.

"We have a bit of time before Cora will be done talking with her dad and comes over. Want to go to the store with me and pick out more food for you to cook me?" I ask her with a smirk.

"Can we get stuff to make this cake?" She asks while pointing at a picture in the cookbook.

"Whatever you like." I tell her.

Meri looks into my eyes, "So, you really like her, huh?" She asks.

I smile, "I love her." I respond.

Meri smiles, "I've always wanted a sister! But aren't you afraid of what will happen once the council finds out you broke your oath?" She asks, now serious.

I look at her, and try to tell her the truth. "I don't know what will happen but I'll take anything they throw at me, as long as I get to be with Cora. Not going to lie, I worry about it from time to time, but Cora is worth everything to me."

Meri smiles with a bit of tears in her eyes, "That's one of the sweetest things I've ever heard." She says.

"Hurry up and finish your waffles so we can go to the store." I child her. She scarfs down the waffles so fast, she almost chokes. "Chew the food, not just swallow it." I laugh at her. She rolls her eyes at me, it reminds me of Cora.

She finishes her last bite. "Ready." She says.

We walk to the car and get in. Meri seems to be handling her legs much better now. The grocery store is a short ten minute drive from the house, I take the long way so Meri can see all the sights. I park in the lot and we walk into the store. Meri looks around fascinated at everything. I grab us a shopping cart and push it around the aisles. Meri is grabbing a lot of things and throwing them into the cart. I let her pick out whatever she wants. Once we've walked the entire store, we check out and pile the food into the car. The back is loaded with groceries. I decide to stop at the local Taco Bell to have her try the burritos. She eats it before we even get back home. She won't shut up about how good it is. It makes me smile.

I'm glad that I got to show Meri land for the first time. Our parents died when we were little, in the war so it's only been us. She missed out on a lot of simple pleasures because of that.

"What have you been up to while I've been away?" I ask her once we pull up in the driveway and we unload the car.

"Mainly studying, I've been hunting with Caol a lot too," she says. *I'm glad I can count on Caol to watch her while I'm away.*

"Good, keep up your studies, maybe you'll be on the council one day." I tell her.

She smiles, "That's the plan!" She says. *The council hasn't had a female member since the Lunafriya days. Cora will become a member now I'm sure. That's if I can get her to join us.*

Meri helps to put all the food away, and cleans up her mess from this morning. "I can't...stop...eating." She says around a bite of a chocolate swiss roll.

I laugh at her, "You better work out more, if you continue to eat like that. I had a hard time at first too. You just have to pace yourself." I remind her.

She groans, "I don't want to exercise." She pouts. My turn to roll my eyes. To keep herself busy for the day, she makes recipe after recipe. I will have too many leftovers at this point. I guess it's ok though, Meri wants to try everything she can before returning to the sea.

Hours go by, and I haven't heard anything from Cora. *I am starting to worry, and hate myself for not being at her side, protecting her in case anything happens. She was almost kidnapped the other day for fuck's sake.* I start to pace the room.

"You ok?" Meri asks. I realize what I'm doing and stop.

"Yea, just worried about Cora, I should be with her at all times as her guardian." I explain. Just then, my phone rings, it's Cora. I answer it on the first ring. "Hey beautiful." I say with a smile. *Finally!*

"Hi, I'm at the lake." She tells me.

"I'll be there in a minute." I say and hang up. "Well, off to get Cora, she's down at the lake, be right back." I salute Meri as I walk out the door.

I walk towards the bushes that separate my yard from the lake, when I hear Cora scream out, "JETT!!" My senses go into overdrive. I'm running the fastest I've ever run before. I see Cora finally and she's running towards me. She's out of breath when she finally reaches me. "Someone...came out...of the lake...he's behind...that tree." She points. "I shot...at him with...my powers. I was scared." She tells me.

I drag her behind my body for protection, while we walk to the tree together. "Show yourself!" I shout. My heart is pounding so fast. I can feel Cora's heartbeat on my back, hers is just as fast.

"Jett? That you?" The man says from behind the tree. I get confused, that's Caol's voice.

"Caol?" I ask. Caol comes out from behind the tree.

"Don't shoot!" He yells with his hands up in the air and a smirk on his face. I smile and push Cora's arm down. She looks at me confused.

"He's a friend." I tell her. We walk towards Caol, and we hug, slapping each other on the back. "What are you doing here?" I ask him.

"Your sister, she's missing." He says with concern.

I shake my head, "No, she's at the house. I couldn't stop her from coming with me last night." I tell him.

Caol lets out a long deep breath. "I was worried." He explains. Then he looks at Cora and smiles. "So, here is the Lunafriya." He exclaims.

Cora smiles back and waves. "Hi, sorry about shooting at you, I'm Cora." She apologizes.

He shakes her hand and doesn't let go, and kneels before her. "Caol, at your service. I offer you my guardian services until the day I die." He says with his head bowed.

Cora says, "Um, thank you."

"Let's go to the house, we've made too much of a commotion already." I state, looking around. *This is a public lake as it is, and I'm sure we're not the only tribe to know about Cora now.* I lead everyone back to the house. I open the door, Meri is still in the kitchen, making even more food.

As soon as Caol see her, he runs to her. "Meri!" He exclaims while they hug. I look at them bewildered, *I didn't know they were on hugging terms.* "Don't ever do that to me again, you hear me? I was scared out of my mind." Caol scolds Meri.

"Sorry, sweetie, but I just had to meet the Lunafriya." She says, then they kiss. *What the fuck! Caol and my sister?*

I start yelling, "Woah, woah, woah! What the fuck! That's my baby sister!" They both look at me. Meri looks down at the floor while Caol has the biggest smirk on his face. *I want to punch that smirk right off his face.* He then wraps his arm around Meri's shoulders.

"And my girlfriend." Caol says.

My face turns a dark shade of red. My fists ball up tight. *I'm about to seriously punch Caol in his smug face. That's my sister, he should know better.* Suddenly, I feel a shock to my arm, it hurts.

"Ouch!" I yell out and look down at Cora, "what was that for?" I ask. My fingers loosen, and I feel the heat leave my face.

"To calm you down. Remember, you can't help who you fall in love with." She pleads at me with her eyes.

My sister is an adult now, she can make her own decisions, and be with anyone she wishes. I have to get that through my head, and really, Caol is a good guy, he's my best friend. My eyes soften and I cup Cora's face in my hands. Now it's Caol's time to look confused.

He gasps, "You broke your oath?" He asks me, shocked. I nod my head. Caol gets a big smile again, "You sly seal!" He says while punching me in the arm.

"So, how long has this been going on?" I point between the two of them, Caol and Meri.

Meri shrugs, "a couple of months." She answers.

I shake my head. "Well, I can't stop you, but know Caol, you hurt her, and I kill you. Or maybe I'll get my girlfriend to do it for me." I say with a laugh. Cora smiles.

Meri looks at her with wide eyes, like she just noticed her. "Hi, I'm Meri, Jett's sister." She tells Cora.

"Hello, name's Cora." She responds.

"She shot at me." Caol tells her with a large grin.

Cora looks sorry for it, "Sorry, I didn't know he was a friend." She explains.

Meri waves her off. "Don't worry about it, you have got to protect yourself, right?" She says. Cora nods. "Can I see your powers?" Meri asks eagerly.

"Later, we don't want any other tribe to know about her and she already might have been seen." I tell everyone. They all nod. Cora looks upset. I try to calm her down while rubbing her back a bit. "Let's eat some food, I'm starving." I say to break the tension.

"I already made a late lunch, some sandwiches and coleslaw." Meri tells us. Cora grabs at her stomach.

We all sit at the kitchen island and make plates, family style. We are all having a good time, talking about old times and laughing. Hopefully these stories are helping Cora decide to come to the sea. Everyone is laughing and we finish our food. We all decide to wait everything out in the house, and watch a movie. I tell Cora that she should pick the movie since we don't know any. She goes over to the movie wall. Only takes a few minutes before she grabs one down. She smiles and starts singing while holding out a movie.

"If there's something strange…in the neighborhood…who you gonna call?…GHOSTBUSTERS!" We all laugh at her. "It is one of my favorites." She tells me.

I pop it in the DVD player and we all sit and watch, by the end of the movie, everyone is dancing to the theme song.

"Well, I should probably head back to the city, Krill is covering for me." Caol says after the movie is finished.

Meri gives him puppy dog eyes, "I'm not leaving. I'll join you when Jett and Cora go." She tells Caol.

He shakes his head. "Alright, not like I can stop you anyways." He says while giving her a kiss on the lips.

I look away, that's still not something I wish to see. "It's almost dark, let's all go swimming and Cora can show you guys her powers before you leave." I suggest. Everyone agrees and we head out to the lake.

I grab Cora's hand and hold it while we walk to the picnic table under the willow tree. I'm proud to show her off as mine. Meri and Caol are following behind us. Once we reach the table, everyone strips out of their clothes and we all have our suits on. I can't help but stare at Cora's body. She notices me and I wink at her. We all walk to the water.

Cora immediately relaxes once we get in the lake. She blows out a deep breath. I grab her hand again and we go deeper into the water. She summons her fin and we all follow suit. We swim around each other, playing in the water, racing each other, trying to catch fish. Cora makes the fish swim around us in a figure eight pattern. It makes me smile at her. Meri and Caol laugh and reach out for the fish. Cora then makes one lay in each of their hands. Meri stares at the fish, and then at Cora, wide eyed with fascination. She lets the fish swim away.

Meri swims up to Cora, "It's been my life's work to study the Lunafriya warriors." She tells her.

Cora smiles, "Glad to have met you then. Maybe you know more than Jett does." She responds.

I look at them with mock pain and scoff. "Everything she knows, she learned from me." I say while jerking my thumb towards my sister. Meri rolls her eyes at the same time that Cora does. "Ok, now that's just weird." I say after seeing that. We all laugh.

Cora looks around and spots the tree branch from before. "Watch this!" She exclaims to Meri. Caol stays back by me, almost getting hit by her powers must have scared him. Cora sends a long string of lightning to the tree branch.

Meri's eyes light up with glee, "Poseidon's Trident! That's wicked!" She yells excitedly.

"Sorry about me and your sister, man" Caol comments lowly. "I really didn't mean it to happen but, we fell in love." He says.

I smile, "It's alright, dude. I couldn't have asked for a better guy for my sister to date." I tell him, we shake hands.

"She's the real deal, huh?" He asks me about Cora.

"She's a fucking Lunafriya." I respond proudly.

We watch as Meri is showing Cora something. Cora creates a ball of lightning. "Now toss it." I hear Meri say.

Cora throws it over to the branch, once it hits, the ball flattens and electrocutes a small area around it, killing a fish in its wake. Cora looks shocked and races over to the fish. It is already starting to float to the top. She looks wildly upset. She grabs the fish, and places two fingers over its side and sobbing uncontrollably.

I swim up beside her fast and grab her shoulders. "Cora. Hey, it's ok. It's just a fish, you didn't mean for it to be a casualty, but things happen sometimes." I tell her.

She shakes her head, sobs are wracking her body. She's shaking and focusing on the fish. Suddenly, the fish twitches. Its eyes change back to black from a milky white, and it swims out of her hands. She stares straight ahead, jaw dropped. I squeeze her shoulders. She looks over at me. My eyes are wide, and I'm in shock. *No one in recorded history has done that before.*

"Cora? Did you just do what I think you just did?" I ask dumbfounded.

She smiles, "If you saw me bringing a fish back to life, then yes!" She exclaims. I look over at Meri and Caol who are also shell-shocked. I begin to laugh, and Cora joins me.

They swim over to us, "What happened?" Caol asks me. I look over and smile at him, an arm still around Cora's shoulders.

"She just brought something back from the dead, no big deal." I joke.

Meri's jaw drops. "But…but that's never been done before." She deadpans. We all smile.

Suddenly, Cora slumps down, she starts to drift down to the bottom of the lake. I direct everyone back to shore. We all summon our legs and I carry Cora back to the table and sit her down. She takes some long deep breathes. I rub her back. Meri and Caol sit across the table from us, watching with concern.

Suddenly, Cora's phone rings. She can't move right now so I check it for her.

"It's Megan." I tell her. She lays her hand out flat on the table.

I set the phone in her hand and she pushes the green answer button, "Hey Megs." She croaks out. She immediately sits up straight, no longer looking tired, she looks flat out scared. "Who is this? Where is Megan?" She demands. She stares at me. Her eyes wide, and tears forming. A few seconds goes by and she gasps for air. The phone drops out of her hands, falling into the sand. "NOOOO!" She yells out. I am pleading with her to tell me what happened, who was on the phone. Cora looks into my eyes, tears flowing down her cheeks. "My dream came true."

Chapter 13

Cora's perspective

I can't control the sobs coming from me, I'm hyperventilating. Jett is rubbing my back, telling me to just breathe, in my ear.

"He…has…Megan." I squeak out through sobs.

"Who?" Jett asks. I try to control myself, I can't help Megan if I'm a wreck. *I'm a badass Lunafriya warrior! First in one hundred and fifty years! If anyone can save Megan, it should be me.* I think about the phone call. I know that I know that voice from somewhere, I gasp!

"Jake!" I shout out. Jett, Meri, and Caol are staring at me. "Jake, the guy that I stabbed in the eye, took Megan. He says I'm to go to North Creek Pier at midnight, alone. Then he'll let Megan go."

Meri looks scared, Caol looks serious and Jett looks furious. "You are not going alone! It is my job to protect you." He seethes. "We will get Megan back and do what we have to with Jake, but we do this together, I can't lose you." He pleads.

I don't want Megan getting hurt, or worse. "I can't risk Megan getting harmed! I have to go alone! You know I can take care of myself. I got away from him before and that was before I developed my powers. He has no chance now." I explain to him.

Jett shakes his head, and repeats, "You are not going alone," through clenched teeth. I roll my eyes, Meri and Caol are staying out of it.

"What do you suggest we do then?" I sigh out. Jett looks around and thinks for a few minutes.

"I'll help! In any way I can!" Meri exclaims.

"I got your back." Caol calls out.

"What time is it now?" Jett asks. I check my phone, it's six in the afternoon.

"Six." I tell him.

"So, we have another six hours before you have to meet that asshole. Let's go check out the pier and see any hiding spots." He says.

We all nod and start to get dressed. We walk back to the house, Jett with his arm around me still. Jett leads all of us to his car and he opens the passenger side door for me. I slide into the car and he shuts the door. Meri and Caol go into the back seat. Jett gets into the driver's side, starts the car and pulls out of the driveway. It's about a twenty minute drive from Jett's house to the pier. I've been staring out the window for the whole drive, thinking, wondering, hoping that Megan is ok, and not being hurt. *I will kill Jake if he does anything to her.*

"Did he say where exactly to meet him?" Jett asks.

I shake my head and clear my thoughts, "No, just said the pier, could be anywhere in this area." I say while gesturing with my hands. He parks the car in the lot, and we all get out.

"Let's spilt up and get the lay-out of the area. Any spots that look good to hide in, report, and meet at the diner in an hour." Jett says to Caol. He's in total guardian mode right now. *I got to say, it's really sexy.*

Caol nods, "Let the water flow freely." He says.

Meri and Jett both chant, "Let the water flow freely" right back. *Huh?* I look at them all confused. They all laugh at me. "It's a saying down in the sea, something the council says after meetings." Jett tells me. I chuckle and shrug.

Meri waves a little before they turn around and walk away from us down the pier, holding hands.

Jett grabs my hand, "Show me around the place." He says with a wink.

We walk around to the fishing boats. The pier is pretty huge. This is a fishing town, after all. Many boats line the pier. There are a lot of shops around, even a big Ferris wheel in the summer, and fair type games.

"One of us could hide in the lake, and keep an eye out, possibly." Jett comments.

I nod, "Yes, but I do have to have the appearance that I'm alone. You can't be at my side during this." I remind him.

"I understand, even if I don't like it. I will only be a few feet away from you at all times. I'm sneaky, Jake won't see me." He says.

I roll my eyes at him. We continue walking, looking for good hiding spots for my friends. We stop at a part of the pier that has shops behind with dark alleyways and the pier goes out straight into the water, clear of boats.

"I think this is where I will wait for him. Someone can hide in the lake, and others in the alleyways, looks like the perfect spot." I tell Jett.

He nods and smiles at me, "I couldn't agree more." He says and leans down to give me a kiss. I kiss him back, passionately. *You never know if it could be our last kiss, our last alone time together. I don't know what's going to happen tonight.* My hands run through his spikey hair, he grabs my ass in his hands and squeezes. *What I wouldn't give to fuck him right now, but we don't have time for that.*

Jett pulls away and we walk back to the diner, where he parked the car, and see Meri and Caol walking towards us from the opposite direction. They are smiling and look happy, but once they notice us, their demeanor changes. Caol gets serious, and Meri, well, she still looks happy.

"We found a spot that will work nicely, let's get some food here and talk over the plan."
Jett tells them.

We walk into the diner together and I tell the waitress that we need a table for four. She
sits us in a booth and we look over the menu. Food is the last thing on my mind right now so I
just order some coffee. I swear, they order almost the whole menu, though. While we wait on
their food, Jett tells them the plan.

"There is a spot at the pier that has many alleyways and is at the water. I will be hiding in
the lake, under the dock, where Cora will be waiting for the asshole." He seethes. "Caol, I want
you in the alleyways closet to the docks." Caol nods his approval. "And Meri, I want you to stay
at the house, you don't need to be here for this." Jett says.

Meri looks pissed. "I want to help!" She pleads. Jett shakes his head at her.

"You have no training, you would only be in the way if anything happens and I don't
want to worry about you too." Jett tries to explain to her.

"Try to stop me from coming with you guys, just try it. You'll see that I can't be
stopped." She whines back like a teenager.

Jett is frustrated. "Please, Meri, don't fight me on this. Just listen to what you're told." He
says. The conversation ends for now because the waitress is bringing their food to the table.
There isn't room on the table for all their food, but they dig in. I sit there and sip my coffee,
watching them devour their meals.

Meri is trying a bite of everything on the table, so giddy over all the food, actually doing
a little happy dance in her seat. Caol and Jett are eating fast. I can't believe it when they both
finish off two coneys each and a cheeseburger, and go back for more. I shake my head in
disbelief.

"How can you guys eat all that?" I ask. Jett smiles with a mouth full of food, then swallows his bite.

"We don't get food like this down in the sea, everything on land has flavor and spices in it, so when mer-people are on land, it's hard to stop eating." He explains.

I nod my head at him and shrug, "Wait, what kind of food do you eat in the sea?" I ask him.

"Fish, plants, grains, and some fruits." He says.

"I don't think I could eat fish, it's been my life's work to save them." I tell him. He looks a bit sad and changes the subject.

"Want some alone time with me before the big fight?" He whispers in my ear. My smile widens and I nod rigorously. He chuckles, and gets the waitresses attention. "Can we get the check, please?" He asks her.

She says, "Right away sir." And walks away.

Meri and Caol are having their own whisper party across the booth from us. "Right, so we are going back to the house, to hang a bit before the fight and drop Meri off. Then Cora can drive her own car to the spot and Caol and I will follow in my car." Jett announces, Meri starts to protest but Jett cuts her off. "Don't fight me please, you are the only family I have left, I need you safe." Meri keeps quiet after that. Jett pays the bill and I leave a very generous tip to the waitress. We all pile into Jett's car and drive back to his house. The drive back was silent. He pulls the car into the driveway and we step into his house.

"Cora, will you join me in my room?" Jett asks, I follow without question.

As soon as the door shuts, I pounce on him. I'm kissing him passionately, rubbing my hands all over his body. *This might be the last time I get to touch him, if things go horribly wrong.* Jett is reacting the same way with me, we can't get enough of each other. I rip off my shirt and Jett follows suit. He's un-zipping my pants and I step out of them. I'm only in my bra and panties now. I rub his cock through his shorts. He's hard as stone, long and thick. He's kissing and sucking on my neck. I stop him and seductively seat him on his bed. He has a smirk on his face. I kneel in front of him and pull out his cock. It's the perfect size. I tentatively lick up and down, giving little kisses on my way.

"Fuck, Cora." He says through clenched teeth. It makes me smile to know I make him feel this good. I put my mouth on his dick and swirl my tongue around the head, under the ridge. He gasps loudly. I slowly push him into my mouth deeper and deeper, up and down. I look up at him. He's looking down at me, his lips parted, then he bites his lower lip. That makes me wet. I suck him off for a few minutes.

"Get up here, baby." He says. I do what he says, and stand up. He lightly grabs me and tosses me down on the bed. He immediately goes for my breasts, popping them out of my bra. He puts my nipple into his mouth, lightly sucking. His hand travels down my stomach to my panties. He finds my clit, rubbing me, seeing how wet I am. I moan out. He switches to the other nipple, rubbing me the whole time. I can't help but be a little noisy, he's making me feel so amazing. He quiets me down by shushing me a little, reminding me that there are other people in the house. He slides his finger into me smoothly, and then another. I'm panting, I want him inside of me now, not his fingers. I want his cock.

"Please, I need you." I say. He rips my panties in two, to get them off faster, it turns me on. He immediately gets on top of me, and shoves his cock into my pussy. I gasp at his fullness, then moan. We kiss passionately while he pumps in and out of me. I'm pouring all my love for him into this. I want him to know I love him, without a doubt. I'm scratching his back with my nails, he moans too.

"Turn over." He whispers in my ear. I bite my lip and turn my body around, wanting him inside me again. I get on my knees and push my ass into the air. He squeezes my ass, then gives it a little smack. It makes a loud noise, and I moan again. He checks to see if I'm wet, which I am, then slides his finger into me. I clench down, it feels good. He replaces his finger with his cock and eases into me. Once he's fully inside, he rocks back and forth, slowly at first. Then it intensifies, he drills me. In and out, in and out. I'm moaning loudly again but I can't help it. I'm so close to climax. I reach my hand down to rub my clit and his balls. In no time at all, I'm coming around his cock. I hear his breathing get ragged, then feel him pulsing inside of me, spilling his seed. He lays his head on my back, both of us trying to catch our breath.

"I love you, Cora." He says.

"I love you too, Jett. With all of my heart." I tell him. Then I start to cry, like full on sobs.

"Oh, baby! What's wrong?" Jett asks full of concern.

I try to calm myself down a bit but it's hard. Jett holds me, just cradles me in his arms, letting me cry on him. Eventually, I calm down and am able to talk.

"I'm scared, what if Megan gets hurt or worse? Or you, or Caol? I could never forgive myself." I tell him, my body shaking. He looks me straight in my eyes and gently strokes my face.

"Cora, you are one bad-ass, amazing woman. You're a fucking Lunafriya. If you really wanted, you could fry that asshole. Megan will be fine. Caol and I will be fine. Don't treat this as a goodbye. I will be with you at the pier. We will save Megan, and hurt Jake, don't worry." Jett reminds me.

He's right, I know he is. Still, his reassurances only help a little. What if we walk into a trap? Since we are planning a trap ourselves, is it so crazy that he would set a trap for us too? I stay in Jett's arms for a while and actually fall asleep. He gently shakes me awake after a while.

"It's almost midnight. We should make our way to the pier." Jett says.

I stretch my limbs, and just for practice, I make a lightning ball. It comes easily to me now, and doesn't even hurt my hands anymore. Jett is watching my every move. I re-absorb the ball, with a smile in my face.

Jett smiles back, "Remember you are a bad-ass." He says. I'm beaming. I get my clothes back on sans underwear, then we walk out of the room together. I hug and kiss Jett quickly, say my goodbyes and walk out the door, dreading what I am about to do. My car is still in the lake parking lot, I have to walk across the beach to it. Meri is sitting at the willow tree table, knees up to her chest, looking very put out.

"What's wrong?" I ask her.

She looks up at me. "I don't like this one bit, if anything happens, to any of you, how am I to know? I can help! I've already helped you develop your powers more. You guys need me!" She exclaims.

I think for a few seconds. *She has helped me. Maybe she knows more tricks that Jett doesn't.* I look around to make sure Jett isn't watching. "Let's go, then." I tell her while gesturing to my car.

"Really?" She asks, positively beaming and following me to my car.

"Yes, you can be my wild card, Jake doesn't know you." I respond.

"Jett won't be happy." She says.

I roll my eyes, "He can be mad at me then, I'm the one who brought you along." I tell her. We get to my car and drive off, heading for the pier.

The drive doesn't take long, there are barely any cars on the road at this time of night. Meri and I talk the whole ride. She tells me that she's never heard of the Lunafriya's having healing powers, or being able to bring things back from the dead. She also tells me that I should be able to call sea-life to help me. Instead of just focusing on one fish or a group of fish, I should focus on asking all the sea-life for help. It's easier to talk about all this stuff than actually do it, but I'll try next time I'm in the water.

We pull into North Creek Pier parking lot and I park the car. I tell her to walk behind me but to not be obvious that she's following me and then hide in an alleyway once I reach the spot. She nods. I walk to the spot we talked about earlier, Meri far behind me. I reach the spot, and wait. I look around, Meri is nowhere to be seen. I'm guessing she is in hiding.

"Psst!" I hear quietly. I take long looks around. "Down here." It's Jett. He's in the water under the docks. "Meri's missing." He says.

I shake my head. "I brought her with me, she's hiding." I tell him quietly.

"What the fuck, Cora!" He exclaims.

I look at him seriously. "Hide, Now. Don't fuck this up." I tell him. He ducks back under the docks, looking angry. I roll my eyes again. He can be as angry as he wants. Meri was right, I need her. She is helping me develop my powers more.

It takes a while, about an hour but eventually, I see a dark shape walking towards me. All of my senses are alive with fear and adrenaline.

"Showtime." I whisper below me so that Jett can hear. The man stops a few feet ahead of me. It's Jake, with his stupid surfer-dude looking haircut, and flannel shirt. He's got an eye patch on his one eye. The eye, I stabbed him in with my keys when he tried to abduct me. *It serves him goddamn right, for trying to kidnap people. He looks like he's trying for a surfer, lumberjack, pirate look.* That thought makes me chuckle inside.

"Where's Megan?" I ask him immediately. His face splits into a sickly evil grin.

"She's safe, for now. I didn't hurt her...much." He says with a chuckle.

This lights my body on fire, I'm so angry, I don't know what I'll do. I grit my teeth and force my fists closed tightly.

"You still didn't answer my question. Where...is...Megan? Let her go!" I seethe.

He chuckles again, "You are in no position to make demands." He says acting all cool, trying to be smooth with a smirk.

I've had enough. *I'm a bad-ass Lunafriya. It's about time he knows this.* I hold my hands up to my chest and make a lightning ball. Jake's eyes get huge, *he wasn't expecting that.*

"Really? Because I will kill you right now, right where you stand, if you don't tell me." I tell him with one eyebrow raised, testing him.

He looks a bit scared and stumbles his words, "You doo...do...do that and you won't ever find her.

My turn to smirk at him, "I guess, that's something I'll have to find out for myself." I toss the ball up above him, to land on an awning. Sparks fall down all around him.

It doesn't hit him but this scares him enough that he jumps into the lake from the docks. I make my move and follow suit, jumping in after him. He's swimming away fast. He summoned his fin and is making a getaway. I summoned my fin as soon as I hit the water, and chase behind him.

Jett swims beside me. "What's going on?" He asks surprised.

"Jake got scared of me, and swam off like a little bitch. He never told me where Megan is, he can't get away! I yell at him.

We race together towards Jake, who never looks back. I try Meri's suggestion, of asking all the sea-life for help instead of individual fish. I focus on the words, *Help me! Stop him! Don't let him get away!* I keep these mantras running through my head while we chase after Jake.

Suddenly, Jake stops. I hear him screaming and see him trying to bat things away with his arms flailing. As I get closer, I see swarms of large fish, biting, and tearing away his flesh. The water around him is tinting pink.

"No! Don't kill him!" I scream.

Jett swims up fast to him and grabs Jake's arms from behind, stopping him from escaping. The fish, which on closer inspection, are snakeheads. Nasty large fish with teeth, which can actually 'walk' on land. I thank the fish for their help and they all scatter away. Jake has bites all over his arms, torso, and fin, some of which are gnarly and deep. I swim around to face Jake, he's breathing heavily.

"Now, where the fuck is Megan? I can do much worse than killing you, ya know?" I tell him with menace dripping out of my voice.

Jake looks genuinely scared but keeps his mouth shut, not saying a word. I look around and see some rope dangling into the water from a ship, I grab it.

"Jett! Put him against this dock post, and tie him up." I yell at Jett. He nods his head and does what I say. Once Jake is tied up and can't escape, I swim in front of him again. "Still don't want to tell me?" I ask him with a sickly sweet smile on my face.

Jake says nothing, just staring ahead. I place my hand on his shoulder and give him a little zap. He screams out loud, but still doesn't break. I let go of his shoulder and grab the end of his fin with both hands.

"It's going to get a lot worse if you don't tell me, just tell me where Megan is and you can be free. I will leave you alone, and let you swim away." I try to reason with him. *I don't like hurting people, and I don't want to hurt him, but I will if I have too.* Jake looks at me pitifully, but still doesn't say anything. "Ok, I warned you." I tell him before unleashing my power into his tail-fin.

The screams coming from Jake must have been heard from above because Caol and Meri jump into the lake at this time. They both see me, holding onto this asshole's fin, with currents of electricity pouring out of me. Their faces display looks of shock and horror. I immediately let go. Luckily for me, Jake is not dead. He is seizing and foaming at the mouth a bit…but not dead. I give him a little break before asking him again.

"Before I get some more of my fishy friends to help me, I'll ask again. Where the fuck is Megan?" I yell in his face.

Jett keeps Meri and Caol back, afraid that they will get hurt. Jake looks up at me. "Nereus city." He coughs out.

"What does that mean?" I ask in general.

Jett swims up beside me, "Nereus is another tribe and mer-city." He tells me.

"Wait, so she's in the ocean?" I ask. Jake nods his head, fighting for strength. "Where in the city? How is she surviving in the water?" I ask again while forming a lightning ball for added effect.

"She's well-guarded in the…council chambers, in the…land training room." Jake sputters out.

I look back at Jett, asking him what I should do, pleading with my eyes.

"We will find her, we don't need him anymore." He nods at me, understanding what I was asking him.

Jake's eyes get huge. I swim in front of him. "But…but you said I'd be free to go!" He pleads with me.

"Yea, I lied. This is what you get for kidnapping people." I tell him while I place my hand over his heart. I let my power flow through me, letting my emotions control me. Jake screams and twitches so badly, it shakes me with him. I continue my on-slaughter until Jake stops moving and goes limp. I let go and swim backwards. "Is he dead?" I ask.

Jett feels for a pulse for a few minutes, "Yes." He says.

Immediately, I get wrecked with guilt. *I killed someone. A deserving someone, but that doesn't make me feel any better.* Jett is by my side in a heartbeat, squeezing me, and reassuring me.

"You had to do it. If you would have let him go, he would have tipped off the Nereus tribe that we were coming. Let's go on land and discuss the new plan." He says while rubbing my arm. *Now, that helps me feel a little bit better.* "Caol, dispose of the body and meet back at the house." Jett orders, and Caol nods before un-tying the dead body. I feel pretty winded from everything.

Jett and Meri help me back onto land. We walk to the car and Jett drives us back to his house. Meri goes straight for the kitchen and starts to cook more food. Jett takes me into his bedroom. I lay on his bed, and he tucks me in, kissing me on the head and turns off the light.

Before he shuts his door, I fall asleep, and luckily my dreams have stopped for the night.

Chapter 14

Jett's perspective

Cora is a mess. She's crying so much that she can barely breathe. I'm rubbing her back, telling her to just breathe, in her ear, trying to calm her down so I can know what the fuck is going on.

"He…has…Megan." She squeaks out through sobs.

"Who?" I ask.

She is trying to calm herself down, then suddenly, she gasps! "Jake!" She shouts out. Meri, Caol, and I are staring at her. "Jake, the guy that I stabbed in his eye, took Megan. He says I'm to go to North Creek Pier at midnight, alone, then he'll let Megan go." She tells us.

Meri looks scared, Caol looks serious and I'm furious. "You are not going alone! It is my job to protect you." I seethe. "We will get Megan back and do what we have to with Jake, but we do this together, I can't lose you!" I plead with her. *There is no way she is going anywhere by herself anymore.*

"I can't risk Megan getting harmed! I have to go alone! You know I can take care of myself. I got away from him before and that was before I developed my powers. He has no chance now." She explains to me.

I shake my head, and repeat, "You are not going alone," through clenched teeth. She rolls her eyes, Meri and Caol are staying out of it.

"What do you suggest we do then?" Cora sighs out. I look around and think for a few minutes. *Maybe, Caol and I can hide out and protect as needed.*

"I'll help! In any way I can!" Meri exclaims.

"I got your back." Caol calls out.

"What time is it now?" I ask. Cora checks her phone.

"Six." She tells me.

"So, we have another six hours before you have to meet that asshole. Let's go check out the pier and see any hiding spots." I tell everyone, which they all nod and start to get dressed.

We walk back to the house, my arm around Cora still, I'm not letting her go. I lead all of us to my car and I open the passenger side door for her. She slides into the car and I shut the door. Meri and Caol go into the back seat. I get into the driver's side, start the car and pull out of the driveway. It's about a twenty minute drive from my house to the pier. Cora is quiet the whole drive there. I don't know how to comfort her, I let her think in silence. We arrive to the North Creek Pier.

"Did he say where exactly to meet him?" I ask Cora.

She shakes her head, "No, just said the pier, could be anywhere in this area." She says while gesturing with her hands in front of her.

I park the car in the lot. We all get out. "Let's spilt up and get the lay-out of the area. Any spots that look good to hide in, report, and meet at the diner in an hour." I tell Caol. I am his superior, but he's also my best friend.

Caol nods, "Let the water flow freely." He says.

Meri and I both chant, "Let the water flow freely" right back. Cora looks at us with a funny look on her face, it makes us all laugh. "It's a saying down in the sea, something the council says after meetings." I tell her. She chuckles and shrugs.

Meri gives us a little wave before they both turn around and walk away from us down the pier, holding hands. *It still bothers me a bit but I guess I will have to get over it. Meri is an adult and can do what she pleases.*

I grab Cora's hand, "Show me around the place." I say with a wink.

We walk around to the fishing boats. The pier is pretty huge. There are many docks with boats lined up. There are shops behind us and even a little bar that the fisherman hang out at.

"One of us could hide in the lake, and keep an eye out, possibly." I comment.

She nods, "Yes, but I do have to have the appearance that I'm alone. You can't be at my side during this." She reminds me.

"I understand, even if I don't like it. I will only be a few feet away from you at all times. I'm sneaky, Jake won't see me." I say.

She rolls her eyes at me. *I love that she is sarcastic.* We continue walking, looking for good hiding spots for us. We stop at a part of the pier that has shops behind with dark alleyways and the docks go out straight into the water, clear of any boats. Cora looks around, her wheels turning in her head.

"I think this is where I will wait for him. Someone can hide in the lake, and others in the alleyways, looks like the perfect spot." She tells me confidently.

I nod and smile at her, *this really does look like the perfect spot.* "I couldn't agree more." I say and lean down to give her a kiss. She kisses me back, passionately. I can't get enough of this woman. Her need for me is seeming desperate right now. Her hands run through my hair, I grab her tight round ass in my hands and squeeze. *What I wouldn't give to fuck her right now.* My dick is getting hard, straining against my pants. I push it against her hips. She sighs and pulls away from me, while shaking her head.

We walk back to the diner, where I parked the car, still holding hands. Meri and Caol are walking towards us from the opposite direction. They are smiling and look happy but once they notice us, their demeanor changes. Caol gets serious, and Meri, well, she still looks happy. *I hope that doesn't mean anything happened between them, I don't want to think about that.* I shake my head to clear those gross thoughts.

"We found a spot that will work nicely, let's get some food here and talk over the plan." I tell them.

We walk into the diner together and Cora tells the waitress that we need a table for four. She seats us in a booth and we look over the menu. Cora only orders a coffee. The rest of us each order about three meals each, with also some appetizers. The bill is going to be huge but I want Meri, and Caol to be able to enjoy being on land, because it's back to the sea for them soon. While we wait for the large amount of food we ordered, I tell them the plan.

"There is a spot at the pier that has many alleyways and is at the water. I will be hiding in the lake, under the dock, where Cora will be waiting for the asshole." I seethe. "Caol, I want you in the alleyway closet to the docks." Caol nods his approval. "And Meri, I want you to stay at the house, you don't need to be here for this." I tell her.

Meri looks pissed. "I want to help!" She pleads. I shake my head at her.

"You have no training, you would only be in the way if anything happens and I don't want to worry about you too." I try to explain to her.

"Try to stop me from coming with you guys, just try it. You'll see that I can't be stopped." She whines back like a teenager. I am getting frustrated.

"Please, Meri, don't fight me on this, just listen to what you're told." I say. *I hate to treat her as a child, but I am the only father figure that she can remember. It has been just her and me since we were very young. How does she not get that she's the only family I have left?* The conversation ends for now because the waitress is bringing our food to the table. There isn't room on the table for all our food, but we dig in. Meri enjoys every bite, trying a bit of food on every plate while dancing a little in her seat. Caol devours his meals fast. I try to pace myself but it's hard when the food is so delicious. Caol and I both finish two meals and still eat some more. Cora looks at us in disbelief.

"How can you guys eat all that?" She asks. I smile with a mouth full of food, then swallow my bite.

"We don't get food like this down in the sea. Everything on land has flavor and spices in it, so when mer-people are on land, it's hard to stop eating." I explain. She nods her head at me and shrugs.

"Wait, what kind of food do you eat in the sea?" She asks again.

"Fish, plants, grains, and some fruits." I explain.

"I don't think I could eat fish, it's been my life's work to save them." She tells me. This makes me quite sad. *What if she doesn't choose the sea because of the food there? Will that be enough of a deterrent for her?* I quickly try to change the subject.

"Want some alone time with me before the big fight?" I whisper into her ear. Her smile widens and she nods rigorously. It makes me laugh so I chuckle a bit, and get the waitresses attention. "Can we get the check please?" I ask her.

She says "right away, sir." And walks away. Meri and Caol are having their own whispers across the booth from us.

"Right, so we are going back to the house, to hang a bit before the fight and drop Meri off, then Cora can drive her own car to the spot and Caol and I will follow in my car." I announce, Meri starts to protest but I stop her right away. "Don't fight me please, you are the only family I have left, I need you safe." Meri keeps quiet after that. I pay the humongous bill and Cora leaves a very generous tip to the waitress. We all pile into my car and drive back to the house. The drive back was silent. I pull the car into the driveway and we step into the house.

"Cora, will you join me in my room?" I ask with a smirk, she follows without question.

I see Caol give me a little wink as I walk by. As soon as the door shuts, she pounces on me. We're kissing passionately, Cora rubs her hands all over my body. I can't get enough of her. My tongue is swirling around hers. She rips off her shirt and I follow suit. I'm un-zipping her pants and she steps out of them. She's only in her bra and panties now. I stare at her perfect body for a minute. She's the sexiest woman I've ever seen. She rubs my hard cock through my shorts. I'm kissing and sucking on her neck. The taste of salt doesn't stop me. Suddenly, she stops me and pushes me onto my bed gently. I have a smirk on my face. I know what she's about to do and I can't wait to have my cock in her mouth. She kneels in front of me and pulls out my cock. My dick jumps at the excitement. She tentatively licks up and down my shaft, giving little kisses along the way. It feels amazing.

"Fuck, Cora." I say through clenched teeth, trying not to be loud. It makes her smile. She puts her mouth around my dick and swirls her tongue around the head, under the ridge. I gasp loudly, probably too loudly. She slowly pushes my dick into her mouth deeper and deeper, up and down. She looks up at me. I'm looking down at her, her blue eyes looking gorgeous. She sucks me off for a few minutes. I can't take it anymore and don't want to blow my load yet. "Get up here, baby." I tell her.

She does what I say, and stands up. I lightly grab her and toss her down on the bed. I immediately go for her tits, popping them out of her bra, so I can see her nipples. I put one of her nipples into my mouth, lightly sucking. My hand travels down her stomach to her panties. I find her clit, rubbing her, seeing how wet she is, she's soaked. It's fucking hot how ready she is for me. She moans out loud. I switch to the other nipple, rubbing her clit the whole time. I shush her a little, trying to remind her that there are other people in the house. I slide my finger into her smoothly, and then another. She's panting.

"Please, I need you." She says. That makes my dick jump again. I rip her panties in two, to get them off faster. She doesn't seem to mind and moans some more.

I immediately get on top on her, and shove my cock into her pussy. She gasps at my fullness, then moans. We kiss passionately while I pump in and out of her. I'm pouring all my love for her into this. I want her to know I love her, without a doubt. She's scratching my back with her nails. It feels amazing, I moan too. It's getting a bit much and I need to slow down or I'll blow my load too early.

"Turn over." I whisper in her ear. She bites her lip and turns her body around. She gets on her knees and pushes her ass into the air. I squeeze her glorious ass, then give it a little smack. It makes a loud smacking noise, she moans again. I check to see if she's still wet, which she is, then slide my finger into her. She clenches down on my finger. *Fuck, she wants my cock bad.* I replace my finger with my cock and ease it into her. Once I'm fully inside, I rock my hips back and forth, slowly at first. Then I intensify, she's clenching down on my cock so tightly. I drill her, faster and faster. In and out, in and out. She's moaning loudly again, but I don't care, let them hear. I'm so close to coming, it feels like she is too. She reaches her hand down to rub her clit and my balls. In no time at all, she's climaxing around my cock. It makes me explode into her, spilling my load. I lay my head on her back, both of us trying to catch our breath.

"I love you, Cora." I say.

"I love you too, Jett, with all of my heart." She tells me, then she starts to cry, full on sobs.

"Oh baby! What's wrong?" I ask full of concern.

She tries to calm herself down but it doesn't work. I hold her, just cradling her in my arms, letting her cry on me. Eventually, she calms down and is able to talk.

"I'm scared, what if Megan gets hurt or worse? Or you, or Caol? I could never forgive myself." She tells me, her body shaking.

I look at her straight in her eyes and gently stroke her face. "Cora, you are one bad-ass, amazing woman. You're a fucking Lunafriya. If you really wanted, you could fry that asshole. Megan will be fine. Caol and I will be fine. Don't treat this as goodbye, I will be with you at the pier. We will save Megan, and hurt Jake, don't worry." I say. *It's cute that she's worried about us, but she doesn't need to be. I'm the one who needs to worry about her. The first Lunafriya within one hundred and fifty years, is bound to attract all the tribes and trouble for Cora.*

Cora stays in my arms for a while and falls asleep. I let her sleep as long as she can before we all have to leave. She needs all her strength. I watch her as she sleeps, she looks so peaceful. I gently shake her awake.

"It's almost midnight, we should make our way to the pier." I say. She stretches her limbs, and makes a lightning ball. I am watching her, purely amazed that she can do these things. She re-absorbs the ball into her hands, with a smile on her face. I smile back, "Remember, you are a bad-ass." I tell her. She's beaming, while she gets her clothes back on, then we walk out of the room together.

She hugs and kisses me quickly, saying her goodbyes to Caol and I before walking out the door. Caol is sitting at the kitchen island looking frustrated.

"What's up with you?" I ask him.

"Meri and I got into it, she won't listen to me and left the house. She's determined to help with the fight." He grunts out.

I get a little anxious, "Do you know where she went?" I ask again.

He shakes his head no. Now, I'm the one who's frustrated. We don't have time to go and look for her if we want to hide out before Jake meets Cora. This is her first time on land, she doesn't know her directions at all and could get lost easily. I run out of the house with Caol behind me. I search the woods around the house quickly, calling her name, no luck. I check the beach at the lake by the house, she's not there. I can see that Cora's car is gone from the parking lot. My heart is starting to squeeze in my chest. I'm getting nervous about Meri missing and the fight coming up.

I look at Caol defeated, "We are going to have to continue the search later. Cora needs us right now." I tell him. Caol nods at me and follows me to the car. The drive to the pier is fast, I might have been speeding. I park the car and we get out. I look around. "I will enter the water here and swim to the meeting spot." I tell Caol.

He nods, "I will use the shadows and go into the alleys." He says. I shake his hand.

"Let the water flow freely." I tell him. Caol chants it back, turns around and walks to the shops. I walk to the docks and make sure no one is around and watching. Once I feel that I am alone, I slip into the water quietly and summon my fin. I swim over to the meeting spot. I pop my head out of the water and see Cora at the docks.

"Psst!" I say quietly. She takes a long look around, searching for the noise. She looks so beautiful. "Down here." I whisper again. Once she notices me, I say the first thing on my mind. "Meri's missing." I say.

She shakes her head. "I brought her with me, she's hiding." She tells me quietly.

"What the fuck, Cora!" I exclaim, she knows that I didn't want Meri to be here. She looks at me seriously.

"Hide. Now. Don't fuck this up." She tells me. I duck back under the docks, feeling livid. *Why are all the women in my life so frustrating?* I can't see anything being under the docks. I won't move since I don't want to get spotted by Jake unless I need too. I can hear everything happening on the docks though.

Suddenly Cora says, "Where's Megan?"

Then I hear a voice, "She's safe, for now. I didn't hurt her...much." Then a sickly evil laugh.

I can hear the anger in Cora's voice, "You still didn't answer my question. Where is Megan? Let her go."

Jake chuckles again, "You are in no position to make demands." He says. My blood is boiling just listening to him. I hear some static start. Cora must have created some lightning.

"Really? Because I will kill you right now, right where you stand, if you don't tell me." She tells him.

Jake's voice starts to waver, he must be scared, "You doo...do...do that and you won't ever find her."

Cora keeps her cool, "I guess, that's something I'll have to find out myself."

I see a bright light suddenly and then someone jumps in the lake with me and swims away fast with their fin. Cora jumps into the water, summons her fin as soon as she is submerged in the water, and chases behind him. I swim up beside her.

"What's going on?" I ask surprised.

"Jake got scared of me and swam off like a little bitch. He never told me where Megan is, he can't get away!" She yells at me. I love how sassy she is. We chase after Jake, swimming as fast as we both can.

Suddenly, Jake stops. We hear him screaming and see him trying to bat things away with his arms flailing. As we get closer, I see swarms of large fish, biting, and tearing away his flesh. Cora must have called for help. The water around him is tinting pink.

"No! Don't kill him!" Cora screams.

I see and hear the panic in her voice. I swim up to him fast and grab Jake's arms from behind, stopping him from escaping. The fish, still giving Jake the occasional bite, and getting me in the process. Cora calls off the fish and they all scatter away. We swim back to the docks, Jake still trapped in my arms. Cora swims around to face Jake, he's breathing heavily.

"Now, where the fuck is Megan? I can do much worse than killing you, ya know?" She tells him with menace dripping out of her voice.

I stare at her face, *glad that I am not at the receiving end of that glare.* Jake says nothing, just staring straight ahead. She looks around and sees some rope dangling into the water from a ship.

She grabs it, "Jett! Put him against this dock post, and tie him up." She yells at me. I nod my head and do what she says.

Once Jake is tied up and can't escape, she swims in front of him again. "Still don't want to tell me?" She asks him with a sickly sweet smile on her face. *She genuinely looks scary, I wouldn't want to be in Jake's position right now.* Jake says nothing, just staring ahead still. *He's got some balls.* She swims closer to him and places her hand on his shoulder. He screams out loud, but still doesn't break. She must be using her power on him. *I personally know what that feels like and it hurts. She didn't do it as hard on me either so Jake must be in pain.* She lets go of his shoulder and grabs the end of his fin with both hands.

"It's going to get a lot worse if you don't tell me, just tell me where Megan is and you can be free. I will leave you alone, and let you swim away." She tries to reason with him. Jake looks at her pitifully, but still doesn't say anything. "Ok, I warned you." She says and releases her power into his fin.

The screams coming from Jake must have been heard from above because Caol and Meri jump into the lake at this time. They both see her, holding onto the asshole's fin, with currents of electricity pouring out of her. Their faces display looks of shock and horror. She immediately lets go once she notices them. Luckily for us, Jake is not dead. Meri and Caol stay back with me, just watching what Cora will do next. She gives him a little break before asking him again.

"Before I get some more of my fishy friends to help me, I'll ask again. Where the fuck is Megan?" She yells in his face.

"She's a bad-ass." Meri says astonished.

Jake looks up at her finally, "Nereus city." He coughs out.

"What does that mean?" She asks. I swim up beside her.

"Nereus is another tribe and mer-city." I tell her.

"Wait, so she's in the ocean?" She asks Jake again. He nods his head, fighting for strength. "Where in the city? How is she surviving in the water?" She asks again looking a bit scared but forming a lightning ball for added effect.

"She's well-guarded in the…council chambers, in the…land training room." Jake sputters out.

She looks back at me, asking me what she should do, pleading with her eyes. Understanding flows through me, *she wants him dead. He can't be let go to warn his brothers in the tribe that we are coming.*

"We will find her, we don't need him anymore." I nod at her. Jake's eyes get huge. She swims in front of him.

"But…but you said I'd be free to go!" He pleads with her.

"Yea, I lied. This is what you get for kidnapping people." She tells him while she places her hand over his heart. She lets her power flow through her, letting her emotions control her. Jake screams and twitches so badly, it shakes her with him. She continues to pump her lightning power into his heart until Jake stops moving and goes limp. She lets go and swims back to me. "Is he dead?" She asks looking slightly freaked out.

I swim up to him and feel for a pulse for a few minutes, "yes." I say. Immediately her body goes slack. The look on her face is pure horror. I swim up by her side in a heartbeat, squeezing her, reassuring her. "You had to do it, if you would have let him go, he would have tipped off the Nereus tribe that we were coming. Let's go on land and discuss the new plan." I say while rubbing her arm. *She has used all her strength today.* She is leaning on me to help her swim. "Caol, dispose of the body and meet back at the house." I order, and Caol nods before untying the dead body from the post.

Meri and I help Cora back onto land. We walk to her car and I drive us back to my house, leaving my car for Caol to take home. Once we enter the house, Meri goes straight for the kitchen and starts to cook more food. I carry Cora into my bedroom. I lay her on my bed, and tuck her in, kissing her on the head and turning off the light. *She needs to get some rest before tomorrow. I know she will want to save Megan and we need to come up with a game plan.*

Meri is busy in the kitchen, "She asleep?" She asks.

I nod, "Yea, she fell asleep as soon as I laid her down. She had an exhausting day." I say while sitting on a stool at the kitchen island. Meri is currently baking the cake from the cookbook she pointed out earlier. She has so much flour on her shirt. She's mixing the batter with a spoon and pours it into a cake pan. Once she's done, she pops it in the oven and sits with me.

"I really like her, Jett. You made a good choice to break your oath." She says.

I shake my head. "I really shouldn't have but I'm glad I did, Cora is an amazing woman." I say. Meri pats my hand in comfort. Just then Caol walks through the door. I look up at him.

He nods at me, "It's taken care of, I took him to a shark cove, and they will finish the rest." He tells me.

I nod back, "Good. Now to make a plan on how to get into Nereus undetected." I say while thinking. We all sit and think for a while.

"We could just use Cora to blow a hole in the city walls, climb in and save her friend." Caol suggests.

"But that wouldn't be undetected, someone would see or hear that, and we would start another battle." I respond.

"They already started the battle by kidnapping. They can't expect to not have retaliation, plus we have Cora on our side." Caol responds right back. *He does have a point, the Nereus tribe started this shit.*

"Why did you let Cora kill that man? He could have helped us get in." Meri says.

I sigh, "She had too, and if she didn't then he would have tipped off the Nereus that we were coming. Plus, I wanted to see her powers in action." I tell her.

She shakes her head, "I see your logic, even if I don't like it." She says.

I nod, "It's how it had to be. Let's get some sleep and talk through a plan tomorrow with Cora, I'm beat and we all need our strength for tomorrow." I tell them.

"Alright man, see you later in the morning." Caol says while wrapping his arms around my sister and dragging her into the spare room.

I shake my head, sigh, and walk to my room with Cora sleeping inside. I strip off all my clothes and slip into bed next to her. She looks so peaceful sleeping there. I wedge my dick on her ass and wrap my arm around her. I fall asleep as soon as I hit the pillow, cuddled with Cora.

Chapter 15

Cora's perspective

I wake up boiling hot with a ton of pressure on me. My hair is sticking to my face. I notice an arm draped around me and a body at my back. No wonder I'm so sweaty. I move a bit and I unstick myself from Jett, who is still sleeping. He looks so handsome lying there. I move slowly off the bed so I don't wake him, who knows when he fell asleep last night. I get dressed silently and go into the kitchen. Meri is sitting at the kitchen island, looking extra happy.

"Good morning!" I say to her.

She notices me, "Morning!" She responds with a huge grin on her face.

"Wake up on the right side of the bed this morning? Why so happy?" I ask her with a smile, her happiness is contagious.

She looks around to make sure the guys aren't around and whispers, "Caol and I had sex last night! For the first time! Well, it was my first time since this is my first time on land." I'm surprised but happy for her. I smile wide, happy that she is comfortable enough to share with me.

"That's great! And I'm glad you enjoyed yourself, my first time was terrible. You will always remember your first time." I tell her.

"Please don't tell Jett, it will only make him mad." She says.

I nod my head, "Your secret is safe with me, plus you're an adult." I say with a smile.

She smiles back, "Want any coffee?" She asks.

"Yes, please!" I respond. Meri starts the coffee machine. "What happened after I went to sleep last night? You guys think of a plan to save Megan?" I decide to ask her.

She shakes her head, "No, not really, Caol suggested that we just find Nereus city and you blow a hole into the wall and we fight our way through to the council chambers. Jett doesn't like that idea." She says.

That doesn't sound like much of a plan. I wish I didn't kill Jake, maybe he could have helped us into the city. I put my face into my hands. "This is all my fault, why did I kill Jake?" I cry softly into my hands. Meri comes over to me and hugs me gently.

"It's not your fault, not at all! You had to kill that man. He would have tipped off the Nereus tribe that we were coming. They started this feud, by kidnapping your friend, and trying to abduct you! You did the right thing." She says while rubbing my back. It makes me feel better, but not by much.

"What's going on?" says a male voice. I look back and it's Caol.

"Nothing sweetie, just making Cora feel better about yesterday." She says.

I dry my tears as best as I can. "Sorry." I say.

"Don't worry about it." Meri says while pouring us all some coffee. She hands Caol and I a cup. I sip mine slowly, I usually don't drink regular coffee like this but I need the caffeine.

Once I finished my cup of joe, I go back into Jett's room. He's still sleeping. I carefully climb under the covers and decide to give him a blowjob to wake him up. He's already naked so it makes this really easy. I lick his cock slowly and I hear him moan. *He's waking up!* I stick his dick into my mouth and swirl my tongue around his tip while working my hands up and down his shaft.

"Morning beautiful!" He says sleepily. I continue my licking and suck him harder. He moans quietly and quickly squirts his seed into my throat. It surprises me but I shallow it, then pop my head out of the blanket and smile at him.

"Good morning!" I say while wiping my mouth with the back of my hand. He runs a hand through my hair and stares into my eyes. "Meri and Caol are awake, waiting for us in the kitchen." I tell him.

He nods his head and starts to get out of bed. I follow him out of bed and stare at him while he gets dressed. We walk into the kitchen together, holding hands.

Meri and Caol are still sitting at the island, eating some pancakes.

"Woo!" I yell out and it makes them both jump and look at me.

Jett is laughing so hard and tells them, "Cora really loves pancakes." I smile and see there are two other plates of pancakes for us. I sit down and start to stuff my face full. Jett still doesn't stop laughing at me, but I don't care, I'm eating my favorite food.

"Any dreams last night?" Jett asks me between bites.

I shake my head, "Nope, it was peaceful. So, what's the plan?" I ask.

Jett looks at me, "Well, we don't really have one yet, Caol made a suggestion but I don't think it's a good idea." He says.

"Whatever the plan is, we have to do it today. I'm not waiting to save Megan any longer." I tell him. He looks at me sadly but nods. We finish our breakfast in relative silence, everyone is thinking. Meri cleans up all our plates and puts them in the sink. "Let's just go with Caol's plan, we have nothing better, so let's go with it." I eventually say.

"Or we go to the council and see what they say." Meri suggests. *I would like to go see Halcyon city, but what if the council decides not to save Megan? What if they order us not to go?* I shake my head.

"I don't want to chance them not letting us go save Megan. We save Megan first, then go to the council." I tell everyone.

"I think it's a good idea. We can get as much information about the Nereus as we can from the council. It's not like they can stop you, Cora." Caol says. *He's right, they can't stop me. I'll go by myself if I really have to.* I look at Jett, asking him what we should do.

"Let's go to the council." He agrees. I shrug my shoulders.

"Fine." I say, "Let's go now then, I'm sick of waiting around." I tell them. They all nod at me. Jett gets up and starts to walk out the door, I follow him. We all go to the beach. "How are we getting there?" I ask curiously. Jett points to the lake.

"There is a portal in the bottom of the lake that takes us right to the city gates." He says. *Now that's just crazy. This whole time, in my lake, there has been a way to get to the ocean.*

Jett and Caol start to walk into the lake. Meri and I follow. We all summon our fins and swim under the water to the bottom of the lake. There is a circle in the bottom of the lake with three crescent shapes on it. *I've seen this thing since I was a little girl, I've always wondered what it was, now I know.* Jett swims up to the portal and traces the crescent shapes with his hand. The circle opens up wide and Jett holds out his hand for me. I take it and we swim through the portal together. *The portal wasn't as cool as I thought it was going to be. It was basically just swimming through a tunnel, no crazy colors or sounds.*

Once we get out, I see a huge glistening city that looks to be made out of crystals. I gasp, and hear Jett chuckle beside me.

"It's beautiful!" I exclaim.

"Just wait till you get inside." Jett says. I follow him to the city gates. "Jett and Caol with the Lunafriya to see the council." Jett tells the gate guards. They nod and open the gates while staring at me in awe.

Jett starts to swim through the gates and I keep a close distance to him. I look at all the buildings while we swim by. *Everything is so beautiful here.* The buildings are tall and pointed, their colors are iridescent. Every building looks to have been built with rainbows. I look around at everything so fast, my head is spinning. Jett points out a particular building.

"That's mine and Meri's place." He says. The front of his house has a shell and coral garden.

"It's amazing looking." I tell him.

He continues his swim till we get to the giant building in the center of the city. We swim down a few hallways and see a guard standing watch at a door.

Jett addresses him, "Hey Krill! How's it going?" He says.

"Fine." Krill grunts out, "Thanks for leaving me to cover for you, Caol." He says while rolling his eyes. "Glad you found Meri though." He says while giving Meri a sheepish little wave. She waves back. "And who is this?" The Krill guy points at me.

"This, my friend," Jett says while putting his arm around my shoulder and boosting me forward, "is Cora, a Lunafriya."

Krill's eyes get wide. "No way! Are you serious?" He asks.

"Yes, now we need to see the council, if you will." Jett responds while waving his arm wide. Krill opens the door behind him and nods us in.

"The council will be with you shortly." Krill says and leaves us alone in the big room.

I look around and see many banners on the walls. The room is a giant circle with many doors and where there isn't a door, there is a banner. The banners are blue with the circle and three crescents inside of it. It must be the Halcyon sigil. It doesn't take long before three old mermen swim in the room with long flowy robes. You can barely see their fins under the robes. One of them is smiling widely at me with what looks like tears in his eyes. The other two look at me warily.

"Welcome! Welcome! Lunafriya!" The smiling elder says. I smile politely and wave. The elders swim closer to me.

"Hello, I'm Cora. Nice to meet you." I say while shaking their hands.

The grumpy looking older gentleman speaks, "I am Master Kae, this is Master Yarrow, and lastly Master Zale. We are the council." Master Zale is still shaking my hand and then reaches in for a hug.

"You have your father's nose and your grandmother's eyes. Even our family colors and swirl in your fin." He whispers in my ear.

I gasp, "Are you my grandpa?" I ask. He shakes his head yes and wipes tears from his eyes. I can't help it, I start to cry too. I've never met anyone on my dad's side of the family before.

We hug for a few minutes then Master Kae states, "That's enough family nonsense, now to business...Please." He sounds grumpy but at least he added the please. I already have a bad vibe about Master Kae. We release each other and my grandpa backs away.

"Can you demonstrate your powers for us please?" Master Yarrow asks.

I raise my hands in front of my chest and make a lightning ball. My palms don't even hurt anymore in the slightest when I use my powers. The Masters all have surprised looks on their faces. I smile and re-absorb the ball.

"What else can you do, dear?" asks Master Zale, my grandpa.

"I can control sea-life, and my dreams sometimes come true. I can shoot lightning out of my hands...Oh and I brought a fish back to life." I tell him, not looking at the other elders while I said all that.

The Masters talk in quiet whispers after that. Jett quickly rubs my back to ease my nervousness, then backs away as soon as the elders turn to face us.

"Have you come to join us in the wars to come?" Master Kae asks directly.

"Well, sir. I have actually come to the sea to save my friend. She's been kidnapped by the Nereus tribe and I plan to get her back. I really only come to you now to see if there is a better way than what we thought up." I blurt out everything, Master Kae makes me nervous. I feel like he already has a problem with me.

"And what was your well-thought out plan?" Master Yarrow asks with a little chuckle.

Jett speaks up now, "It's not a very good idea but we thought that maybe Cora could blow a hole in the city wall and we fight our way through. We know that Megan is being held in the land training room, she is human." I nod my head at Jett.

Some of the elders laugh, "You are right, that is not a very good idea. You realize that will start another war with the Nereus tribe, right?" Master Kae asks.

I'm a little frustrated. *The old fools are not helping so far.* "To be all honest with you...Sir. The Nereus started the war already, by kidnapping my friend and trying to kidnap me. I got away but Megan wasn't so lucky. This isn't a laughing matter. Either you guys help us come up with a new plan or I go on my own." I say with my fists closed into hard balls.

I can feel my powers surging through me. I am quite livid right now. Sparks are starting to come out of my hands. Jett puts his hand on my shoulder to calm me down, it works. I'm able to open my palms and stretch out my hands. The Masters are all staring at me. Kae is throwing daggers at me with his eyes. *I don't think he's used to getting talked to like that.* Yarrow just has the same glazed look in his eye, like always. But my grandpa, Master Zale, he looks slightly amused at me, just a hint of a smile brushes his lips.

"Let us talk this over, and we will let you be known when we come up with a decision." Master Yarrow yawns out. Jett and Caol nod their heads, I follow suit.

"Let the water flow freely!" Grandpa says happily. We all chant right back and are dismissed from the room. We all swim out of the council chambers.

"Now what?" I ask feeling defeated.

"Now, we wait until summoned. You can come see my dwelling, if you would like." Jett says.

I shake my head yes vigorously. We swim out of the city center. There are a group of mer-people gathered and waiting. *I guess news travels fast, being the first Lunafriya in one hundred and fifty years. I kind of expected something along these lines.* Everyone is staring at me. My face is flushing, I can feel the heat on my cheeks.

I subconsciously ask for help, I guess because at that moment a large sting ray comes to my rescue and swims in front of me so I am hidden from the crowd. Everyone ooohs and aaahs at it, some even clap. I hear Jett chuckle beside me. We hurry and swim faster to make it to Jett's dwelling without more interruptions. The coral garden in front of the house looks amazingly cute.

"All my idea." Meri says after I comment on it. Jett opens the door and lets us all inside. The space doesn't have much, a few hard looking chairs, a table. Then the house splits off down the hallway and I can't tell how many rooms there are. You can slightly make out the outside through the walls, it actually looks pretty cool.

Jett grabs my hand, "Let me show you around." He says and pulls me along with him. He takes me into his bedroom first. Once the door is closed, he pulls me into a giant bear hug. "You did well in there." He says while not letting go.

"They are not going to help us, we just need to go ourselves. And Master Kae is a dick." I vent my frustrations to him, soaking up his body warmth.

He chuckles, "You will get used to him. I don't think anyone's ever talked to him the way you did." He says.

I let go from the hug. "He needs a reality check, just because he's an elder, doesn't give him the right to boss me around." I tell him.

Jett smiles widely, "Spoken like a true Lunafriya, I think Kae is just intimidated by you. Technically, you have more power and authority than him." Jett mentions.

I nod my head and finally look around his room. The bed looks hard and uncomfortable. There are pictures on the walls, on closer inspection, they are old Lunafriya drawings, of the first Lunafriya tribe, looks to be done by his own hand. He has glowing algae for lights all around the room. Jett is watching me while I survey his room. He also has a small anemone garden by his window, I go to touch it.

"I wouldn't do that if I were you." He says before I put my hand on it.

"Why? It might not sting me. Maybe because of my powers, I'm like a clown fish." I smirk at him.

He shakes his head and rolls his eyes. "Go ahead then." He says with his eyebrows raised. I still have a smirk on my face and I run my fingers through the anemone while staring at him. Nothing happens.

"Told you, I'm a clown fish." I laugh out.

He comes closer to me, brushes my hair behind my ear and says, "You are amazing, you know that?" while giving me a soft kiss on the lips.

I smile, "Yup, I knew that." I chuckle again. He shakes his head and laughs.

There is a soft knock on the door, "Sorry to interrupt, but the council has summoned us." Meri says.

"Wow, that was fast." Jett comments. I nod my head and follow him out of the room, hand in hand. Krill is waiting for us in the front room to escort us back to the council chamber. Jett immediately lets go of my hand, once he sees him. It makes me a little sad but I do understand. We wanted to wait to reveal our relationship. I flex my hand and a few sparks come out.

Krill stares at me for a minute, until I clear my throat. He then shakes his head and leaves the dwelling. We all follow Krill to the city center. Jett follows very closely behind me. It doesn't take too long to get there.

"Please wait in the chambers for the council members." Krill speaks.

We all enter and wait. After about ten minutes, I start to 'swim pace' the room. *It's ridiculous that they summoned us, just for us to wait on them more. They should have waited to call on us if they weren't ready for an audience.*

Another thirty minutes goes by, and none of the Masters arrive. I am so frustrated. I squeeze my fists into tight balls, they are sparking like mad. Jett tries to calm me down, but without touching me. He doesn't want to expose that he broke his oath just yet, and being in the council chambers would be a shitty place to have someone find out.

Finally, the back door opens and the three Masters swim in. Master Kae has a sickly evil grin on his face. Master Yarrow still looks tired, but Master Zale, my grandfather, looks down right sad.

"We have some important matters to discuss with you first, before we discuss the war with the Nereus tribe." Master Kae says, his voice dripping with malice. I look up at him with confusion.

"It has come to our attention, that you, Jett, have broken your oath for dear Cora." Master Zale says sadly. Jett looks horrified. *How they fuck did they know?*

"You know the punishment for this crime already, I assume." Master Kae says, still with that evil fucking smile. Jett nods his head quietly. *I don't know though, Jett said it wasn't a big deal.*

"What?" I ask, still squeezing my hands into fists, sparks flying out of them.

Master Yarrow answers with only one word, "Exile."

I roll my eyes at them, "Seriously? You are going to exile Jett because we fell in love? How ridiculous is that?" I spit out.

Master Kae chuckles, "He knew the consequences of his actions."

My body convulses. I am so livid that I can't help myself. I explode with showers of lightning from my hands, it falls all around me. Caol and Meri back up so they won't get hit with my powers. Jett does the opposite, he clings to my body, whispering in my ear, trying to get me to stop. I eventually do and see the damage that I created on his body. He has scorch marks all over his arms and torso.

"I'm sorry, I couldn't help myself." I whisper to him.

He grabs my chin, "It's ok now." He says. I turn my back to the horrified council members.

"Just so you know, if you are exiling Jett, you are exiling me. I will not help you with the wars to come. And if you are not on my side, then you are against me and I can't wait to do battle with you on the field." I say all of this to Master Kae, since I have a feeling this decision is all on him.

I start to swim out of the room. "Please Cora! Don't leave!" My grandfather yells after me.

I turn around to face him and with a sad face, I tell him, "I'm sorry, you can't help who you love, and I have a friend to save." Then I swim very fast out of the city center. I don't stop swimming until I feel a tug on my tail fin. I halt and turn around, we are out of the city, quite far from it actually. Jett is holding onto my tail with Caol and Meri far behind.

"Hold up, baby." Jett says while grabbing me into his arms and giving me another giant hug. "Thanks for sticking up for us in there." He whispers into my ear.

I kiss his neck, "Of course. I told you they wouldn't help us. I'm doing this my way." I tell him. I feel his head nod on me. "Now where the hell is Nereus city. I'm saving Megan now. I'm not waiting any longer." I say. Jett pulls away from the hug and stares into my eyes.

"It's actually quite far, we will have to swim there." He tells me. Meri and Caol finally catch up to us.

"I can't believe the council is being such pricks about this." Caol says to us.

"I'm following you Jett, wherever you go." Meri tells him. Caol nods with her.

"See, they lost three of their people and a Lunafriya over the matter." I say while pointing to myself, "I bet Kae is pissed." I comment. Jett chuckles a bit. "How did he know anyways?" I ask.

Jett looks put down, "I don't know but I'm guessing Krill told them. He saw us holding hands coming out of my room. He never liked me much, and jealousy, I think." He says.

"Well, anyways, what's done is done and like I said before, I'm going to save Megan. Point the way to Nereus city." I say. Caol and Jett both point east. I start to swim that way, "You guys coming?" I say and everyone starts to follow. Jett catches up with me and swims by my side, grabbing my hand. We swim like this for a long time, hand in hand. It's peaceful. Jett keeps scanning the area around us, his guardian duties never quit. I look behind us and Meri and Caol are following not too far behind with their hands linked as well.

At some point in our journey, we stop to take a break. Which is good because I'm exhausted and starving, realizing that I haven't eaten since breakfast. Jett finds us a nice little cave that we can rest without being noticed. Meri and Caol decide to find us some food while Jett and I take the first rest break. He keeps watch and tells me to try to sleep, which won't happen unless I get some food. I still try though. I float on my side in the water, not really touching the ground but close to it and close my eyes. Sleep never comes but just the relaxation of lying there, helps.

Eventually, I hear Meri and Caol come back into the cave. My eyes pop open and I sit up. I watch as they come in, their arms are full of things. They lay their bounty in the middle of all of us. I look over everything and it's mostly seaweed, some crabs, and sea cucumbers.

"Cora, would you mind calling us some fish for our dinner." Meri says to me.

I look a little shocked at first but shrug, *we have to eat and fish is the main diet for a mermaid*. I think in my head. *Ok fish, who would like to be eaten around here, I'm hungry*, being the smartass self that I am. Nothing happens. I focus, for real this time. I think, *I need a sacrifice, fish willing to be eaten, join me*. I wait before I try again. Soon, a small school of tuna swim into the cave and stop in front of me. I look at Jett and he is smiling. Everyone is, in fact.

"Now what?" I ask. Jett grabs a fish and splits it open with a knife.

"Cora, try zapping them with your powers, and the crabs. I think they might cook that way." Meri says.

That's not a bad idea, so I try it, being careful not to hit anyone. First, I shoot the tuna. They drop down, their eyes showing no life in them. Then I shoot the crabs, I hold my powers a little longer on the crabs, to break through their tough shell. Meri and Jett are busy preparing our meal the rest of the way. Jett cleans the scales off the fish while Meri rolls the meat into the seaweed. We each get a crab and some seaweed rolls. I try the roll first and it's really not bad at all. I finish them quickly and break into my crab. *I've always liked crab legs on land, just wish I had some butter to go with it*. I'm the first one done with my portion of the food.

"You know, I was a little nervous about the food down here, but I got to say that was pretty delicious." I tell them. Jett smiles at me, finishing his food too.

I let everyone else take a rest before we head out again. I insisted that Jett sleep and let me stand guard. I'm a Lunafriya, I can take care of myself. I think everyone is asleep, Jett is snoring a bit actually. I poke my head out of the cave, to view my surroundings, when I see something move beside me out the corner of my eye. I turn my head quickly and without much warning, I feel tremendous pain in my face and everything goes black.

I wake with a fright, trying to remember the dream I just had. Only thing I can remember is someone gets hurt, badly. My face hurts, so I instinctively go to touch it. It stings to the touch at the bridge of my nose and eyes, *I bet there is a nasty mark there.* I wince loudly and open my eyes, wondering where the fuck I am. The room is bare, just a door and a bed made of sand, looks like a prison cell to me. *What the fuck happened? How did I get here? Are Jett and the others ok?* I start to panic a bit. My breathing is low and fast, sparks are shooting out of my palms. I try to control my breathing. I think, *Help! Help me! I don't know where I am.* I close my hands tightly and just focus on breathing.

Suddenly, the door latch starts to move. This scares me enough to stop my breathing all together and watch, with my hands ready to strike whoever opens that door. Finally, the latch moves all the way down and the door starts to open. But to my surprise, an octopus is what swims in. I look aghast and stare. *I guess my call for help worked.* The octopus looks at me and with one of its tentacles, starts to play with the sand. It writes out the word 'Nereus'. *Perfect, so I'm right where I need to be.*

Thank you, I think. Octopi are such amazing creatures, so smart. *Can you show me where they are keeping a human?* I ask him in my head. The octopus grabs my arm with one of its tentacles and pulls me along with him out the door. I follow along the corridor.

Occasionally, there are guards that swim by. The octopus hides me with his camouflage against the wall, every time. The guards never expect a thing. We reach a door that has a placard on it. It reads,

'Land training room

Caution: water-free zone'

This is it! Where Jake said Megan would be. *Thank you.* I think to the octopus and he swims off. I open the door and it's a tiny room with another door. Once I close the door, a red light turns on and the water starts to drain out. The water gets to my waist and I summon back my legs, still in my swim gear. The light turns green once all the water drains out of the room. I open the next door, walking a little shaky on my legs. The room is giant with a couple of other doors at the back. It's filled with exercise equipment, mats on the floor and drawings all over the walls. Not a single person is in the room though. I walk to a door and try to open it, it's unlocked but empty inside, except for a mop and broom. I try the next door and once I open it, I gasp!

There are four passed out females laying on cots on the floor. I run to the first one, and it's Penelope Guzhar. I recognize her from her picture on the news. She's one of the missing women from town. I look at the next woman, it's Kristy Webbing. These are all the missing girls! Megan is lying next to Kristy.

I shout "Megs!" with pure relief. I try to shake her awake but she doesn't. I panic a little, and slap her on the face a couple of times, yelling "Megan! Wake up!" I check to see if she's still breathing, and she is, to my relief. "Ok Megs, I'm going to get us out of here." I tell her, looking around. "I'm going to get all of us out of here." I say to all of them, who knows if they can hear me or not.

I find some long rope in the main room and come back to tie us all together. They are heavy now but once we get into the water, I'm sure the weight will lesson. I just have to be quick to the surface once I get into the water, I don't want any of them to drown.

Now what? How will I get out of this room without being detected or stopped? I think for a few minutes. *If Caol wanted me to blow a hole through the city walls, why couldn't I blow a hole through the ceiling and swim out to the surface? I can also ask for help from the sea-life when we get into open water, hopefully something will listen.* I gear up the girls and tie them to my waist. I point my hands above me, focusing on one point of the ceiling.

I release my power with force. Water starts to pour heavily into the room. I summon my fin and bolt out of the hole I just created. *Help! Help me to the surface quickly!* I yell in my head over and over.

The same octopus swims up to me, grabs my arm with a tentacle and pulls us, shooting up faster than I could have myself, and I pride myself on my fast swimming. I look back, everyone is still tied to my waist, so that's good. But the city below is in chaos, it looks like I might have started a battle. There are mer-people swimming around, some fighting a small group of people. Some are fleeing the danger.

Everything is getting smaller and smaller by the second. I was hoping to see if Jett was among the fighters but I can't make out people anymore, they all look like dots now. We reach the surface and the octopus flings us all out of the water. Once I break through the surface, I summon my legs. It wouldn't be good if anyone saw me with my fin.

We all land on a row boat. Lucky for us, it was here and empty. I paddle the boat to the nearest shore I can find. Everyone else is still knocked out. It takes a long while but I eventually reach a beach and untie myself from the group. I pull the boat up on the deserted beach. I scan around my surroundings and see an emergency phone. I sprint to it and pick up the receiver.

"Nine one one, where is your emergency?" Asks the operator.

"I don't know where I am, a beach I guess but I found a boat with four unconscious women tied together in it on the shore." I hastily tell the operator, sobbing a little.

"Ok ma'am. We pinpointed the call location, we have a patrol car and an ambulance on the way." The operator says.

"Thank you." I say before hanging up the phone.

Megan and the rest of the girls should be ok. I need to go help with the fight. I check the women once more, to make sure they won't float away. I hear sirens getting closer before jumping back into the water. I summon my fin and swim to the pink tinted water of the city nearby.

Chapter 16

Jett's perspective

I wake to the best feeling. My dick is hard and getting licked. I moan, and open my eyes a little. I see Cora putting my dick into her mouth and swirl her tongue around the tip while working her hands up and down my shaft.

"Morning beautiful!" I say sleepily. She continues her licking and sucks me harder. It doesn't take long for me to come, especially with morning wood. I moan quietly and quickly squirt into her throat. She takes it like a champ and shallows it, then pops her head out of the blanket and smiles at me.

"Good morning!" She says while wiping her mouth off with the back of her hand. I run a hand through her hair and stare into her beautiful eyes. "Meri and Caol are awake, waiting for us in the kitchen." She tells me.

I nod my head and start to get out of bed. She follows me out of bed and stares at me while I get dressed. We walk into the kitchen together, holding hands.

Meri and Caol are sitting at the kitchen island eating some pancakes. "Woo!" Cora yells out and it makes them both look at her funny.

I bust out laughing so hard, remembering the first time I made Cora some pancakes, and tell them, "Cora really loves pancakes."

She smiles and we sit down. Cora starts to eat the pancakes that Meri made us but she does it so fast, like she isn't even chewing them. I still can't stop laughing at her, but she shrugs it off.

"Any dreams last night?" I ask her between bites.

She shakes her head, "Nope, it was peaceful. So what's the plan?" She asks.

I look at her, "Well, we don't really have one yet, Caol made a suggestion but I don't think it's a good idea." I say.

"Whatever the plan is, we have to do it today, I'm not waiting to save Megan any longer." She tells me. I nod at her, but not liking this at all. *We need a better plan before we attempt anything.* We finish our breakfast in relative silence. Meri cleans up all our plates and puts them in the sink. "Let's just go with Caol's plan, we have nothing better, so let's go with it." Cora eventually says.

"Or we go to the council and see what they say." Meri suggests. *That actually doesn't sound like a bad idea. The council should be able to help us, at least get some more fighters on our side.*

Cora shakes her head. "I don't want to chance them not letting us go save Megan. We go save Megan first, then go to the council." She tells everyone.

"I think it's a good idea, we can get as much information about the Nereus as we can from the council. It's not like they can stop you, Cora." Caol says. Cora looks at me, letting me decide what we ultimately do.

"Let's go to the council." I agree. She shrugs her shoulders.

"Fine." She says, "Let's go now then. I'm sick of waiting around." She tells us. All of us nod at her. I get up and start to walk out the door, with Cora following very closely behind. We all go to the beach. "How are we getting there?" She asks curiously.

I point to the lake. "There is a portal in the bottom of the lake that takes us right to the city gates." I say. Cora looks a bit disbelieving at me.

Caol and I start to walk into the lake first. Meri and Cora follow us. We all summon our fins and swim under water to the bottom of the lake. I swim up to the portal and trace the crescent shapes with my hand to open it. The portal opens up wide and I hold out my hand for Cora. She takes it and we swim through the portal together. Once we get out the other side, I hear Cora gasp, and I chuckle beside her. I couldn't wait to see her reaction to Halcyon city.

"It's beautiful! She exclaims.

"Just wait till you get inside." I say. She follows me to the city gates, with Meri and Caol close behind. There are two guards standing watch at the gates. "Jett and Caol with the Lunafriya to see the council." I tell the gate guards.

They nod and open the gates while staring at Cora with their mouths agape. I start to swim through the gates and she keeps a close distance to me. We let our hands drop away from each other before we left the portal. I don't want to take any chances of someone seeing us like that until later, after Megan has been found. She looks at all the buildings while we swim by. After swimming for a few minutes, I point out a particular building.

"That's mine and Meri's place." I say.

Her face lights up, "It's amazing looking." Cora tells me.

I continue my swim without stopping again till we get to the council chambers. Krill is keeping watch, doing Caol's normal job.

I address him, "Hey Krill! How's it going?" I say.

"Fine." Krill grunts out, "Thanks for leaving me to cover for you, Caol." He says while rolling his eyes. "Glad you found Meri though." He says while giving Meri an awkward little wave. *He always had a thing for Meri, well at least that was always my suspicion.* She waves nervously back. "And who is this?" Krill points at Cora, checking out her body. *I can read those little thoughts in his eyes.* This pisses me off.

"This, my friend." I say sarcastically while putting my arm around her shoulders, trying to convey that she is taken, "is Cora, a Lunafriya."

Krill's eyes get wide. "No way! Are you serious?" He asks.

"Yes, now we need to see the council, if you will." I respond while waving my arm wide. Krill opens the door behind him and nods us in.

"The council will be with you shortly." Krill says and leaves us alone in the big room.

Cora is busy looking around the room, taking everything in. It doesn't take long for the council to arrive.

"Welcome! Welcome! Lunafriya!" Master Zale says with a wide smile, he looks to be excited to meet his granddaughter. Cora smiles politely and waves.

The Masters swim closer to her, "Hello, I'm Cora. Nice to meet you." She says while shaking their hands.

Master Kae addresses her first, "I am Master Kae, and this is Master Yarrow and lastly Master Zale. We are the council."

Master Zale is still shaking her hand and then reaches in for a hug. They are whispering to each other and I can't make out the words, but they both start to cry. Master Zale wipes tears from his eyes. They hug for a few minutes, Cora crying into his shoulder.

Then Master Kae states, "That's enough family nonsense, now to business…Please." He sounds grumpier than usual. They release each other and Master Zale backs away to the rest of the council.

"Can you demonstrate your powers for us please?" Master Yarrow asks Cora.

I back away, putting an arm out to signal to the others to back up too. Cora raises her hands in front of her chest and makes a lightning ball. The Masters all have surprised looks on their faces. *What did they expect? I've told them I found a Lunafriya. They should remember what the Lunafriya's were capable of.* Cora re-absorbs the ball.

"What else can you do, dear?" asks Master Zale sweetly.

"I can control sea-life, and my dreams sometimes come true. I can shoot lightning out of my hands...Oh and I brought a fish back to life." She tells the council.

The Masters huddle together and talk in quiet whispers after that. I quickly rub her back to ease her nervousness, then back away as soon as the elders turn to face us.

"Have you come to join us in the wars to come?" Master Kae asks her directly, getting straight to the point.

"Well, sir, I have actually come to the sea to save my friend. She's been kidnapped by the Nereus tribe and I plan to get her back. I really only come to you now to see if there is a better way than what we thought up." She blurts out everything. Master Kae looks at her with distain.

"And what was your well-thought out plan?" Master Yarrow asks with a little chuckle.

I speak up now, "It's not a very good idea but we thought that maybe Cora could blow a hole in the city wall and we fight our way through. We know that Megan is being held in the land training room, she is human." Cora nods her head at me.

Some of the Masters suddenly laugh. "You are right, that is not a very good idea. You realize that will start another war with the Nereus tribe, right?" Master Kae asks in a belittling sort of way. Cora is getting a little frustrated, I can tell. She rolls her eyes and puts her hand on her hip. *I know this look, here comes her attitude.*

"To be all honest with you…sir, the Nereus started the war already. By kidnapping my friend and trying to kidnap me. I got away but Megan wasn't so lucky. This isn't a laughing matter. Either you guys help us come up with a new plan or I go on my own." She says with her fists closed into tight little balls.

Sparks are starting to come out of her hands. She is getting angry and losing control. I put my hand on her shoulder to help calm her down, it works. She opens her palms and stretches out her hands. The Masters are all staring at her. I let go of her immediately. Master Kae looks livid. I don't think he's used to getting talked to like that. Yarrow just has the same glazed look in his eye like he always does, but Master Zale, he looks slightly amused at her, and just a small smirk lays on his lips.

"Let us talk this over and we will let you be known when we come up with a decision." Master Yarrow yawns out. Caol and I nod our heads, Cora follows suit.

"Let the water flow freely!" Master Zale says happily. We all chant right back, even Cora and we are dismissed from the room.

We all swim out of the council chambers. "Now what?" Cora asks looking defeated.

"Now, we wait until summoned. You can come see my dwelling if you would like." I say. She shakes her head yes vigorously.

We swim out of the city center. There are a group of mer-people gathered and waiting. *I guess Krill or the gate guards must have let the news out. I kind of expected something like this.* Everyone is staring at Cora. Her face is flushing. Suddenly, a large sting ray comes to rest in front of us, blocking us from view of the group. Everyone oohs and aahs at it. I chuckle, knowing it was Cora who called the sting ray to cover her. I hurry and swim faster to make it to my dwelling without more interruptions. Cora stops in front of my place to check out the garden.

"All my idea." Meri says after Cora comments on it. I open the door and let everyone inside. Cora looks around, awe in her eyes.

Once the door is shut, I grab her hand. "Let me show you around." I say while pulling her along with me. I take her into my bedroom first. Once the door is closed, I pull her into a tight hug. "You did well in there." I say while not letting go.

"They are not going to help us. We just need to go ourselves…And Master Kae is a dick." She vents her frustrations to me.

I chuckle, "You will get used to him. I don't think anyone's ever talked to him the way you did." I state.

She lets go from the hug. "He needs a reality check, just because he's an elder, doesn't give him the right to boss me around." She tells me.

I smile widely, "Spoken like a true Lunafriya. I think Kae is just intimidated by you. Technically, you have more power and authority than him." I mention.

She nods her head and looks around my room for a while. I watch her while she surveys my room. She swims up to my anemone garden at the window. She reaches out her hand to touch it.

"I wouldn't do that if I were you." I say before she does.

"Why? It might not sting me, maybe because of my powers, I'm like a clown fish." She smirks at me.

I shake my head and roll my eyes. "Go ahead, then." I say with eyebrows raised, watching her. She still has a smirk on her face and she runs her finger though the anemone while staring at me. Nothing happens.

"Told you, I'm a clown fish." She laughs out.

I go closer to her, and brush her hair behind her ear and say, "You are amazing, you know that?" while giving her soft kisses on her lips.

She smiles, "Yup, I knew that." And chuckles again. I shake my head and laugh, I love her silly, sarcastic nature.

There is a soft knock on the door, "Sorry to interrupt, but the council has summoned us." Meri says.

"Wow, that was fast." I comment, looking surprised. She nods her head and follows me out of the room, hand in hand. Krill is waiting for us in the front room to escort us back to the council chamber. I immediately let go of her hand, once I see him. I see a tiny smile in the corner of Krill's lips. Cora flexes her hand and a few sparks come out.

Krill stares at her for a minute, watching her hands, until she clears her throat. He then shakes his head and leaves the dwelling. We all follow Krill to the city center. I follow very closely behind her. It doesn't take too long to get there.

"Please wait in the chambers for the council members." Krill speaks and *I swear he gives me a tiny wink before we enter the room.* Now, all we have to do is wait for the council members. After about ten minutes, Cora starts to 'swim pace' the room, looking nervous.

Another thirty minutes goes by, and none of the Masters arrive. Cora is getting frustrated. She squeezes her fists into tight balls, they are sparking like crazy. I try to calm her down, but without touching her. I don't want to expose that I broke my oath just yet.

Finally, the back door opens and the three Masters swim in. Master Kae has a sickly evil grin on his face. Master Yarrow, still looks tired, but Master Zale looks sad. Now I'm starting to get nervous too.

"We have some important matters to discuss with you first, before we discuss the war with the Nereus tribe." Master Kae says, his voice dripping with malice. We look up at him with confusion.

"It has come to our attention, that you, Jett, have broken your oath for dear Cora." Master Zale says sadly. I get sick to my stomach. *Fucking Krill, that asshole told the council what he saw. I'll have to hurt him next time I see him.*

"You know the punishment for this crime already, I assume." Master Kae says, still with that evil fucking smile. I nod my head quietly, *knowing full well, that they will banish me from the city and the tribe.*

"What?" Cora asks, still squeezing her hands into fists, sparks flying out of them.

Master Yarrow answers with only one word, "Exile."

She rolls her eyes at them. "Seriously? You are going to exile Jett because we fell in love? How ridiculous is that?" She yells out.

Master Kae chuckles, "He knew the consequences of his actions."

Her body convulses and she screams. A shower of lightning is pouring down around her. She lost control of herself. Caol and Meri back up so they won't get hit with her powers, but I don't. I need to stop her before she hurts anyone or herself. I cling myself to her body, whispering in her ear, trying to get her to stop, to calm down and control herself.

My body is on fire, my skin feeling like it will peel off of me. She is pouring her power out at full strength. She eventually registers me pleading in her ear to stop and she does. She looks me over with shock on her face. I look down to see the sorry state I'm in. I have scorch marks all over my body.

"I'm sorry, I couldn't help myself." She whispers to me.

I grab her chin, looking deep in her eyes, "It's ok now." I say. She turns back to the horrified council members.

"Just so you know, if you are exiling Jett, you are exiling me. I will not help you with the wars to come. And if you are not on my side then you are against me and I can't wait to do battle with you on the field." She says and starts to swim out of the room.

"Please! Cora! Don't leave!" Master Zale yells after her.

She turns around to face him and with a sad face, tells him, "I'm sorry, you can't help who you love, and I have a friend to save." Then she swims very fast out of the city center.

We follow her out, me hot on her tail. She doesn't stop swimming until I pull on her tail fin. She halts and turns around and sees me holding onto her tail with Meri and Caol far behind.

"Hold up baby." I say while grabbing her into my arms and giving her another hug. "Thanks for sticking up for us in there." I whisper into her ear.

She kisses my neck, "Of course. I told you they wouldn't help us. I'm doing this my way." She tells me. I nod my head. "Now, where the hell is Nereus city? I'm saving Megan now, I'm not waiting any longer." She says. I pull away from the hug and stare into her eyes.

"It's actually quite far, we will have to swim there." I tell her. Meri and Caol finally catch up to us.

"I can't believe the council is being such pricks about this." Caol says to us.

"I'm following you Jett, wherever you go." Meri tells me. Caol nods with her.

"See, they lost three of their people and a Lunafriya over the matter." Cora says while pointing to herself, "I bet Kae is pissed." She comments. I chuckle a bit. "How did he know anyways?" She asks.

"I don't know but I'm guessing Krill told them, he saw us holding hands coming out of my room. He never liked me much, and jealousy, I think." I say.

"Well, anyways, what's done is done and like I said before, I'm going to save Megan, point the way to Nereus city." She says. Caol and I both point east. She starts to swim away, "You guys coming?" She says and everyone starts to follow her. I catch up with her and swim by her side, grabbing her hand. We swim like this for a long time, hand in hand. It's peaceful. I keep scanning the area around us, making sure we aren't followed or being hunted.

Cora starts to look extra tired so I suggest we stop for a while to rest. I find us a nice little cave that we can rest in without being noticed. Meri and Caol decide to find us some food while Cora and I take the first rest break. I keep watch and tell her to try to get some sleep. She lays down and I go to the cave entrance to keep watch. It doesn't take too long but Meri and Caol come back with their arms full. Cora sits up once we enter the cave, *I wonder if she got any sleep.* They drop their load of food on the ground.

"Cora, would you mind calling us some fish for our dinner." Meri says to her.

She looks a little shocked at first but shrugs. It takes a little while but soon, a small school of tuna swim into the cave and stop in front of her. She looks at me and I smile, simply amazed by her. Everyone is, in fact.

"Now what?" She asks. I grab a fish and split it open with my knife.

"Cora, try zapping them with your power, and the crabs. I think they might cook that way." Meri says.

She tries it, being careful not to hit anyone. First she shoots the tuna. They drop down, their eyes showing no sign of life in them. Then she shoots the crabs, she holds her power a little longer on the crabs, to break through their tough shells. Meri and I are busy preparing our meal the rest of the way. I clean the scales off the fish while Meri rolls the meat up in the seaweed. We each get a crab and some seaweed rolls.

Cora tries the rolls first and finishes them quickly and breaks into her crab. Everything is perfectly cooked, just like on land. Cora is the first one done with her portion of the food.

"You know, I was a little nervous about the food down here, but I got to say that was pretty delicious." She tells us. I smile at her, finishing my food too.

Cora lets everyone else take a rest before we head out again. She insisted that I sleep and let her stand guard, telling me that she's a Lunafriya, and can take care of herself. I let her and lay down beside my sister and best friend. It doesn't take long before I feel myself falling asleep.

▪▪

I awaken after what seems like a really long nap. I open my eyes and see that Meri and Caol are still sleeping beside me. I look around for Cora but I don't see her. I get up to check the mouth of the cave, maybe she went out to keep watch, like I did.

Once I get to the cave entrance, I look around and see no Cora. My heart starts to constrict in my chest. I panic, "Cora! Where are you?" I yell.

I don't get an answer. I swim back inside the cave and wake up Caol and Meri. "Cora is gone!" I scream at them.

They both wake up with a start and help me look for Cora. Caol has excellent tracking ability. He looks around the cave entrance for a few minutes.

"Jett! See here." Caol says while pointing to the ground. "It looks to me that someone was dragged off from here. You can see the fin mark dragging along the sand here." He says.

Oh no! Cora's been captured! That's the only explanation. I don't even think, I just follow the trail with Caol and Meri behind me.

Caol stops me before we get too close to a city, Nereus city to be exact. We hide behind a giant rock in the sand.

"Now what?" I ask Caol, hoping he will find us a way into the city, I can't think straight right now.

He shrugs, "We need a way in, either knock out the guards at the gates or find a weakness in the walls. Someone might catch us. Either way, it's risky." He says.

I nod my head, showing my agreement. At this moment, I look around, wondering what we should do, when I notice something. A small group of five armed mer-men are swimming towards us. They have the Halcyon crest on their chest plates. Caol notices them too and we swim to meet up with them. I immediately notice who a few of them are. They trained with me at the guardian academy.

"What are you doing here?" I ask them.

One of the tallest mer-men I've ever seen states, "Master Zale sent us to help the Lunafriya in her mission.

My heart rises with a bit of hope, the council is still going to help us. "Well, now it's a rescue mission, the Lunafriya's been taken by the Nereus." I tell them.

They in turn each nod their heads and click their tridents on the sand.

"Our best plan was to knock out the gate guards and sneak in." I say.

The tall guardian asks, "Would you like us to distract them while you three sneak in?"

That's probably the best idea, we don't have armor and can sneak around the city without getting noticed as fast. "Yes, let the water flow freely." I say with a bow.

"Let the water flow freely." Everyone else chants.

The guardians go on ahead of us, we are staying in the shadows. I can hear the guardians being rowdy, but not what they are actually saying. They start to swim differently, acting like they ate too much rotten fruit, or drank too much alcohol, if we were on land. It sounds like they are arguing, getting closer to the city gates. Meri is in between Caol and me.

"What are they doing?" She whispers to us.

"My guess is that they are acting drunk to distract the guards away from the gates." I whisper back.

"Not a bad idea." She says.

I nod my head and motion to her to keep quiet. The guardians stop in front of the gates and start to fight with each other in the group. This gets the gate guards attention and they swim over to stop the fight.

"Now's our chance, let's go!" Caol says and we swim as fast as we can to the gates, while staying in the shadows. The guards don't see us slip through the gates.

Now we must be careful not to attract unwanted attention. We swim slowly around the city, looking for where the Nereus tribe keeps the council chambers. This city is different from Halcyon. The buildings and dwellings aren't made out of crystals like ours. They are made out of mud and sand. Everything is bland here. We make our way to the center of the city, just guessing the chambers will be in the center. When we hear a big commotion behind us. The armored guardians are now in the city, fighting off some other Nereus guards. They get surrounded.

"They need our help!" I yell to Caol.

He nods his head and follows me. I grab a fallen soldier's weapon, a long curved blade, and start to attack the Nereus from behind. I down a few of them before the Nereus realize the fight is on both sides of them.

Suddenly, a large boom echoes throughout the city. Everyone looks up to where the noise came from. Sand and dust are floating like a mushroom cloud above the largest building, I see a mermaid, swim out with four humans attached in a line behind her. My heart swells as it has to be Cora, I can see purple and green on the tail fin. An octopus swims up in front of her and pulls her up to the surface faster than I could imagine. At least she's safe, and it looks like she found Megan. I wonder who the other people she had were.

A sharp pain cuts at my abdomen. I wince and focus back on the fight to see a Nereus guard in front of me with his sword sticking into my belly. I power through the pain and grab my blade tight, swinging it to the Nereus's throat. It connects with the guard and sticks into his neck, like butter. I rip my blade out and blood oozes into the water, making everything a shade of pink. I pull the sword out of my stomach and continue to hack away at any Nereus that dares to come at me. I see Caol fighting around me and even Meri has joined the fight. She has picked up a fallen trident, stabbing anyone who gets in arm's length. My arms start to feel heavy. The blade drops out of my hand. My world starts to darken. I collapse on the ground and the last thing I see and hear is Meri dropping her trident, racing towards me and screaming my name.

End of book 1 Sea Secret.

Book 2 Sea Storm coming soon.

Thank you for taking this journey with me! This is the first book I have ever written. I hope you love it as much as I did. Please join my Facebook page, Elise H. Ford-author. To get news of my upcoming books.

Made in the USA
Middletown, DE
04 February 2019